SOUTHERN GODS

SOUTHERN GODS

JOHN HORNOR JACOBS

NIGHT SHADE BOOKS

Cover art by Rodrigo Luff
Cover design by Claudia Noble
Interior layout and design by Amy Popovich

ISBN: 978-1-59780-285-7
eISBN: 978-1-59780-353-3

Printed in the United States of America

For my father who told me the stories of Achilles and Odysseus
On the drive to Michigan, after midnight,
Sometime in 1979.

And for my mother, who let him.

'As flies to wanton boys are we to th' gods,
They kill us for their sport.'

—*William Shakespeare,*
King Lear Act 4, scene 1, 32–37

Prologue

1878, Rheinhart Plantation

The black thing walked from the forest and took the shape of a man. Wilhelm watched it through the window, from his sickbed.

At first the creature shuffled, a thing of gristle, all angular joints and thick sinew. It moved erratically, in a herky-jerky fashion that reminded the boy of a circus performance; each limb's movement was prolonged, drawn out, as if for dramatic effect. The legs lifted, paused, wavered, and then placed themselves, each one moving independently of the others. It was hard to tell if its appendages ended in hands, or hooves, or claws. Even in the slanting afternoon light, its features were indistinct, blurry. The creature moved into the stubble of the empty field and stopped.

The boy thought it might be *wildschwein*—one of the vicious boars that foraged the dark wood and edges of fields—until the thing shifted. Its skin became mottled, rippled, and then faded back to black.

It rose. The black creature looked as though its spine had cracked and reorganized itself, and a man stood where the creature had.

But it was still black. Still inhuman. And faceless.

It turned and looked at the boy.

How he knew it perceived him, the boy couldn't say. The entity's head remained featureless, like an ebony mannequin's. Wilhelm's breath caught in his chest and he could feel the impeding frenzy of coughs building. With it would come the blood, at first just flecking his lips, then a fine spray that would speckle his handkerchief, drip on his dressing gown, soil his linens.

Der Erlkönig, he thought, remembering.

He had started coughing in the winter and never stopped. To ease the tightness in his chest, the Rheinhart servants began placing boiling pots of water in his room at night. The steam would fog the windows and in the morning, the boy would be able to hear the farm come to life around him: the clucking of the chickens, the braying of mules being harnessed, the screeches of peafowl, the clatter of pans and cutlery in the kitchen. But he would not be able to see it.

By spring, his mother moved him out of the room he shared with his brother and into the small bedroom at the back of the plantation house, near the sleeping porch. He'd cried and thrashed and tried to talk her out of it, but she stood pale-faced at the door, tears streaming down her cheeks, and shook her head. Wilhelm fought as the servants entered the room and began bundling his clothes; he swung his fists wildly, but he'd already lost enough strength to be easily winded. He hit one serving man's back with his small, hard fists, but the man ignored him except to pull his shirt over his mouth and nose. His younger brother, Karl, watched from behind their mother's skirts as the burly servant grasped Wilhelm's arms, turned his face away, and drew the crying boy out of the room, down the hall and stairway, and firmly placed the boy in a vacant servant's quarters, behind the kitchen. He cried then, and hated.

At night, he dreamt of killing his brother, and his mother, for banishing him. For abandoning him.

He grew weak and pale.

One morning his father had come to his new room, bundled

Wilhelm in a blanket, and carried him through the house with a blank expression. The boy watched, partly bemused, as he passed through the house in his father's arms, staring up at the vaulted ceilings and crystal chandeliers as they passed overhead in a strange procession. His father placed him in a harnessed carriage and drove east at a furious pace until they came to a wide, massive river.

They boarded a ferry, their horse nickering, the carriage swaying on its wheels. After an hour of stevedores straining against the Mississippi's current, they gained the eastern shore. That evening they pulled into the courtyard of a beautiful building, a place strewn with light and laughter and fine gentlemen and ladies walking on the grass, the smoke from cigars wafting on the evening air like a warm memory. The sign read Gayoso House, although the building, to the boy's eyes, seemed palatial.

"Where are we?" he had asked.

"Memphis."

"But why?"

"Why? You mean why are we here?"

He nodded. His father jumped down from the carriage and handed the reins to a stable attendant. When his father lifted him, again, the gentlemen and ladies turned to look. Wilhelm felt his cheeks grow red. He coughed into the blanket as quietly as possible.

"Here," said his father, handing him a handkerchief. "Cough into this. It's very important."

"Why are we here?"

"You're sick."

"I'm feeling better. I've stopped coughing. See?"

"Yes." His father carried him across the lawn and into the hotel. He set Wilhelm down in an ornate chair in the lobby as he paid for a room. Then he lifted him again. The boy was growing accustomed to staring at ceilings.

That night, silent men came into his darkened bedroom and touched him with cold hands. With soft, papery voices, they asked him to cough and listened to his chest. They frowned and regarded him solemnly, eyes devoid of hope.

Consumption, they called it, as they spoke with his father in hushed voices. His father's face grew somber and even paler than before, and he glanced at Wilhelm and smiled at him, weakly.

Wilhelm's breath came in short gasps, and his eyelids felt leaded and heavy. He closed his eyes.

When he awoke, it was still night and his father sat beside him, reading by lantern light.

"What are you reading?"

"A story."

The boy fought the cough building in his chest. He didn't want his father to pity him.

"Will you read to me?"

"It's in German."

"Memaw taught me some. I know a few words."

"I'll translate. How's that?"

Wilhelm nodded and nestled further down into the bed.

"This is *Der Erlkönig*, a poem by a man named Göethe, written a long time ago. It's a story about a father and his son, traveling home on horseback through a dark forest. The boy is sick, and the father is frantic to get him home. As they ride, the boy becomes delirious and sees a frightening man in the woods."

His father began to read, haltingly at first. Sometimes he'd sound out the German and then translate.

My son, oh why do you look so afraid?
See Father, don't you see the Elf king is there?
The Elf king, Elf king with crown and cloak?
My son, it's a wisp of mist.

He paused. "How much of this do you understand, Wil?" he asked.

"I don't know. Enough. It's scary."

His father smiled. "Very scary to me. And very sad. I'm sorry I never taught you how to speak or read German." He rubbed his eyes. "I should stop. The ending might be too frightening for you right now."

"No, it isn't. I just don't understand everything."

"Let's see if I can explain it." His father shifted in his chair. "The man can't see the elf king, only trees. The Erlkönig promises things to the dying boy, the love of his daughter, if only the boy will come with him. In the end, the boy dies. The poem doesn't make it clear whether the boy is hallucinating the Erlkönig or if he's really there, stealing away the child's life." He bowed his head for a moment, then pulled a pipe from his vest, packed it with tobacco, and lit it from a match. "I don't know why I'm reading this to you at all. Maybe it was on my mind."

"I thought elves and fairies were good. At least in all the stories Memaw read me they were." Wilhelm coughed again, and his father looked at his pipe, turned, and set it down in a crystal ashtray.

"What is good?" his father asked. "In the old wives' tales and stories they steal away children and raise them up to be kings and queens of distant lands. The grumpkins help cobblers mend shoes and find lost jewelry for young ladies. But those are children's stories. The interesting thing about the Erlkönig is that he's not some sweet little fairy. He's a monster. And monsters make for good stories." His father smiled wanly. He passed his hand over his eyes and yawned.

After a moment, his father took Wilhelm's small hand in his warm large one and squeezed. Then, he lifted the book and continued reading. It was the last time the boy felt truly happy, lying in a Memphis hotel room as his father read to him about a dying boy.

But now, the creature—the awareness—cocked what passed for a head and stared at him. Wilhelm, at that moment, didn't think monsters made for good stories at all.

The entity took several long, sweeping strides—seeming to flow across the field—and suddenly, it was at the window, filling the frame.

The boy gasped and then began to cough. He felt wetness on his lips. Blood.

When he regained control of his body, he realized it was cold now, with the upright man-thing peering in at him. The morning's warmth had vanished, and Wilhelm shivered and tried his best to hold back another coughing fit. He felt blood dripping from his lower lip onto his dressing gown.

For long moments the boy and the thing matched gazes—watery blue eyes staring into an eyeless, blank face—and then the thing broke the gaze by stepping into the room. Through the window, through the wall, it was as if one second the creature stood outside and then as the boy blinked, it moved through glass and wall to loom above him at the foot of the bed.

I'm going to die, thought the boy. Having lived for months with the terrible knowledge of his disease, the boy was strangely non-plussed by this realization. *Something ripped in my chest when I coughed and now my lungs are full of blood. I'm going to die now, and Death is here to collect me.*

"What?" He hesitated, because the Death-thing did wear the shape of a man. He *could* be a man. "Who are you?" the boy asked.

The black figure stood absolutely still. For a moment the child thought it was just an illusion of shadows, the dying afternoon light playing strangely on the walls of his sick room. But then the thing cocked its head again and the illusion was broken.

I come before. I prepare the way, it spoke directly into his mind. *I am the herald. All you know will pass.*

The boy looked at the figure and began to tremble. He breathed, short quick breaths, chest tightening, and he could feel blood in the back of his throat, burbling and popping.

You are dying.

The boy nodded. This thing spoke what everyone else ignored for so long. For an instant he was grateful to it for being honest, stating the situation so simply. His mother danced around the obvious for months and his brother, Karl, avoided him totally. His father was always traveling, taking grain or cotton to market. The serving woman who brought him food, emptied his chamber-pot, and washed his soiled linens, she wore a bandana around her face and couldn't meet his eye. Even when he cried.

As he looked at the creature, he felt an overwhelming hatred for his family, those who had put him aside to die. And the burning feeling in his chest, the itch that would erupt into a frenzy of bloody coughing now, felt like a warm rage suffusing his being. His body was learning to hate.

Would you serve and live? Or end this suffering and die?

The words thundered in his mind. Something was offered here that went beyond words, went beyond his comprehension.

The black creature moved, filling the room with darkness, even though the sun streamed through the window.

Rise, then, if you would serve.

The boy began coughing again. More blood dripped from his mouth, but now the pain burned with something more akin to lust.

As he drew himself up in the dark thing's shadow, the boy could feel himself hardening, becoming recalcitrant and cold and strengthening, becoming ever stronger. Becoming something... else.

If you would serve, take up your father's sword.

The black thing turned, stepping through the wall, back into the field.

If you would not die, remove your mask.

The boy watched as the figure flowed back across the barren fields toward the dark wood.

If you would not be weak, consume the strong.

It was gone.

Wilhelm Rheinhart stood panting in the gathering darkness, blood dripping from his lower lip. He remained still for a long time and then, squaring his shoulders, opened the door to the long hall and walked out of his sickroom.

He found the old sword—his father always called it a gladius—in a cabinet in the library. The leather-bound books spanned to the ceiling, muffling the clank of the sword as he drew it from its short scabbard, its edges as sharp as when the sword had been issued to his father in the War Between the States. A short wide blade, a stabbing blade, it lay heavy and inert in the boy's hand.

His mother sat in the parlor, at the piano, when he found her. Holding the blade flat, the boy came up behind her and drove the sword into her back with a violent movement, piercing her heart. She arched her back and drew in one surprised breath, and never exhaled. Pitching forward onto the keyboard, her body made a jangled, minor chord. The flounces of her dress discolored with blood.

Turning, the boy walked from the room, face hard.

He found Karl in the kitchen with a serving woman. His brother ate raw sugar from a bowl, dipping wet fingers into the brown stuff, smiling at the serving woman who looked on.

Wilhelm chopped once with the sword, driving the blade deep into the woman's neck, then roughly jerked it out. Thick arterial blood sprayed across the kitchen. Her eyes bulged and blood frothed at her mouth. She toppled onto the floorboards near the stove.

Karl swung around from where he sat at the kitchen table and stared at his brother, caked in gore. He opened his mouth and brought sugar-rimed hands to his face, his eyes wide. He began to scream.

"Goodbye, brother," Wilhelm croaked as he drove the sword through Karl's open mouth. The scream died to a gurgle. Karl skittered on the end of the sword, vibrating as his body, with instincts of its own, tried to shake itself loose. Karl flopped backward onto the table, eyes vacant, body slack.

After Wilhelm cut his brother open, he ate Karl's heart with great wrenching, tearing bites, chewing each mouthful until he could swallow it, the salt and iron of the blood making him gag, so much so that he thought he might vomit it up in a clotted mess. He managed to keep it down, his aching jaws working strongly, the muscles grinding in his blood-smeared cheek, until it was finally gone.

Afterward, Wilhelm swooned, standing uneasily in a growing pool of blood. He cried, weeping like a boy alone in the woods, weeping for what he'd lost, and for what he'd gained. Tears streaked his face and, after a while, he started to feel a burning in his chest again.

Wilhelm stood and looked around at the kitchen in amazement, the sword slipping from numb fingers. It fell to the floor with a clatter. The sobs coming from his chest were so loud it took a while for Wilhelm to realize they were his own.

When his thoughts finally turned to his father, he made his way out into the night, the cicadas whirring their night-songs, the oaks throwing up black branches against the canopy of starry sky.

The thing that had once been a boy wiped his tears and moved forward into the night, into the dark wood, looking for his master.

Chapter 1

Memphis, 1951

"A man will uproot his life, move his home, his family, to avoid paying back one large. A measly grand. But he won't really *change*," Gene Corso said around his Havana, passing Ingram a slip of paper.

Ingram sat in the office, on a cul-de-sac off Poplar, facing Corso over an expanse of mahogany desk. Ceiling fans stirred the smoke in the air. At the far end of the office, beyond a plate-glass window, three men played cards and laughed at a joke.

Corso tapped a thick, ringed finger on the desk blotter.

Ingram glanced at the slip of paper. A name and license plate number. Ronald Meerchamp.

"He drives a blue Packard, white trim, they tell me. Got his license from the DMV. Just called up and asked for it, pretty as you please." Corso drew on his cigar. He looked at the tip and blew on the cherry. "This guy's a pussy hound. He likes the dark meat. And that means Pauline's."

Ingram knew the place. Off Gayoso and Pearl.

"You gonna be able to recognize him?"

"Yeah. He sat in on Wilson's poker game last week. Got took for a bundle."

"That was my fucking money. Tellya what, Bull. I'll give you ten percent of what you get back. And another job in a coupla days. Got a guy needing someone found in Arkansas. Weird job but it pays."

Corso brought a bottle out of his desk and poured whiskey into a crystal tumbler.

"We're done here. Send Mickey in on your way out." He sipped his drink.

Ingram stood and took his hat from the rack. He walked over to the three men playing cards.

The dour one sniffed and looked up at Ingram, a cigarette dangling from his lower lip.

"What? We got a game going here."

"Corso asked for you."

Mickey stood, cursing.

"Goddamn, you're a fucking big one, ain'tcha? They call you Bull cause you're so big? Or did your mother fuck cattle?"

Ingram put his hand on Mickey's shoulder.

"I wouldn't." The words were flat, inflectionless. Mickey coughed.

"Yeah, well, the boss wants me."

Ingram walked out into the Memphis heat.

His 1949 Plymouth Coupe sat sweltering at the curb. He threw his hat and jacket into the passenger seat. Sliding behind the wheel, he felt the sticky heat of the leather seats.

Driving east, Ingram smoked and hung his arm out the window to dry the armpits of his shirt. He twisted the knob on the radio until he found Nat King Cole on WDIA, crooning about a buzzard and a monkey.

The sun dipped in the west, casting long shadows across the street. Ingram turned off Union onto Gayoso, slowing, the coupe rumbling in low gear. He found the brothel on the corner of Pearl. No sign, just a line of cars parked down the street.

No blue Packard in sight.

He parked the coupe caddy-corner and watched as men wandered in and out of the large, frame house. Occasionally, a whore wandered out on the upper gallery to smoke. As the sun went down, the house brightened, the red curtains filtering bloody electric light onto the yard, the street. Ingram checked his watch. Drawing a pint from beneath his seat, he cracked the Federal Papers on the whiskey and sipped.

At 7:30, Ingram started the coupe and drove past Pauline's. He found a diner a few blocks away. After a porterhouse and fried potatoes, he drank coffee, chatting with the waitress. She had an ex-husband and a kid at Sewanee.

"He's a smart little kid, that Stephen. Always quoting stuff." Bad teeth and breath that smelled like shrimp.

Ingram nodded.

"You single?"

"Sure."

"Oh. Me too."

"That's nice."

"You serve?"

Ingram shook out a cigarette and tamped the loose tobacco on his wrist. She lit the tip with a match.

"Thanks."

"You see some action?"

"Pacific."

"My ex was a reporter." She snorted and put her hands on her hips. "Instead of a gun, they gave him a camera. He stayed in Washington. You believe that? The cheap bastard."

"Can't say I wouldn't have traded places with him."

She scratched at her hair with one lacquered fingernail.

"You want some more coffee?"

He threw down a five, smiled, shaking his head, and ducked through the door.

Back at Pauline's, he drove around the block until he spotted the blue Packard. Someone had done a poor job on the white racing stripes. He stopped long enough to match license numbers, then continued down the block. Ingram turned around and found a spot to park within twenty feet of the Packard. He smoked and watched Pauline's, taking an occasional sip from the whiskey.

The street was empty by the time Meerchamp staggered out onto the porch and toward his car. Untucked suspenders dangling at his sides, he walked with the rubbery gait of a sailor on leave, drunk and recently vigorous. At the car door, he fumbled with his keys. *I could do this now. But he might not have the dough on him.*

Meerchamp pulled onto Pearl and headed south.

Bugs made tracers in Ingram's headlights as he tailed the Packard. Meerchamp parked at a large apartment building. Ingram cruised the block before parking.

From the glove-compartment, he took a snub-nosed .38 and slipped it to the small of his back, followed by a foot-long leather-bound rod that he flattened to his forearm.

He entered the building, passed the elevator, and checked the mailboxes. Meerchamp 713A. He entered the stairwell and bounded up the steps by threes until he reached the seventh floor.

At apartment 713A, he stopped, scanned the hallway. No one. He rapped on the door.

The voice, when it came, was hesitant. "Who is it?"

Ingram kicked in the door, splintering the locks. He heard a satisfying *oof* as the door banged open.

Ingram moved into the apartment, ducking his head. Meerchamp lay on the floor in his shirt-sleeves and boxers, blinking.

"No!" the man screeched. "Help!"

Ingram clubbed Meerchamp's head with the sap, toppling the smaller man forward. He caught him by the neck with one big hand. Meerchamp's breath whooshed out as Ingram yanked him into his chest.

Desperate, he clawed at Ingram's eyes.

Ingram jerked his head back, snarling, holding Meerchamp out at arm's length. He tossed him through the door, into the kitchen. Meerchamp slammed into the cabinets, head-first, and slumped to the floor.

In a flash, Ingram was on him again, and dragged him to the sink, shoving the man's head under the spigot. He cranked the water on. Meerchamp spluttered and screamed, fighting Ingram's grip.

"Goddammit, you son of a whore! What do you want?"

Ingram banged Meerchamp's head in the sink. "Stop playing games. You know why I'm here. Where's the money?"

"What?" The man's voice pitched up an octave. "What money, what—"

Ingram pulled him from the sink and smashed his face with the sap. The nose went flat, and the blood started coming.

"The money. Where is it? Last chance."

"I don't know what you're talking about!"

A ceramic pitcher sat on the counter, filled with wooden spoons, spatulas, whisks, and a meat tenderizer. Ingram grabbed the tenderizer and forced Meerchamp's hand onto the counter.

"Where's the fucking money? Last chance."

"You already said last chance, you sonofabi—"

Ingram slammed down the pewter mallet. The first blow sank into Meerchamp's flesh and flattened the hand against the counter. The second blow pulped the man's little finger. Meerchamp's screams became frantic. No neighbors in sight but the man was getting too loud.

Ingram bashed his head against the counter to quiet him.

Meerchamp slumped to the kitchenette floor, face a bloody mess, eyes unfocused, barely moving. Ingram grabbed one of the dinette chairs and sat down, straddling it backward.

"You got whiskey?" Ingram said. "Left mine in the car."

Meerchamp glanced at the ice-box. Ingram found a fifth of vodka in the freezer. He twisted off the cap and placed the open bottle at his mouth. Meerchamp sucked greedily.

"You're gonna lose those fingers." Pulling the bottle away, Ingram brought it to his own lips and took a drink. "I can't understand why you don't just cough up the dough."

Meerchamp closed his eyes, leaning forward. Ingram propped the man up and patted his cheek.

"Goddamn. Why didn't you just pony it up?" Ingram shook his head. "Fuck. Put out your hand."

The smaller man looked at Ingram blankly.

Ingram stood up and grabbed a dish towel. "You can die from wounds like that, soldier. Put out your hand."

The man stuck out his paw, and Ingram poured vodka over the man's hand. Meerchamp screamed, but weakly now.

"Ssshhhh, hush."

He fished his cigarettes out of his pocket, shook two out of the pack. He lit them with a Zippo, the hard metal sound of it bright in the kitchenette.

Ingram removed a cigarette from his mouth, reversed it, and placed it in Meerchamp's bloody maw. Smoke drifted weakly from his nostrils.

"Listen. Here's how it is. You owe Mr. Corso a grand. I don't know how or why you borrowed it. I don't care. All I know is that Mr. Corso sent me here to collect."

Ingram took a deep drag on his smoke. "Now, I'm not a torturer. There's things I won't do. But I've been told to either get the money, make you see some reason, or throw you out the window. So why don't you smoke your cigarette and think about it. Here, have another drink."

Ingram put the vodka bottle again to the wounded man's lips. Liquor and blood drooled from the corners of the man's mouth. They smoked in silence until Ingram, taking one last drag, ground out his cigarette.

"Okay, where's the dough? If you don't pony up, you'll fly."

The man's eyes grew wide and shifted left.

"In there?" Ingram snatched him up like a doll, and pushed him into the living room.

"Where is it?"

"Ooovah deerah. Pest oo waresh."

"What? Chest of drawers?" He spotted a chest with a radio on top. "There?"

The man nodded. Ingram sat him on the couch, and went to the bureau and rifled through it. He found a wad of money in a clip, a pint of cheap brandy and a military issue .45, and Meerchamp's car keys. Ingram counted the money. Eight hundred dollars. He pocketed the cash and keys.

The little man was unconscious. Ingram searched the apartment.

In the bathroom, he found some Vaseline and rubbing alcohol. He poured rubbing alcohol over the man's mangled hand, smeared it with Vaseline, then bound the mess as best he could with the shredded linens.

Corso won't be pleased at the short change. But that's not my fault. I just collect.

Chapter 2

"**M**r. Ingram! You gots a telephone call!"
An insistent voice from the hall.
"Telephone, Bull! Mr. Phelps from Helios Studios on the line!"

A band of light stabbed into the darkness of the room from a dormer window.

"Mr. Phelps is on the party line for you! You best get up and get it." The voice was thick, feminine, familiar.

He rose slowly, hair tousled and back hunched. He hobbled over to the wash basin atop his chest of drawers. Ingram's scars shone silver in the half-light of the room. He splashed water on his face, grabbed a shirt and pulled it on.

"Hold on, Maggie! Go tell him I'm coming, willya? That's a girl." He winced at the sound of his own voice.

Downstairs, standing rumpled and bleary in the kitchen, Ingram took up the telephone receiver and said, "This is Ingram."

"Hold the line, sir. Mr. Phelps will be with you in a moment."

18

Female, young, and shapely if her voice was any indication.

After a moment of rustling, a man came on the line.

"This Bull Ingram?" The voice was bright and articulate.

"Lewis, sir. And yes, that's me."

"My name is Sam Phelps. I want you to come to my studio to discuss a little job." It all came out quick but measured, each word popping easily, distinct and forceful, firing down the wire, through the receiver into Ingram's ear.

"Well, Sam—"

"Mr. Phelps to you, son. I know something about you. I'm... friends...with Gene Corso, who you've been freelancing for. He recommended you to me."

"OK, Mr. Phelps. That's aces with me. Where are you?"

"We're at 706 Union. I'll expect you here at three." He hung up.

In the kitchen, Ingram looked around. Maggie bustled in the communal dining room, cleaning up the remains of breakfast.

"There any way I can get something to eat? Some milk or bread or something?"

Maggie looked at Ingram with lidded, amused eyes.

"Bull, a man as big as you ought get up in time for breakfast. You know Mrs. Fahey's rules; breakfast is served when breakfast is served. No sneakin' and no favorites."

"I was out late."

"You always out late." Maggie looked around theatrically, checking to see if an obviously absent Mrs. Fahey was about. "It don't matter. You go get cleaned up, and I'll put a plate in your room. There's some ham and cornbread left."

For a moment Ingram just stood in the kitchen, helpless, his brain pounding, and marveled at the kindness of near strangers.

"Thanks, Maggie. That's real...well, thanks."

Maggie put her hands on her ample hips and looked at him, a little curious, a little sad. Her dark skin shone luminous in the light of the kitchen window.

Voice softer, she said, "Bull, that's all right. I know you a good boy. You was in the war over there. I'd be a bad person if I didn't help you out, everything you done for us."

"I haven't done anything," he said.

"Go on, Bull. Go get cleaned up, and I'll bring you a little plate."

After a shower in the communal bathroom, Ingram took his time grooming, the white of the shaving cream contrasting starkly with the deep black circles under his eyes. From his closet he withdrew cuffed slacks and a crisp white shirt, open collared. Dressed, he pulled the shades and sat smoking in the dark, filling the small room with smoke, thinking.

Strange man, that Phelps, brusque yet friendly, forceful yet jovial. Ingram remembered Captain Haptic from the USS *Cleveland*, a similar kind of man. Flinty hard, yet able to tell jokes so profane that men had trouble holding in their laughter doing pushups. Forty-five miles out of Borneo, the crew carrier came across that fucking Jap sub with escort, perforating the sides of the cruiser, making her as carious as some rotten tooth. The Marines—doing exercises on the deck—glistened in the sun, Cap Hap bellowing at their side, a continuous froth of good natured bile, vinegar for the soul of the Marine doomed to die. Then the world wrenched, and the *gahn gahn gahn* of 50 cals came, at first distant but growing. Men cursing and bellowing with fear and exaltation after months of boredom, the *gahn gahn gahn* growing louder until it filled all perception and men fell out, scattered in fear. Marines, mean sons of bitches, bailing and scattering, and people yelling, "Bull, get yer ass up!" But he was immobile, still frozen in the half-lunge of a pushup, head cocked and looking up at Cap Hap who, fully reg, still loomed over Ingram, finger pointed, making some profane point about the virtue of a Jakartan whore. The whole world wrenched horribly once more. Ingram looked back at the Cap. He'd been replaced by a mist, a billowing and intangible ghost, drifting up all crimson, rising up into the Pacific air, rising and dissipating into the yellow light, dispersing on the wind while the growl and scream of klaxons beat thinly at the air.

A soft rap sounded at the door. Maggie entered, carrying a wax-paper-covered plate. She placed it on his chest of drawers and looked around the room. Clothes, ashtrays, and empty bottles littered the floor. Out of date newspapers covered the room's single chair.

She waved her hands in the air dramatically, clearing the smoke, and walked to the window. She drew back the curtains. Light flooded the room, bringing grimaces to both Ingram's and Maggie's faces.

"Oooh-ee, you sure ain't got no house training," she said. "I've been here at Mrs. Fahey's since before the war, seen many young men, just like you. But none as big. Or as messy."

She paused, putting her hand on her hip. "I was thinking, Bull."

"Congratulations."

She laughed, waving off his comment.

"Bull, you know I got grandchildren."

He grunted.

"I'd be happy to take care of this room for you, make sure you eat and sleep right, for just a little bit extra."

Ingram stubbed his cigarette out into an already overflowing ashtray.

"What're their names?"

"What?"

"Your grandchildren. Their names. What are they?"

Maggie paused. "Fisk and Lenora."

"Lenora is a pretty name."

"She's a pretty girl. So how 'bout it?"

"What're we talking about?"

"Five dollars. Every two weeks. I make sure your room is clean, even if you're out late. You'll have food in the morning, whenever you need it." Maggie thought for a moment. "But I ain't gonna cover up nothing for you, or get you no sauce. And I'll make sure the house is safe. Lord, I do that already."

"I can take care of myself."

"Whoo-ee. And this room sure looks it."

Ingram stood, paused for a moment.

"Deal."

Ingram smiled as mischievously as his blunt face would allow. With a great flourish, he spat into his fist. "Shake on it."

Spitting into her palm, Maggie grinned back, showing empty teeth.

Ingram laughed, and they shook. Maggie said, "A bargain, then. Five dollars in advance."

❧

Later that day, Ingram pulled his coupe to the curb at Helios Studios, 706 Union, feeling quite underwhelmed. As Ingram approached, two Negroes with guitars exited the front door, shaded by a Bradford Pear. Both men looked upset and angry, faces pulled down in distaste.

What pissed those fellas off?

One of the black men made the sign of the cross, removed a necklace from his open collar, and kissed it.

Out of the coupe, Ingram's white shirt began to discolor. The thick summer air was oppressive, stifling. The haze felt almost palpable. The slow-moving Mississippi cast water into the air like some long brown moccasin sloughing off its skin as it crawled downstream.

Inside, the air conditioning beaded the windows with condensation. A blonde woman with heavy eye shadow attended the phone, chewing gum. She looked up as he entered.

"Bull Ingram?"

"Yeah. Lewis Ingram, ma'am."

"Mr. Phelps is waiting for you in the control room. Right over there." Her bracelets jangled as she pointed. "Please refer to Mr. Phelps as Mr. Phelps. That is his preference."

Ingram stopped. "OK, will do. Any other advice?"

She laughed. "Hell yes, sugar. Tell the bastard to give me a raise. And if he asks you to do something, go ahead and do it. It's easier that way, and nobody gets hurt."

Ingram smiled, then pulled his shoulders back, brushing his head against the ceiling.

"Hurt?"

"Figure of speech."

In the control room, Phelps listened to music, strange dark music.

In the Marines, Ingram heard whatever played at the USO Dances and even, when the *Cleveland* was East Indes-bound, the broadcasts of Tokyo Rose. Jensen, Ingram's bunk-mate, built a quartz radio from Quaker Oatmeal cans and crystals, carefully feeding an antenna from the lower bunk to the floor and then the hull. The metal of the ship itself worked amazingly well as a receiver. In the deeps of Pacific night Jensen and Ingram would listen to the far-off broadcasts of Tokyo Rose, her soft taunting voice loathsome and exciting. But the USO dames and even Tokyo Rose would play music as tame and sanitized as any government meal. Ingram heard this new dark music and felt moved and upset and aroused all at once. The deep beats and rhythms, the mournful wails from Negro mouths singing such plain rhymes so heartfelt, so stark and true, they struck him powerfully. For a moment he felt like he had never really heard music before, like he had been missing some component of his soul that had not come shipped in the original package.

In the room a man sat staring at a pad of paper filled with scribbles and figures. Electronics and speakers cluttered the space; the gray control panels butted up against a large plate window that opened into another room full of cords and microphones and instruments.

Phelps noticed him standing near the door, twisted a knob on the tape machine, silenced the music, and stood up. Phelps wore a dark suit with a thin black tie, hair slicked back into a greasy pompadour. He had an alert, quick face and a compact frame with large hands.

They shook, and Phelps motioned him in.

"Bull? Goddammit, son, Corso wasn't lying when he said you was a big one. You think that chair will hold you?"

Ingram sat down in answer.

"All right, Bull. Man of few words. I can appreciate that."

Phelps patted his chest pocket searching for his cigarettes. He flipped a Pall Mall up to his mouth and lit it, watching Ingram.

"Tell me about yourself, Bull. I like to get to know a man before I start giving him orders."

"Not much to tell. Born in Mississippi, joined the Marines in '43 when I was seventeen. After the war, came back to the States and knocked around for a little bit, saw some of the country. Bought a car and drove out to California. Didn't like it there so I came back here. Been here ever since."

"In the war, huh? That's good. You see much action over there?"

"No more than anybody else. Wouldn't want to do it again."

Phelps laughed a little too hard. "I'll bet... I'll bet. So what've you been doing since you got back? You stay employed?"

"Sure, Mr. Phelps. I keep busy. I run errands for Mr. Corso, the usual stuff."

Phelps eyes brightened, and he leaned a little closer to Ingram in his seat.

"You go out and find folks who owe Corso money?"

Ingram remained silent.

"How hard is it to find folks?"

Ingram looked around the room. It was a mess. He thought about it for a moment and then said, "Not too hard. People can't help talking. Nobody's gonna uproot their life for a couple hundred bucks. And that's what you'd have to do to get away from Mr. Corso. He's gonna find you."

"But you're the one who does the finding?"

"Sometimes."

Phelps smiled at the admission. He kept staring at Ingram intently, calculating. Then, as if he'd come to some conclusion in his internal dialogue, Phelps stubbed out his cigarette in the ashtray.

"OK, hoss. That's fine. Lemme tellya a little bit about what we do around here, and then I'll tellya what you're gonna do for me."

Phelps took a deep breath. "I come from Alabama, used to DJ down there. Didn't come from no rich parents, and I worked hard every day growing up, out in the field, helping my family raise the crops. But I knew sure as shit from a very early age that I wasn't going to be a farmer. I was too smart for that; I was a listener. I could hear things other people couldn't hear, changes in voices, true meanings behind the words."

Phelps smoothed his pants, stretched his back a bit, and resumed. "Now, I ain't saying I was some kinda psychic or anything like that. I just got a good knack of hearing what's behind the words, the tones, that people say... you know, son?"

Ingram found it strange to be called son by a man who, from the looks of him, couldn't be more than three or four years older than him.

"You ever spoken with someone, and knew, just knew, that he was lying, or he was telling the truth but there was something behind that truth that he wasn't telling? Or you just knew from the sound of his voice that he didn't wish you no good? Huh?"

Ingram thought about some of the men he served with. "I reckon so. Couple of times at least."

"Well, I'm good at it. Better than most. Might be the reason I became a DJ."

He pulled open a drawer and removed a bottle of Wild Turkey. Phelps poured them both generous glasses.

Phelps drained his glass. "I've got some trouble I need you to take care of for me. The first is one of my boys is missing and I need you to find him."

He pulled a picture from the same drawer and threw it on Ingram's lap with a quick jerk of his wrist. Startled, Ingram took the picture carefully in his hand, trying not to smudge the glossy surface. In the picture, a lean man with a goofy smile and a blond crew-cut stood next to a black man in a shiny suit, guitar in hand. Obviously taken in the studio.

"Which one am I supposed to find?" Ingram asked.

"The white one, of course, son. Keep up with me. His name is Earle Freeman. We call him Early cause he's always late. He's a good kid, one of my scouts. Served in the Army, did his time and got through it, knows how to handle himself in a fight, and in general, a good man to have around. I sent him out hitting all the stations in Arkansas with the new presses of Sonny Burgess and Billy Lee Riley. Forty-fives."

At the blank look on Ingram's face, Phelps said, "Bull, it's rhythm and blues. Ain't you ever heard of it? Negro music. And it's pure gold, let me tell you, gonna make me rich and Sonny and Billy too."

He paused. "Don't you know what I do here, son?" He sighed and then took another drag off of his cigarette. "What I do here is record black music. The boys come in, I flip this switch right here, and the microphones pick up all the sounds around them. Then we get records made of the songs we recorded. We send 'em out all over the South, to all the radio stations we can find.

"I started this company last year, and we're going cannonballs right now. I sent out Early with a box of forty-fives of this music—"

"That the music you were listening to when I came in?"

"You like that? Yes, that's the music. I sent Early out with a box of these here forty-fives and two grand to hit as many radio stations as he can. Now he's two weeks late getting back and his wife hasn't heard from him for a least ten days. I'm out a good man and two thousand dollars."

"Two thousand dollars seems like a lot of money for traveling around Arkansas. Ain't like there's nice hotels over there."

"Well, the money isn't all for traveling, if you know what I mean." Phelps smiled. "It's for promoting Helios artists and Helios products, that's what it's for."

"I don't follow, Mr. Phelps."

"Well," Phelps drawled, "Early drives around, might be Arkansas, might be Mississippi, might be Louisiana, just wherever we need more of a radio presence, and he visits every station, big or small—and, son, there's some goddamned small stations peppering the countryside, especially in Arkansas. You go west and cross the 70 bridge, it's like you're entering a whole different country over there, and it ain't friendly and it ain't even making any attempts at joining the rest of the civilized world, except for buying radios. But they sure do love their race music. So Early drives around and visits all the station owners, makes the deliveries of the forty-fives, and he might take the owner out to dinner, or maybe throw a little party for him, or maybe just give him a little green to hold him over. You know, son, one hand washing the other."

Ingram knew what Phelps was talking about; he'd seen it every day since arriving in Memphis. And Mr. Phelps had enough Memphis clout to arrange this meeting through Ingram's boss, who wasn't a man to trifle with.

"I understand," Ingram said.

"I'm sure you do." Phelps poured himself more whiskey. "So I need you to find Early and get back whatever forty-fives or money's left over and bring him back here. I'll split whatever is left of the dough with you. But it's not the dough that's the important part; Early's a good kid, and I don't think he'd run off. Or abandon his wife. So I'm a little worried about the goddamned idiot."

"Why didn't you just call the cops, put in a missing person's report?"

"Well, son, we did. But we're having a hard time figuring out who to call. We called the Arkansas State Troopers and let them know, and they said they'd keep an eye open for anyone matching Early's description, but we couldn't tell them a place to look because Early drives all over Arkansas. And maybe he hadn't been too diligent about checking in with me, which is my fault; I should've ridden him harder about that. Then we called the police station at Brinkley—which is Early's last known whereabouts, about four days old from the point he went missing—and the Brinkley police force has got a whopping two men, the sheriff and his deputy, and they sounded like they was going to tear up the earth looking for Early, at least once they got through with lunch. I tell you, it's backward over there. So we need you to find him for us; we need somebody, if Corso is to be believed, who can get the job done quick and professionally, not pass on any word of the payola and entertainment aspects of Early's job, and most important, keep his mouth shut. You got that, son?"

Ingram nodded.

Phelps pulled out his wallet and laid out five crisp twenty dollar bills on the studio's console. "Here's some operating cash, for gas, lodging, food. There's juke joints and barrelhouses all over eastern Arkansas that Early would go to and scout talent when he was on the road. Maybe you can get wind of his trail either there or at the stations. The last station I could find record of him visiting was in Brinkley, a boil on the ass of the South, that's for sure. KBRI is its call letters, broadcasting at 1570 AM. Man by the name of Couch was Early's contact there. You might want to talk to Early's wife, get the low down on his last call. Here's her address. After that, I want you to report to me twice a week."

"See Early's wife. Couch in Brinkley. WBRI. Report twice a week. Got it."

The older man drank, shivered with the alcohol, and said, "That's the first part of the job. Here's the second. Come over here and listen to this."

Phelps moved his chair over and manipulated the controls of a reel-to-reel recorder. The tape hissed on the spindles. Phelps turned to Ingram, hand on the machine's controls, and said, "The past month or so, we've been picking up a radio station out of Arkansas. It's a pirate radio station, which means it doesn't obey FCC regulations, doesn't broadcast its call letters every hour. I want you to find out where it's coming from. Who runs it."

Phelps gave Ingram a penetrating look. "You'll understand a little bit more after I play this for you." He flipped the switch, and the machine began to play.

From the speakers came harsh fumbling noises. Then silence. More noises and then Phelps' voice saying, "Get it over here. Just get the goddamned mic and put it by the radio's speaker! Right there—"

Scared. He's frightened.

More thumps and static sounded. Then Phelps screeched, "Turn up the volume! Turn up the radio!"

There were more hisses and scratches, then sound came from the speakers. A guitar, liquid and buzzing. But something else was layered over it, under it.

The guitar slurred out a melody, the player's fingers obviously dexterous, quickly alternating from finger picking to buzzing the slide, always returning to a minor melody. The guitarist kept time by stomping his feet.

Ingram shifted in his seat, fists balled into hard knots. Something was coming with the sound that he couldn't understand.

The stomps went beyond dull treads reverberating on wood. The percussion sounded like the foot of a slave still shackled and possessed. The percussive beat held the sound of a thousand slaves, bloody and broken and murderous, each walking forward with the rattle and clank of their broken shackles, knives whisking in their hands, walking through the night under black skies. The guitar's atonal buzz reached places in Ingram that had been deaf until then, each note curdled with madness and hatred, each measure meted out in some ethereal range that was perceived by more than ears—as if Ingram, not the radio, were the receiver and the invisible transmissions emanating out of the deep and dark fields of Arkansas held some frightening and terrible message just for him. As he listened, Ingram's skin grew clammy, and each hair stood on end.

Beyond the sun, beyond the stars
Beyond the long black veil
It whispers in the dark
Where light and love both fail
Where do you sleep?
Where did you fall?
Beyond the sun, beyond the stars
Waiting for our call
Beyond the sun, beyond the stars
Waiting for our call

The voice sounded hurt and reluctant. The lyrics repeated until they became a chant, rising and falling over the guitar and beat, rising and falling with little variation other than a growing sense of dread. More than the rhythm, more than the guitar, the man's voice made Ingram feel like something was wrong, like something was not right with the world and this man's words were the first outward sign of a deeply buried, world-spanning cancer.

Whoever is singing that horrible song... he doesn't want to. Those words hurt him. Jesus Christ.

The chanting continued, Ingram clenching his fists, grinding his jaws. He reached for his glass and downed the whiskey. He felt like the only way to make this feeling go away was to kill. Phelps or himself, it didn't really matter.

Behind the man's voice Ingram perceived another voice, a voice singing the same words in a harmony that made a mockery of any song that came before, that mocked any idea of love, or light or warmth.

He brought is hands in front of his face, tried to lower them, but they seemed to have a mind of their own. He turned toward Phelps.

A hiss started building, static in the signal, and Ingram heard the recording-Phelps cursing, adding his own chant. "Goddamn. Goddamn. Goddamn." The music crescendoed, the guitar fluttering and buzzing higher and higher, the voice (or voices, Ingram couldn't tell) pitching higher and more frantic, the percussion thumping frenetically like a body spasming on the floor.

Then silence.

Ingram breathed a sigh of relief and lowered his hands.

What was I about to do there? Kill him?

A voice, a man with polished tones, came on the recording. "That was 'Long Black Veil,' by Ramblin' John Hastur, a fella known about these parts. And a perfect tune to finish the night with. To finish all nights with." A few clicks and pops sounded, then hissing.

Phelps turned off the tape machine and looked at Ingram.

"Kinda curdles your milk, don't it?"

"I'll say. Never heard anything like that before. Don't know if I ever wanna hear anything like it again."

Phelps grinned, showing uneven teeth. "I want you to find out where that radio station is, and who made that recording. I had a couple of fellows come in here earlier today, they're from Arkansas, and players too, and they've never heard of John Hastur, nor heard that tune neither. And that's a little strange. Blues musicians are about the most unoriginal people to walk God's green earth. They won't write their own song if they can play someone else's, and they know every soul that came within a hundred mile of themselves, I guess from being so vain. Anyway, neither Hubert nor Jimmy had ever heard of the 'Long Black Veil' before. Not this version, at least. So I want you to find this Ramblin' John if you can. Best way to do that is to find out who's broadcasting him. So find that radio station, and from there, we'll find Ramblin' John."

"Why'd you want to put that kind of music on a record? Don't think anyone would want to buy it."

Phelps sucked his teeth. "Well, you're wrong about that. People would buy it. Maybe not in droves, but they'd buy it. Cause it's powerful, son. It's got that something. I watched you listening to it. It got to you." He fanned his hands out, like a child framing the sky. "And someone who can write a song that powerful, well... maybe he's got other songs... nicer songs."

"Or maybe songs that aren't so nice. But you're right, it does got something, and it's something I don't want."

Phelps guffawed, slapping Ingram on the shoulder. "But you'll do the job anyway, won't you, son?"

Chapter 3

"Look, Mommy! A barn *and* a tractor!" Franny cried, pointing out the car's window.

Sarah looked at the farmlands on both sides of the highway. "Yes, baby. I see."

Perched beside Sarah on the bench seat of the sedan, Franny smiled and watched the country rolling past her window. Dressed in a pink frock with white trim, hair pulled into a bun at the back of her head with a red bow, she kicked her legs aimlessly, her heels thumping on the car seat. She grinned at Sarah, eyes sparkling, and exclaimed at the passing animals and buildings as they drove.

Sarah sneaked glances at her daughter as she drove. Little Rock diminished behind them; before them lay Gethsemane, her family home. Little Rock was the only home Franny had ever known.

Sarah's hand went to the bruise on the line of her cheek, the tenderness there. Luckily, it hadn't discolored too much, just yellowed a bit and that was easily covered by concealer. He'd been dead drunk and insensible. When she refused his embrace, turning her

32

face away from his gin-laced breath, he'd swung, his fist catching her on the chin, sending her reeling. She had hit the wall and sat down, hard, on her ass. He dragged her by the hair to the bed, but when he mounted her, he couldn't get hard. The booze had finally unmanned him.

When he was sleeping, she went to the kitchen and stood there for a long time with a knife in her hand, looking at the ceiling. Finally, she shoved the knife back in the drawer and gathered up as many suitcases as she could find. By morning, she and Franny were packed.

He came down the stairs like he was in some war-torn European country, wary and tense. She was waiting for him. In measured tones, Sarah informed Jim that she was taking Franny home to Gethsemane, to the Big House, the house she grew up in, to help take care of her mother, dying of lupus and beginning to suffer from dementia.

There was no mention of the bruises on her face. She felt like a coward for not confronting him, but the only thing that kept her coherent was the thought of what Franny might think of her, of Jim, of herself.

Sarah's eyes remained dry as she told him they were leaving, and Franny looked back and forth between her parents trying to discern what was actually being said. Jim cursed her, picked up his paper, and opened it with a pop. He remained sitting, and slowly drank his coffee as Sarah gathered up their bags, loaded Franny into the car, and drove away.

She couldn't understand why their marriage took this sorry course; it seemed so wonderful and bright when he'd first come back from overseas—wounded, yes, but alive and the whole world celebrating victory. Sarah held that victory close to her heart and took ownership of it, as if it were her own. And in some ways it was her victory. She'd stayed chaste and worked at the local radio factory, assembling pieces of communications equipment, radios, receivers, speakers. There were always men wanting to sleep with her—and some she wanted in return—but she remained firmly and obviously married, as steadfast as Penelope. She'd written to her husband every day, filling her letters with happiness and the minutia of life at home, at the radio factory, ending each letter with a smear of lipstick and a spray of perfume. At Jim's homecoming there was happiness and love and warm nights spent sweating in bed, his body over hers, arms pinioning her to the mattress, waist to waist, and she'd never felt anything like it before. She'd loved that; his body, how he moved with such freedom on top of her. He inspired her, he changed her. She found she could discard the matronly inhibitions that the world—her society and relations—exacted upon her, and in the bedroom be free, free of thought and speech, everything distilled down to the slap of flesh on flesh, sweat pouring, lips finding lips.

But the war took its toll on Jim too, the silvery scars on his chest and legs, his nightmares and hollow-eyed days. And as those days passed, then the months, Jim's drinking grew deeper and his work, running the printing company his father founded, made demands on him that became harder for both him and Sarah to bear—the lonely nights, the horrible aftermath mornings. When he was home, he drank, and demanded things of her she couldn't—or wouldn't—do. Then one morning—Jim seething in his hangover, angry at her, angry at the world—Sarah stood up, bolted to the bathroom, and retched over the toilet. He looked simultaneously surprised and chagrined. For that day, he felt like a man again, now that the baby was testament to his virility. But the next night he didn't come home until the early morning, stinking of gin and cigarettes. The baby saved Sarah. But nothing could save Jim.

From the moment she laid eyes on her daughter, Sarah marveled at the beauty that had come from her own body. When Sarah looked into the mirror, she saw tired eyes and a crooked nose, the scar on her eyelid and the gray at her temples. *Not so gray, and my figure is still good.* And Franny, now small for her age, had flaxen hair that was almost white, thin delicate features, slim forearms, and a long neck traced by bluish veins that ran to her temples—translucent and filled with so much light that it suffused her underneath her skin. Sarah felt as though she could see Fran's insides, the hard skeleton framing the foam-like flesh, letting the light through. That child was her care and her heart.

"Look, Mommy, a cow!" Franny cried, and then, "We're going to Mimi's!" She had said that over and over. "Mimi's!"

"Yes, baby. Mimi's sick."

"She's turning into a wolf, daddy says, like in *Little Red Riding Hood*."

Damn him.

"No, baby, she's not turning into a wolf. She's just sick, and she's been sick for a while. And the sickness Mimi's got makes her skin look funny. We're going to help her get better."

They drove in silence until Franny said, "Ooh, look, Mommy! A cow and a dog!"

They left Little Rock that morning, and now, three hours later, they neared Gethsemane. Sarah pulled the sedan off Highway 31 and took the small dirt road through the orchard, the road lined with pecan trees littering the ground with their seed, the fields half obscured by the diagonal rows of trees.

They called the Rheinhart estate the Big House. The field hands and laborers who worked the land, ministered the tractors and ushered the grain into silos—to them all, it was the Big House. As Fran and Sarah approached the old beauty, with its high dormered windows, deep shadows among the galleries behind tall columns, the Big House stood half in darkness and half in the fierce light of noon.

How many summer afternoons did I spend on that porch? With Daddy and Baird and Uncle Gregor, books and lemonade and then boys and later Jim before he was sent off to the war? On that porch he courted me, and Daddy brought out the courting candle and set it to burn a long time because Jim was going into OCS. But Jim was hours away now, surely drinking at his office or at the nearby bar, and tonight she wouldn't have to sleep with Franny for fear of marital obligations or of strange midnight rants on the iniquities of men and women. The Big House was home, and Sarah felt welcomed and surrounded by it, driving down the pecan-lined lane.

Now closer, Sarah observed the decay of the old family estate, the scaling paint, the wisteria eating at a column on the front porch, crumbling the molding and slumping the porch downward. *That wasn't there the last time I was here, but wisteria grows fast.*

As the sedan rumbled up in the graveled drive, Alice came out the front door and waved, smiling big, her apron white against her dark skin. Sarah had known Alice as long as she had lived. When she was five, Sarah, laughing, gave Alice one of her china dolls, the Negro one from Germany that she'd received from Uncle Gregor that Christmas. With that act, she won Alice's love and they became friends, the daughters of servant and landowner. They had grown up together under Alice's mother's watchful eye, until the day that Alice had grown old enough to assist her mother and Maggie needed to go home to Memphis to attend her parents.

Sarah exited the car. Alice ran down the steps, and they hugged fiercely, holding each other for a long while. Alice said, "Ooh, girl. It's been too long since you been back. Come on inside, I've made your favorite. And who might this be?"

Alice broke from Sarah and turned toward the car; Fran stood frozen on the white gravel of the drive, a hesitant smile curling her lips.

"Alice, let me introduce you to my daughter, Franny." Sarah nodded from woman to child and said, "And Franny, this here's Alice, who I told you about."

"Mommy says you talk in your sleep."

The women laughed, and Alice said to her while looking at Sarah, "Only when your momma ain't here to kick me. But, Lord, girl, are you fair." Alice reached out and touched Franny's shining hair. "Child, you look like you swallowed a hundred-watt bulb." Alice squatted on her knees and whispered, mock theatrical, "Franny, can I tell you a secret?"

Franny nodded, her eyes big.

"There's some kids hiding on that side of the house," Alice said, flipping her head toward the corner. "And they've been waiting to show you the peafowl."

Squeals and laughter came from the side of the house, children caught hiding. Then, with yelps and high-pitched whoops, two children rounded the corner of the old house and barreled toward the driveway, jumping and waving their arms. Franny ran to meet them, squealing too. When she neared the two older children, she stopped short, like a puppy encountering a larger, unfamiliar dog. The girl put her hands on her hips proudly, while the boy did a nervous dance, hopping from one foot to the other.

"My name's Fisk, and she's—"

"Fool! I can introduce myself. My name's—"

"Lenora," Fisk said, beaming. "She's my sister."

"And he's my idiot brother, Fisk."

Fisk turned on his older sister. "It gonna be real funny when Fran watches me knock you on your butt."

Lenora stepped away, and looked at Fisk, down her nose. "Yeah. Go on and try it, lil man. Fran here'll be laughing when I put you on *your* back."

Lenora raised a fist as though she was going to hit her brother in the face; Fisk stared at her, unblinking.

"You gonna do it?" he asked. Lenora turned away, shaking her head. Franny turned to glance at Sarah with a look that said, "What am I supposed to do here?"

The children, caught in a patch of sunlight, took turns shaking Franny's small hand, grinning big. They matched, somehow, the dark-skinned brother and sister and the bright, luminous little girl.

Fisk jittered, moving left and right, hopping.

"We got some peafowl," he said, sticking out his chest.

"We ain't got no peafowl, Fisk. Her gramma do, and we just take care of 'em."

"Well, there's some peafowl here. You're gonna love 'em, though don't mess with the big boy, Ole Phemus. Only got one eye, and he's meaner than the Devil."

Franny asked, "Peafowl?"

"Yeah, you know. Peacocks? Big fan tail, all green and blue and pink. Come on, we'll show you."

Franny looked at her mother again. Sarah mouthed the word "go," giving a shooing motion with her hands. The children dashed off, running back around the house, flapping arms, singing, laughing.

Alice called, "Stay by the Big House, y'all! And there's a yellow jacket nest by the shed! Make sure Franny don't get near them! You hear me Fisk? Lenora!"

Sarah followed Alice up onto the porch, into the house, walking through the quiet rooms, footfalls soft on the ancient weathered rugs. She'd heard those soft sounds a million times before but now they seemed new. She looked at her old home as if she'd never seen it before. And in a way, she hadn't. There was a lot of water under that particular bridge.

Alice led Sarah into the kitchen and said, "Your momma's having a bad day today. Chest hurting and short of breath. You can go up there in a little bit. First, come over here and let me look at you."

Alice drew Sarah by her hands and turned her to face the light spilling into the kitchen from the window above the sink. "Girl, you look tired here." Alice touched Sarah's temple lightly. "And here." Touched her heart, above her breast. "I see he's been rough with you." Her hand went to the bruise at Sarah's cheek.

"Alice…" Sarah didn't know what to say.

"All men unman themselves, eventually. They don't even need us to help them. They'll do it on their own. But when they're limp, when they're powerless, they're the most dangerous."

"Alice… I don't—"

"Sssh. Don't worry. He won't ever touch you again. You're home now, and I'm gonna take care of you, just like I always did. You're my girl. Always was. Always will be." Alice smiled, then hugged Sarah fiercely. Sarah remembered.

When she was younger, Alice watched after her, a glorified babysitter, a companion, vigilant and ever-watchful for dangers to body and soul and virtue. Once, when the Alexander boy asked to go walking with Sarah in the grove, and Sarah's father nodded once in response, the boy took her hand and they walked into the trees, the smell of burning fields filling the autumn air. Out of sight of the Big House, they kissed, even though Sarah had been a little too young to understand the demands of a young man's body. He held her close, pressing his body tightly to hers, his mouth heavy. He had tasted of peppermints and tobacco, not altogether unpleasant, and Sarah hadn't really minded the kissing, the tight embrace. But then his hands moved on her back and she felt a little uncomfortable, then more uncomfortable when he pressed his pelvis tight to her waist. She pushed him away, just a little too hard, and he fell on his back, face clouding with anger, then surprise, his eyes locked on something behind her. Sarah almost knew, when she turned, what she would see. Alice, standing quietly by a pecan tree not ten feet away, staring at the Alexander boy, a heavy branch clasped in her fist, her calico dress ruffling slightly with the breeze. There was no doubt in Sarah's mind what she'd have done with the branch if he'd gone too far. The boy had run away.

Best of friends, Sarah heard them say, the folks in the town's main street, as she walked by, that Rheinhart girl and her colored servant. Like she got herself a slave. Which hurt Sarah more than anything. She had never asked Alice for anything—protection, service—nothing except love and that was all she offered in return. Indeed, Sarah thought, if anyone owns anyone in this relationship, she owns me. I'm her girl, always returning to her, coming back to the home she provides.

Now, in the kitchen, Alice gripped her tight and said, "You know, I ain't gone let nothing happen to my girl. And that Franny! Whoo-ee. You sure make a pretty baby." She shook her head. "Jim weren't always so hard, was he? It'd kill me if all this time you spent away from me was... I don't know... wasted."

"He's... all right. He works hard." She tried to keep the tears back. "I love him, but... no more. He's not the man I married. Something in him was broken. Over there. In the war."

"Drinks too much as well, I hear."

"How can you hear that? You're three hours away."

"Shoot, girl, you know I got my doodlebugs." An old joke between them; Alice, since she was a child, claimed she had the *gris-gris*, the hoodoo charms that her grandmother and mother passed down to her. And the doodlebugs were, as far as Sarah could understand, the invisible familiars that Alice used to discover things. Sarah imagined them as little floating points of light that wafted out into the world and took in information, then returned to Alice and reported, like sentient will-o-wisps.

Sarah, suddenly glad to be home and with Jim behind her, laughed.

Alice joined her, laughing. "Well, you know I gotta check in on you every once in a while, since you run away from me... Shoot, girl, I understood why, though. That Jim, ain't been a better lookin' man round these parts in an age. Hard to believe he'd go so sour."

Sarah blushed; yes, Jim had been gorgeous, but less so every day. "He's fair seeming."

"Easy to seem fair." Alice sucked her teeth. "If I ever see him again, he'll find a knife in his damned belly."

Sarah was caught between worry and gratitude; she had no doubt Alice would do what she said.

"So, you ever hear from... Calvin?" Sarah hoped that was the right name.

"Shoot, he ran off with some other woman, I guess. I shouldn't never have fallen in love with no blues man. Always on the road. Every night, a different town, different juke joint, lots of ladies to choose from. He vanished a couple of years ago."

"I'm sorry," Sarah said.

"Only person who's sorry should be Calvin."

"But what about the kids, don't they miss him?"

"He weren't ever around here enough for them to give a damn. Occasionally Fisk asks after him, takes out the guitar Calvin left and picks a little bit, but he's the youngest and didn't have his heart broken as much as Lenora."

Alice paused, then moved to the counter.

"Coffee?" she asked.

"No. I better go see my mother."

"Ain't no easy way to say this, but she looks horrible. Her skin has got all dark, you know, how the disease works. Doc Polk said this might happen. Anywho, it's tight and hard, her voice is all ripped up, and well… she's dying, ain't no secret. She's been drinking plenty too. To ease the pain, you know?"

"How much?"

Alice brushed her apron and looked down. "I guess maybe 'bout… oh… maybe a bottle of port every couple of days." Alice wouldn't meet Sarah's eyes.

Sarah nodded. A strange numbness came on her; her mother was dying and a drunk now as well. "She due for another dose, Alice? And why doesn't the doctor prescribe something for her, to ease the pain?"

"Doc Polk did, but it made her vomit and he ain't been back since. Might've been that your momma might've acted like your momma."

"What, haughty and imperious?" Sarah said.

"What? No, just bossy and rude, you know, like she always been." Alice smiled.

Sarah laughed. "Yes. Well, show me where the port is and I'll take it up there. If you could check on Franny, I'd really appreciate it."

Alice touched Sarah's hand, resting on the block. "It's gonna be all right. You be strong, and when you come back down, I'll have you a nice piece of minced meat pie and a pot of some strong hot coffee. How's that sound?"

Sarah smiled, and put her other hand on top of Alice's and squeezed. "Alice… I'm so glad to be home. With you."

Alice winked at her and said, "Go on, now. It's a hard thing you have to do, so you better go on and do it. The port's in the library, where it's always been. There's a tray there, clean glasses and the bottle. There's extra bottles below the dry bar."

Sarah walked down the hall, away from the kitchen, toward the library. The library doors stood shut like she remembered from childhood. How many times had she walked this hall with dread?

Waiting for her father or, when she was even younger, her grandfather? Or her Uncle Geeg? Happy Gregor.

She slid the doors back, into the pockets in the walls. The library was still, filled with light slanting in from the big bay windows facing the south fields. On the northern wall stood books—hundreds, thousands of books from floor to ceiling—their dark bindings gathering weight and gloom in the otherwise bright room. A desk, solid cherry wood with lion's paws for feet, sat in the center of the room with a small green shaded light and leather chair.

Sarah remembered when she was a little girl and her grandfather, Gregor, and her father closeted themselves in here, surrounded by books, pipes filling the room with smoke redolent of cherry and brimstone. Her mother would bring her in once the sun set, and she kissed each man in turn, their whiskers tickling her nose, the musky smell of the books mixing with their pipes and the Scotch they drank in leaded tumblers. Gregor, brightly dressed in greens contrasting with his red hair, his pot-belly popping over his belt, forked beard jutting wildly, would exclaim over her. He would touch her cheek, or her hair—which had been at least as flaxen as Franny's—and then grab her in a big bear hug and twirl her around until she felt dizzy, laughing while her father watched, unspeaking. Daddy would often turn back to his book then, while Gregor spoke to her with soft questions and smiles, asking about her days, what she had learned at school. And then he'd cocoon her in his arms, lift her up, and carry her to bed. As her eyelids drooped and breath came heavy, he'd sing, sometimes in French, sometimes in German, sometimes in English, a big silhouette sitting comfortably by her in the dark.

Don't say a word. Mockingbird. Don't sing. Diamond ring. Don't shine. Silver mine. Her Gregor, her Ungle Geeg.

As she grew older, she'd listen at the doors before going in, eavesdropping on their conversations; but she never understood. Gregor had a keen interest in books and spices and language while her father always seemed to want to find something or someone. Her grandfather just seemed lost.

*I wish Gregor was here now, to kiss me with his whiskers and take
me upstairs and tuck me in.*

She sighed and walked over to the dry bar, a small waist-high
cabinet inset into the vast wall of books. Inside she found a row of
crystal decanters, each bearing a wrought silver tag. Scotch. Bourbon. Port. Brandy. And, alone, a name-brand bottle. *Wellings Fine,
A Spanish Fortified Wine* read the label. It sat on a tray with a
delicate stemmed glass, rimed with gold. Sarah took the tray and
went back toward the kitchen, through the dining room to the
great stair.

She walked up the grand staircase, moving down the gallery
overlooking the first floor atrium, the fine Persian rugs lining the
wooden floors and muffling her footsteps. Sarah had forgotten the
beauty of her old home, the delicate *fleur di lis* and intricate trellis
work adorning the wood of the upper gallery, the crystal facets of
the now-dark chandelier hanging parallel with her as she looked
down over the front atrium, the rich paintings of the old scions
and merchantmen of the Rheinhart clan. Her ancestors.

At her mother's door, she stopped, breathing deeply, the silence
of the house surrounding her, calming her. She knocked twice,
softly, and entered.

The room smelled foul, like alcohol and urine.

It was dark, the curtain drawn, and as she moved forward, her
foot caught on something that went clattering.

"*Unn.* Alice? That you? What time is it?" The voice was scratchy
and hoarse, but still her mother.

Sarah realized she was holding her breath and exhaled. "No,
Momma. It's not Alice. It's me."

Silence. Then an indrawn breath. "Sarah? *My* Sarah? It's been so
long. I don't know if I even remember what you look like."

Sarah placed the tray on the bed and went to draw the curtains.
For a moment, just before she pulled them apart, Sarah had the
most bizarre feeling. A phantom of her lonely mind maybe, but
she was certain that instead of her mother, there was a grinning,
slavering wolf panting there in the dark, grinning at her. Sarah

grabbed the curtains, the small of her back itching, and pulled them aside, flooding the room with light.

It wasn't as bad as she had imagined, but the lupus had taken its toll on her mother. Elizabeth Werner Rheinhart's face had darkened into a leather mask, the flesh of her cheeks, her nose and chin and lips a dark, mottled red. Elizabeth's eyes were crimson as well, throughout what would have normally been the white part of the eye. Her body was wasted, thin. But the only truly frightening thing about her mother, was, as always, her gaze, the intense scrutiny that stripped Sarah to bone, seeing through her, judging.

"Oh, baby, it's okay. The doctor said this is just passing. Just a passing phase. I'm gonna get over this. Did you bring up my afternoon sip?"

"Yes, Momma. Here it is." Sarah poured the glass full of amber liquid and placed it in her mother's white hand.

Her mother downed it quickly, and said, "Ah," and settled deeper into the cushions of the bed. "One more." Elizabeth nodded at the bottle.

As Sarah refilled the glass, she asked, "How are you... um... how are you feeling?"

Elizabeth took the glass and looked at Sarah, face inscrutable from the mask of lupus. "How the hell you think I feel, you ninny? Like hammered shit."

The older woman blinked owlishly, shook her head, then said, "I'm sorry, baby. I've always been such an old crab-apple to you. And now... now that I'm sick, I haven't gotten any better."

Sarah looked down at her mother's hands, resting on the comforter.

Elizabeth shook her head, sighed, and said softly, "It's bad, honey. I can feel my heart twitching in my chest, and it's hard to breathe sometimes. My joints have all swollen to the size of grapefruits, and it's a bitch to walk, even to my vanity. But I've got my peafowl, and I've got Alice, who's a savior, though she don't know it and I'm not gonna tell her." Elizabeth downed the second glass of port and put the glass on the tray.

She looked around the room as if checking for visitors. "And I've been seeing things," she whispered. "Bloody footprints all through the house. Sometimes I hear someone banging on the piano. At first—"

She held out her hand for another glass. Sarah refilled it and handed it to Elizabeth.

"At first I just thought it was Fisk or Lenora, but Alice assures me that they're prohibited from going into the parlor. I told her I'd terminate her employment if I ever found them in there."

"Momma! You didn't."

"Hell, yes, I did, Sarah. They have to know some limits." She sipped. "Sometimes I hear whisperings, coming from the library. But when I go in, they stop."

Sarah slowly shook her head.

"Momma, you're just tired is all. And in pain."

"No, you ninny. There's something going on." She gave a weak smile, showing yellow teeth. "Sorry."

Sarah reached out and touched her mother on the cheek, the dark part.

"Don't cry, baby. I'm gonna be all right."

Sarah reached up and discovered her own cheek wet with tears.

"Baby, it's gonna be okay," her mother said. "We'll figure it out, now that you're here. Maybe it's just my imagination."

Sarah bowed her head like a child. She pressed her cheek to her mother's breast, found bone where she had once found soft flesh, and wept. Her mother shushed her and brushed her hair. "Sssh, baby. It's gonna be okay, we're gonna be all right. Everything's gonna be all right now that we're together."

Sarah cried into her mother's breast, hoping with all her heart it was true.

Chapter 4

The morning after the Meerchamp collection, Ingram called Ruth Freeman on the kitchen phone. She sounded happy, eager even, to see him as soon as possible. She gave him directions to their bungalow on Bellevue, off Poplar. An infant squealed in the background.

Maggie, bustling about in the kitchen, smiled at Ingram. He placed the phone's receiver on the cradle.

"You been busy, I see. Hope you found your room to your liking. Must've come in late; I didn't hear you come in last night."

Ingram smiled back, resting his haunches on the counter near the phone.

"I got in pretty late. Usual. Had a job to do, and it took a while to get paid."

"Well, long as you got paid. That's all that matters, don't it?" Maggie's smile grew larger, and she gave Ingram a wink as she wiped an invisible speck from the center isle of the kitchen. "Coffee?"

"That'd be great, Maggie. Oh, that reminds me. Here's next week's money for... well... for our arrangement." Ingram withdrew his wallet and gave Maggie a five dollar bill. "I got a job that's gonna take me out of town."

"That's good you got more work. Where you going?"

"Believe it or not, to Arkansas. Drove through there once on the way to California. Can't remember it much."

"Well, there's not much to remember about Arkansas, if you're lucky."

"No, I guess not."

Maggie stopped wiping the counter, opened a cabinet, and removed a coffee cup. "Milk and sugar?" She lifted her head. Ingram nodded. She continued, "I'm from Arkansas, Bull. Can you believe that? Born and raised there."

"Really?"

"Yessir. Now, a lotta folk think Arkansas is the most backward state known to mankind, and that'd be true, if it wasn't for Mississippi." Maggie leaned her head back and laughed at her own joke. Her teeth shone white against the darkness of her skin. Ingram frowned. "I came here to look after an aunty and never left. But I want you to look after yourself over there. It's a whole different place. People think different, act different. There's deep places in the earth over there, places that man knows only a little, deep tracks of forest that no white nor black man has walked on still since the Indians held the land. Someone who doesn't know their way can get lost real easy."

"Deep places in the—"

She waved her hand dismissively. "You get into any trouble, I want you to try and find Gethsemane, that's the town I come from. My daughter, Alice, she still lives there and can help you if you need it. I'll send her a letter and tell her you might be through that way."

"Maggie, I'm only going to be over there about a week, at most. No need to do any of that, I'll just—"

"Bull, I'm trying to tell you something. Over there, in Arkansas, things don't go the same way they go everywhere else. Things take longer, things go wrong. Roads are bad, bridges go out. It's backward, Bull. But it's got its strong points too."

"Like what?"

"Well, it's a garden, really. The soil is rich and red like blood, or brown like chocolate, least where I come from. Things take root and grow real easy, game gets fat off the land, and sometimes, it seems like all a man or woman has to do is stretch out her hand, God's bounty is there for the taking. I guess I ain't making much sense, but it's important you watch yourself. People think that place is just a bunch of hicks, and yes, that's what they are, but they're more than that too. Just stick to the villages and towns, stay away from the little places away from the main roads and cities. Stay in the lighted areas."

Ingram grinned. "You'd think I was going into Transylvania or something from the way you talk, Maggie."

Maggie handed Bull his coffee, and said, "There's worse things than getting bit on the neck. Come on, I'll help you get packed. I did some of your laundry last night while you was out carousing, should be dry by now."

❧

Early and Ruth Freeman kept a tidy little cottage on Bellevue Avenue, nestled in a copse of oak and birch trees.

Ingram pulled the coupe into the drive. A small, tawny woman came out on the house's front porch at the sound of Ingram's car. She was slight, high breasted, and modestly dressed in a maroon skirt and white blouse.

As he walked toward the house from the coupe, she began to appear older, lines of worry and stress stenciling their way into her skin. Her eyes were puffy and red. She wrung her hands as he approached.

"Mr. Ingram?"

"Yes, ma'am. That's me."

"Tell me it's true, you're gonna find my Early."

Ingram took off his hat and stopped. "Well, I'm gonna do my best. That's why Mr. Phelps sent me over here. Maybe we should go inside and talk about it."

Inside, Ruth poured Ingram a glass of sweet tea, two ice cubes. Yellow flowers decorated the sides of the glass. An infant babbled in another room. Ruth glanced toward the back bedroom, and said, "Supposed to be nap time, but the little tiger doesn't know what's good for him."

Ingram sipped his tea. "Mm. That's good tea, ma'am."

She twisted a dishrag in her hands. "Please tell me what you're gonna do to find my Early. *Please*." Her eyes welled with tears.

Ingram had no true experience with weeping women. The only time he'd seen his mother cry was on his seventeenth birthday, when he'd boarded the train that took him to Tuscaloosa and basic training. He'd been packing his duffel bag and his mother appeared at his bedroom door, apron white in the light from the window. She embraced him, grabbing him fiercely like she'd had when he was a little boy, when it was easier to wrap her arms around him. She stood back, her hands on his biceps, and looked up at him, staring hard into his face. "You'll be careful, won't you?" Tears came to her eyes, and she wiped them with her apron. By '45 when the war was over, she'd died of cancer, and he still lived when, over and over in the Pacific, he thought the opposite would surely be true.

Ingram said, "I'm gonna try and pick up his trail in Brinkley, ma'am. Maybe he just got sick and holed up in a hotel until it passed over."

Ruth shook her head. "For ten days? No. But maybe he's been tossed in jail. Early drinks sometimes to sickness. Or maybe he's shacked up with some woman... and you know... that's fine if he is. At this point I'd rather him be doing that than... well—"

She didn't want to be a widow just yet, and he couldn't blame her.

"Ma'am," Ingram began again, as gently as he knew how, "I came over here to see if you could tell me anything about his last phone call, what he might've said or mentioned."

She sniffed and wiped her eyes. "Well, he didn't say much, just told me he loved me and for me to kiss little Billy for him. He said he'd stayed in England and Stuttgart and laughed, saying all he needed now was to stay in Paris and London. Oh. He did say one more thing, said he had heard about a blues man Mr. Phelps might be interested in and was gonna try to see the man play at a roadhouse, but he didn't say where."

"Did he mention the blues man's name? Was it Ramblin' John Hastur?"

Ruth paused, looking uncertain. "Could've been. I'm sorry, Mr. Ingram, I can't remember. Right about then little Billy started crying."

"That's okay. So let me get this straight." He cleared his throat. "Early had been to England and Stuttgart the day or night before his call. That's good to know." Ingram grabbed his hat off the kitchen table and moved back toward the door. "I'll do my best to find him, ma'am. Shouldn't be no problem."

Ruth began crying then for real, not just sniffles and welling tears. A flush came to her face, her eyes hitched up in pain, and she moaned. A soft blubbery sound. Tears poured down her cheeks, her mouth pulled down at the corners into a grimace.

"Please find him. He's all we got," she wailed, and she threw herself against Ingram's chest.

Ingram felt her body pressed against his, her breasts pushing into his stomach, and wondered if she'd already begun planning for her husband's demise.

On the way out of town, Ingram stopped, filled his tank, and bought a map of Arkansas. As he paid, the clerk at the counter said, "Going hunting?"

"Maybe. Why'd you ask?"

"Only couple of things to go to Arkansas for. One's hunting and t'other's fishing. That's all."

"Well, then, I guess I'm going hunting."

The man behind the counter handed Ingram his map. "Good luck."

Flipping the brim of his hat, Ingram said, "Thanks. Looks like I'll need it."

Ingram drove west on Highway 70 into Arkansas. Crossing the Mississippi, its turgid brown waters taking their swift, inevitable course south past Helena, past Greenville, even further south into the Louisiana swamps and tributaries, the French parishes, Ingram felt connected to something larger than himself. The slats of the wooden trestle-bridge rattled and clattered as he drove the coupe over them, his window down, the smoke from his cigarette whisking out into the freshening afternoon air, the slanting rays of the afternoon sun dappling the highway. The trees stood dark at the roadside in the afternoon light, but Ingram made out oak and cypress, bone-white birch, each one slowly passing. Particles of cottonwood hung suspended in the air, rising and falling, flashing by Ingram's open window. He smoked and drove west in the gathering gloom of the dying afternoon, the greens becoming black.

The deep forest and swamps lining the Mississippi broke and leveled into flatter landscape. Fields and farmhouses slowly drew by his windows. The tires of the coupe thumped on the brown concrete slabs of the highway, each section's tar seam thudding and rocking the coupe on its shocks. Outside his window furrowed fields rolled past, the rows of beans and cotton passing like spokes of an enormous wheel, its hub far off past the horizon, the rim meeting the road.

He passed through small towns, buildings clustered around a railroad or a granary. Not much traffic on the highway, very few people in the fields barring an occasional lone tractor turning over the earth, a combine trundling across a dusty plot, a battered and beaten truck rolling down a gravel road, throwing dust against the sky. The country seemed nearly abandoned, as if all the people had been spirited away and left their homes and fields to turn to dust.

Ingram flipped on the radio and scanned the AM band, rolling the knob slowly from left to right and then back, searching for signals. Hisses and pops, signal squelches, then the infrequent clear reception of broadcast filled the car and whisked out the window like Ingram's cigarette smoke. Each station crackled like a procession of avaricious ghosts; pastors fervently preaching, adverts and jingles hawking soap and dishwashing detergents, plaintive country music, the drone of news.

He dialed in 1570, the frequency Phelps indicated was Mr. Couch's station. At first that frequency was just static, the occasional word rising through the noise like a fish rising to the surface of a murky pond, pale and indistinct. Closer to Brinkley, the signal gained clarity, coalescing into something understandable.

KBRI played swing and big band platters, Lawrence Welk, Jimmy Dorsey, Johnny Mercer, and Vaughn Monroe—Ingram thought of this music as the drone of the USO.

The more Ingram listened, the more he thought of the music at Helios Studios. Rhythm and blues, Phelps had called it. A driving beat married to raw emotion that Ingram found the big band music lacked. And then Ingram remembered Hastur and the "Long Black Veil." The chanting and sound of slaves marching, the sound of knives and pain and hatred.

Despite the heat of afternoon, Ingram shivered. He switched off the radio and drove in silence.

The coupe devoured the miles. Before dark, Ingram rolled into Brinkley, a hundred miles west of Memphis. Driving down the main drag, Ingram scanned the buildings looking for the KBRI call signs. He spotted them near a nexus of power lines and transformers running into a short narrow building with a large plate glass window. The door read:

WHERE
THREE DINGS MEANS
GOOD THINGS!

KBRI

BROADCASTING AT 1570 KHZ
BRINKLEY'S ONLY SOURCE FOR
NEWS, WEATHER AND FAMILY ENTERTAINMENT

DAYTIME FORMAT - 5A.M. TO 3P.M.
NEWS, LOCAL ANNOUNCEMENTS, FAMILY ENTERTAINMENT

EVENING FORMAT - 3P.M. TO 8P.M.
FAMILY ENTERTAINMENT AND COMEDY

NIGHT-TIME FORMAT - 8P.M. TO 10P.M.
DANCE AND POPULAR RECORDINGS

NEGRO GOSPEL, FOLK, CONTEMPORARY MUSIC 10P.M. TO 12A.M.
WITH DERWOOD MILLER

Behind the building was a steel tower stabbing into blue sky. Ingram pulled the coupe into a diagonal parking space, put on his hat, and went inside.

At a small front desk, the secretary sat smacking gum, twirling a pony-tail, and reading a biology book. She couldn't have been more than fifteen. She looked up brightly as Ingram entered the door.

"Hi! Can I help you?"

Ingram had assumed the KBRI radio station premises would not be too dissimilar to the Helios Studio space—cluttered, smoky, full of interesting photographs and musical paraphernalia. Quite the opposite; the KBRI office was near bare, a small desk with phone (and teenager), a couch and side tables littered with newspapers, then a long unbroken space of fifteen to twenty feet of empty hardwood floors that met a back wall with a large plate glass. An older man sat at controls in front of a microphone. Ridged waffle-like material covered the walls of both the front office and sound-booth.

The KBRI broadcast played softly throughout the front office, emanating from fabric-lined speakers mounted on the wall.

Ingram walked closer to the girl at the front desk and said, "Hi. My name's Lewis Ingram. I'd like to speak with Mr. Couch, if I may."

The girl turned in the chair, hooked a thumb back at the sound booth, and said, "Daddy? He's just about to do a round of advertisements. Once he finishes them, he should have time to talk with you. You can have a seat over there."

She stood, faced the sound booth, and waved her arms over her head like she was flagging down a passing airplane. Mr. Couch looked up, irritated, and then shook his head. He spotted Ingram standing in front of the desk. The girl pointed to Ingram's chest, then made talking motions with her hands. Couch nodded, returning to his work. Ingram took a seat.

When Couch finished with the announcements and advertisements—the Cotton, Grain, and Stock Report, messages from the London Woolen Company, Immanuel Baptist Church, the Clifford and Weldon Piano Service company—he walked briskly to the front office, adjusting his glasses. He approached Ingram, hand out, ready to shake. A thin, even scrawny, man, Couch was buttoned down and buttoned up, wearing a bow tie and suspenders.

"Martin Couch, sir. I'm the owner and operator of KBRI. What can I help you with?"

Ingram stood and took Couch's hand. "I'm trying to find someone, Mr. Couch."

Couch withdrew his hand from Ingram's grasp. "Are you a policeman?"

"No sir, I've been hired to find Early Freeman. Early's boss, Mr. Phelps, mentioned you saw him last."

"Oh. Yes, I spoke with Mr. Phelps on the phone. And just the other day, Sheriff Grazer came by and asked me some questions. I told them everything I know."

"Do you think *I* could ask you just a few questions? We think Early moved on to other towns with stations, and I'm trying to find out where those might be."

"Sure. Shoot."

"OK, then. When was the last time you saw him?"

"I think it was July eighteenth, a Thursday. He dropped off a couple of forty-fives for Derwood, our night DJ, and then took Lisa and me over to the dime store for a malted and a sandwich." He nodded toward his daughter.

"So you're pretty familiar with Early, huh?"

"You could say so. He comes by and drops off records for Derwood to play. You know, Negro folk music… very primitive. We only play that at night when we drop the wattage and limit the broadcast area."

"I see," Ingram paused. "Do you know if Early had any contact with Derwood? You think I could talk to him?"

"I don't see any problem with that, Mr. Ingram. But he hasn't got a phone. Lisa, can you write down Derwood's address for Mr. Ingram?" Lisa flipped through a Rolodex and jotted some information on a 3x5 card, bringing it over and handing it to Ingram.

"Thanks. Did Early say where he was heading next?"

"No. I'm sorry. We just talked about children. Early was quite worried about being a father. He confided in me that his father was not the most pleasant of men and he feared making that same mistake. Of course I reassured him; someone who worries about those things doesn't become it."

Couch took off his glasses and polished the lens with a white handkerchief. "In my own way, I guess I was his friend. I never accepted any money from him, nor his offers of 'entertainment.' He's been coming round here for the last year at least, once a month. And recently, he's been questioning me about being a good father." Couch looked at Lisa, who rolled her eyes at this last statement. "Which I tried to answer to the best of my ability, though my being a 'good father' is constantly up for review." Couch grinned at his little joke, and the girl rolled her eyes again and sighed heavily.

"Well, I appreciate it, Mr. Couch, and I know Early appreciates it too." Ingram put his hat back on and said, "Thanks for taking the time to answer my questions."

"Not at all, Mr. Ingram. I'm glad to have been of help."

Ingram turned to the door and stopped.

"Oh, there's one more thing. Did Early mention anything about a pirate radio station broadcasting out of these part? Or anything about a fella named John Hastur?"

Couch blanched, and he blinked several times rapidly. "No," he said, hesitantly. "He didn't. I'm sorry."

Ingram furrowed his brow. He glanced over at the girl, who had retrieved a fingernail file and was busily grooming her nails.

Ingram turned back to face Couch. He took a quick step toward the man, forcing him to look up, using his sheer size as a tool of coercion.

"I guess I should phrase that another way," Ingram said. "Do you know anything about a pirate radio station located around here? You ever heard of John Hastur?"

Couch looked down at his hands holding the glasses and handkerchief as if he'd just discovered something brand new. He placed the glasses on his face and said, "No, Mr. Ingram, I have no knowledge of any of this. I'm sorry, really. But I have to get back to the booth and finish up the afternoon broadcast. Sorry I couldn't be any more help. Good day."

The girl glanced at Ingram on his way out, and around her gum said, "Thanks for stopping by. Be sure to tune in to KBRI on Sundays for the Sunny Sunday Sermon's with Maddox Bradley." She gestured back toward the booth. "He makes me say that."

Ingram grinned. "Stick in there."

❧

The 3x5 card Lisa gave Ingram read, "D. Miller, 200 Cherrylog Road, Brinkley. P.S. I think you're cute."

Chuckling, Ingram got back into the coupe and headed toward the filling station he'd seen earlier as he entered Brinkley's main street. The station attendant pointed him in the right direction.

Brinkley, Ingram realized, was just Main Street and one other block of modern houses: four walls, a roof, a driveway, porch, backyard, maybe even a second story. Once he drove beyond that block, he passed overgrown lots next to small, low-slung houses and shacks with no discernible line between driveway and lawn. Derelict cars lolled on cinder blocks and scarred tree trunks; stacks of tires teetered by front doors. Beyond stood hovels held together with galvanized tin and bailing wire.

It was dark now, and Ingram drove into unknown country, the electric lights illuminating Main Street diminishing in his rear view mirror. As he drove past the tar-paper shacks, he saw candles and lanterns lighting bare rooms with shadowy figures.

Ingram followed the station attendant's directions and eventually his headlights found the hand-painted sign for Cherrylog Road. Flat fields surrounded his car. Corn blocked his view to the left and right. Rustling with the breeze, the stalks stood taller than even Ingram underneath a sky salted with starlight. His tires crunched on the gravel, and the road wound among the fields, passing corn, then cotton, then a stand of trees, then more fields until Ingram crossed a small concrete bridge.

Ingram saw a farmhouse, dormered and gabled, with a porch and a gallery, passably maintained except for the soft decay of scaling paint. Bean fields ran up and kissed the yard. Ingram parked his car, angling the headlights onto the porch and front windows.

He shut down the coupe, leaving the headlights on, and opened the door. It was quiet, except for the rustle of the wind and the tick-tick-tick of the coupe's engine as it cooled. Each footstep crackled dry grass, each footfall on porch-step creaked abnormally loud. Ingram hunched his shoulder blades with the noise.

Knocking on the front door, he bellowed, "Hello?" He walked

around the house's lower level, shielding his eyes, and peered through the windows. The interior of the house was dark, shadows and looming patches of blackness appearing as furniture. The stars didn't give enough light to see, and the coupe's headlights didn't reach. Ingram moved back to the front of the house, squinting his eyes in the glare, and considered heading back to town to get dinner.

The headlights died.

Suddenly, he was blind. From behind the coupe, Ingram heard footsteps and low-pitched sounds like garbled speech.

Oun tulu dundu nub sheb tulu onnu ia denu fin de nulu sheb lar stir rub neb.

Ingram paused, listening. His body tightened, arms out as if fending something away.

He jumped off the porch, landing in the grass in front of the coupe. Still blind, he crouched as low as possible, and balled his hands into fists. He thought of his gun.

Still the bizarre words came. Ingram edged out to the side of the coupe so that he might be able to get into his car, retrieve his .38 under the front seat. Anything. He felt his back prickling in the same sense he'd had years ago in the Pacific, the sense of impending danger. For a moment he felt a strange dislocation and he closed his eyes, thinking that when he opened them he'd smell the smoke and gunpowder, hear the screams of his men and the report of their rifles. Even now he felt the thick jungle undergrowth of years before, lost in the darkness of Guadalcanal.

Oun tulu dundu nub sheb tulu onnu ia denu fin de nulu sheb lar stir rub neb.

The sound of the voices pulled him away from his reverie. Ingram opened his eyes, and could see again, dimly. Shapes formed out of the blackness: the coupe, a bush, the line of overgrown lawn.

A tall, black figure watched him from across the rural road, the silhouette of a man, lean and angular. The darkness concentrated down to two specks, the creature's eyes. They watched him, unblinking.

Ingram remained locked in the thing's gaze as the guttural

sounds continued, coming in harsh, pounding rhythms. Layered above and beyond the voices came a sound like the tearing of the dark; beyond sound, it rocked Ingram's frame, shook his bones.

Something bad's gonna happen. Something bad...

His mind felt disjointed; his thoughts careened around and dashed away unchecked. He gritted his teeth. His shoulders rose, and he raised his fists, every muscle taut.

The sound grew—*Hastur!* he thought, remembering the recording from Phelp's studio—widening and expanding. He felt like he could taste an oily blackness invading his mouth.

Desperate, he dug his keys from his pocket and leapt forward toward the coupe's door. He fumbled at the handle. The keys flipped away, slipping from his fingers. His hands were numb, unresponsive. The hideous sound filled all his senses. Eyes full of night, the reek of the dark in his nose and on his hair, the oily taste of blindness on his tongue, Ingram's senses filled with noise and blackness and pain.

"Come on, then, bastard. *Come on,*" he bellowed into the approaching dark, swinging his fists.

The shadow overwhelmed him.

Ingram screamed with rage, ripping at his own face. The black noise grew, rising. He felt the red sensation possess him, the fury of battle-madness gripping him like long ago, and he *hated.* The dark thing standing across the road, himself, the world—he felt unbounded hatred for everything. He staggered forward, trying to get to the black figure still watching him, eyes like congealed darkness, to kill it, rip it to shreds, pound it to a pulp. If anything came between Ingram and the loathsome figure across the road, it would die too.

Ingram fought desperately to remain standing and sane, but his ears rang from the screams. The strange, high-pitched sound ripped at his mind again, and his sanity skittered away like butter on a hot pan. He keeled over into the grass and ripped at his eyes, his ears; anything to stop the sound, stop the darkness. Blackness pushed in from all sides, invading his body, and he knew no more.

Chapter 5

Ingram awoke to stars.

He'd dreamed of Captain Haptic, his old captain. They'd been on leave, in Hawaii, drinking and singing old country folk songs, off key. A real memory. But in the dream, Cap Hap had been dressed as a Roman centurion, like in the movies, with a breast plate and plumed helmet. He drank like Ingram remembered him, though.

From where he lay on the lawn, the black curtain of sky above him was strewn with millions of twinkling points of light. He looked down at himself. Dried blood streaked his fingers and palms. His face felt raw.

Ingram lay there on his back, half-under his coupe, face throbbing. He watched the heavens turn above him as he breathed in the grass, chest rising and falling.

The sound of cicadas ebbed and peaked, accompanied by the hoot of an owl and the faint far-off bark of some lonely, chained dog.

Ingram brought his hand up to his cheek, and his fingers came

60

away sticky. He rolled over on hands and knees and patted at the grass in the darkness until he found his keys. He rose painfully, and levered himself into the coupe. He turned the key, and the engine growled into life. Ingram discovered that the light switch for the headlights had been depressed to the off position.

Ingram pulled out a smoke and lit it with trembling hands.

Why did he stop? Let me live?

Ingram felt his anger building—a strange echo of the feeling he'd had with the rough sound of the silhouette—his resolve to see this job through calcifying to some rock-hard permanence. With every throb of ripped face, his anger grew.

I'm gonna find that bastard if it's the last thing I ever do, so help me God.

It was Ingram's version of prayer, and he didn't know even if he meant Early Freeman or Derwood Miller or the silhouette by the side of the road.

The coupe trundled through the night, crunching its way back Cherrylog Road.

On Main Street, Dougan's pharmacy was closed, but KBRI was still lit. Ingram drove the coupe slowly past the building. Couch was in the booth window, head bent, ministering to his flock, an electric priest sending out his blessings at 1570 kilohertz with one thousand watts of power. But Ingram wanted no more conversing with Couch, no more dissembling; thinking about it now, he realized it was only the girl's presence that had kept him from forcing the truth out of Couch. With cracked bones and blood. Maybe too much blood.

He pulled the coupe around the back of the KBRI building, parking in the shadows of the tower. Ingram exited the coupe and tested the building's rear doors; both were locked. He went back to the car, lit a cigarette, and sat fiddling with the radio, tuning in KBRI.

Ingram watched for Derwood, smoking and taking sips from the pint of whiskey he kept under his seat. From his bag he took a white undershirt, poured some whiskey on it, and dabbed at the scratches on his face.

Jesus. Did a number on myself. What the hell happened back there?
Couch's voice sounded sonorous and lulling even through the
speakers of the coupe. Ingram leaned back in his seat and dozed.

When Derwood took the air at 10 PM, Ingram sat upright and
cursed, looking around the lot, wishing he had watched the front
door.

"Welcome, ya'll, to KBRI's evening programming. I'm Derwood
Millah, and tonight we got a real treat for you, the new single from
Little Rock's own Jim Cannon. Later we'll spin some of the Memphis favorites but right now I don't want you to forget that everybody needs some plumbing work sometimes. Pipes get clogged,
food gets down the drain and not to mention hair and other stuff...
ooh. But there's a solution to all of these problems. That's right, if
you need help with your plumbing, be sure to call W.T. Grant and
Son Plumbers, right here in Brinkley, and they'll come by and—"

Derwood's voice wasn't as smooth as Couch's but what he lacked
in polish, he made up for with enthusiasm. When Derwood began
playing music, Ingram sat upright.

Rhythm and blues, he called it.

It came through the speakers like a dream, a deep pulsing dream.
He started with Sister Rosetta Tharpe, who sang a throaty spiritual.
He followed it with Robert Johnson, who cried of hell hounds and
debt. When Derwood announced a Helios artist, Hubert Washington, Ingram started the coupe, maneuvered it out of the parking lot, and drove back to Cherrylog Road.

He parked the coupe away from the house, out of sight, and
walked back down the road, his footsteps crunching on gravel. It
was dark now, an intermittent cloud-cover partially obscuring the
stars. The sap rested easily in his hand, the .38 cold and reassuring
in the small of his back.

He went around to the back of the house, found a door, and
smashed the window with the sap. Inside, he flipped a kitchen
light and looked around. A picture of a man with a woman and infant, bundled in winter clothes. Nothing more to indicate family.

Might be his ex. Miller, a shabby, solitary male. The house reeked with the stench of unwashed bodies and trash, yet it was relatively clean. Ingram walked around the first floor, flipping on lights and opening closets, cabinets, anything. Finding nothing of interest, he went back to the kitchen, turning off lights as he went, and pulled a fresh bottle of milk and a wedge of cheese from the main compartment of the ice box. He sat his .38 down beside the milk bottle, and took a seat facing the kitchen door. Using his pocket knife, he curled slices away from the cheddar and popped them into his mouth, chewing thoughtfully.

He sat sipping milk, eating cheese, at the flimsy wooden table until he heard the car pull up to the front of the house. He hummed the Sister Rosetta Tharpe song he'd heard earlier.

Ingram waited. He heard creaks on the porch steps, the ratchet of the key in the front door, and then heavy footfalls coming toward the kitchen.

Derwood Miller walked into the kitchen with his mouth open, eyes wide in unbelief. A stringy man, dressed in cheap clothes that hung loose on his frame, Derwood nervously ran a hand through over-greased hair and glanced from Ingram, to the milk and cheese, to the gun.

Ingram smiled, nodding at the opposite chair.

"Derwood?"

He didn't bother with exclamations of protest. Derwood crossed his arms over his narrow chest, standing in a yellow pool of light, eyes boring in to Ingram.

"Yeah. That's me. What're you doing in my house?"

"Waiting for you," Ingram said, hooking the chair with his foot and sliding it toward Miller. "Have a seat."

His eyes shifted from the gun to the milk then Ingram again. He sat down on the offered chair like a dog sitting down to a meal from an unknown hand.

"Derwood, earlier tonight, I was attacked right out in front of your house by... someone—something—I can't explain." He pointed toward the bloody streaks on his face. "You can see I got the short end of that stick."

Ingram reached forward and pulled the pack of cigarettes out of Derwood's shirt pocket. He took one for himself and offered one to the other man. Derwood shook his head. Ingram lit his.

"I can't explain it, so I won't even try." He blew the smoke toward Miller and dropped the match on the floor.

Ingram sat quietly for a long while, smoking, blowing the smoke into the other man's face. He picked a loose fleck of tobacco from his teeth. He took a speck of lint from his slacks and smoothed the fabric.

Eventually, he raised his head, looked at Derwood, and said, "Tell me everything you know about a man named Early Freeman. If you lie, if you leave anything out, you'll regret it."

Miller swallowed, his Adam's apple bobbing in his throat.

"I know Early through work, deejaying at KBRI. He comes through about once a month, takes Mr. Couch to lunch and drops off some forty-fives, then moves on to the next radio station, the next town. That's about it."

"Mr. Couch said you've spent some time with him. Tell me."

"Well..." Miller's eyes flicked around the kitchen looking for something, some way out of this unexpected domestic interrogation. "Sometimes, we'd go drinking, you know, roll out to the Stockyard tonk, out near the county line, and Early would always do the buying, long as I made sure I spun his records. Which was fine with me cause I would've spun 'em anyway. They're good."

"Tonk?"

"Yeah. Honky-tonk. A blues joint. We'd listen to the blues, drink beer, or Coke and whiskey."

"It a Negro establishment?"

"Yeah, but they know me there. They play the best blues, even on the juke. Most weekends, there's a player, or a band. It's good. Folks don't know what they're missing."

Ingram paused to think, flicking the ash of his cigarette onto the floor. "So, when was the last time you saw Early?"

"Same day Mr. Couch did. He told me you'd been by asking after Early."

"He take you drinking that night?"

"Yeah, he did. We went out to the tonk, like I was telling you, and pretty much got our bellies tight, you know?"

"He mention where he was off to next?"

"Said he was gonna head down to England, visit the folks over at KENG."

That matched what Ruth Freeman had told him about Early's last phone call.

"What do you know about Ramblin' John Hastur?"

The outraged flush of red drained from his cheeks like water from a cracked glass, his eyes pulled tight as if to ward off a blow. Miller brought his hands into his lap, like a schoolboy, and clasped them together.

"Nothin.' I don't know nothing 'bout him."

Ingram clubbed Miller across the face with the sap. Miller looked at Ingram with surprise, an expression of pure bewilderment on his face. He toppled onto the linoleum of the kitchen floor.

Ingram snatched the front of Miller's shirt, lifted him, then placed him back in his chair.

"What do you know about Ramblin' John Hastur?" Ingram said slowly.

Miller swayed in his chair and reached a hand up to touch his rapidly swelling cheek. His hand came away bloody.

"I know... I don't know nothing," Miller said, looking Ingram straight in the eyes and saying it slowly. "Nothing."

Ingram rapped Derwood's head twice with the sap, and the man slumped back into the chair, unconscious.

Ingram stood. He moved across the room and rummaged in the kitchen cabinets and closets. In an adjoining hall, he found a cylinder of nylon rope and returned to the kitchen. He bound Miller's hands and feet. He tied his body to the chair. Taking a pot from an open cabinet, he filled it with water and dumped it on Miller's head.

Miller spluttered. He twisted his body, looked down in surprise at the rope binding him.

Ingram patted Miller's cheek. "Here's the deal, pard. I'm not gonna hit you again. You're gonna tell me everything you know about Ramblin' John Hastur or I'm gonna pick up this chair, with you in it, and take you outside, where that fucking thing attacked me. I'm gonna set you down on the edge of the wood, out of sight of the road, and let you think about what you know and you don't know. I'll come back tomorrow and we'll have this conversation again, if there's anything left of you."

A growing horror filled Miller's face as Ingram spoke, and Ingram felt it too. The blackness. The memory of a silhouette approaching. A black, open mouth, emanating sound. The idea of leaving Miller out there, on the edge of the woods like a sacrifice—no, an offering, he thought suddenly—horrified him. And just as suddenly, Ingram knew—*he knew*—that if he did leave Miller on the wood's edge, the offering would be accepted and he'd be able to parlay with the black creature.

"No," Miller said. "I'll spill."

"Then spill, goddammit. I'm tired of waiting. And I might not like it—you definitely won't—but I'll do as I fucking say and put you out there." Ingram motioned toward the dark windows at the front of the house.

"They call him the Yellow King. Or the Tattered Man. He plays and sings his songs with the Devil's voice."

"Who's they?"

"Negroes. Black folk all around. Poor white folk who work the fields. Sharecroppers and wood folk, you know, them that live on the edges of the bayou, or the river, and fish for a living. You hear 'em sometimes, talking 'bout him, when you're at the store, or passing 'em on the street. You know? His name just sorta starts getting heard."

Ingram nodded. *It's the fucking middle ages out here. No Errol Flynn in sight.*

"And what do they say?"

"That Ramblin' John sings with the Devil's voice and plays with the Devil's hands. That when he sings, it's like he's casting a spell.

That he's got songs that if you heard them, they'd drive you mad. That his songs can raise the dead." Miller paused here, uncertain. "They say his voice can get a woman with child if she hears it full." Ingram grew cold, remembering the song on the pirated radio station. The black thing in the dark, making that unholy sound. He reached up to touch his face and caught himself.

"Did Early ask you about him?"

Miller looked as sheepish as was possible with a swelling, bloody cheek, and said, "Yes."

"And you told him just what you told me, didn't you?"

Miller nodded.

Ingram grunted. "OK, Derwood. One more question. What do you know about this radio station? The pirate radio station."

Miller exhaled, almost relieved. "Early asked me about that too. I heard it... I heard it once, late at night after my shift. I went... wild. Before I could stop myself, I went to her bedroom. My wife." He bowed his head. He sobbed. "She left the next day, took the kids."

"That's tough, soldier."

Derwood stayed that way for a long while. Finally, he sniffed and raised his head.

"It's always on a different frequency. It's always on at a different time of night and that... well... they play Ramblin' John songs. Full ones. If everything they say is true, it's a good thing they shift frequencies every time they broadcast because if you always knew where you could tune in to 'em, the whole world might go crazy, or fall under Ramblin' John's spell." Miller smiled as he said this, recognizing the absurdity of the statement. He winced with the pain of his skin drawing tight on his cheek.

Ingram dropped his smoke to the kitchen floor and crushed it with his wingtip. "OK, Derwood. That'll do. You got any candles?"

"Yeah," Miller said, looking toward a cabinet. "There's a box of 'em right in there. What'dya need candles for?"

Ingram stood and retrieved the box. He stopped, and turned back to Miller. "Lemme ask you one more thing, and I guess you don't have to answer if you don't want to."

Ingram sat down in the opposite chair and said, "Have you seen him? You know, the dark thing."

Miller looked at Ingram. The two men locked gazes for an instant.

That answers that.

"Okay, Derwood, here you go." Ingram used the matches again and lit a candle. Moving behind Miller, Ingram dripped a pool of red wax onto the linoleum floor directly behind his chair. He seated the base of the candle in the wax, the candle standing upright and only an inch or two below where Miller's hands were tied. Miller moved his hands as far away from the candle flame as he could.

"It's gonna take you a while, and hurt like hell, but you should be able to burn your way out of there before morning, if you start right now. I'll be seeing you."

Ingram walked out of the kitchen, out the front door, and back to the coupe. He drove back through Brinkley, now dark in the early hours of the morning, back through the night and away from the town, regaining Highway 70 and heading west again until he came to Lonoke.

At the first church he could find, Ingram parked the coupe as near as possible to the front doors, locked the car, and fell across the front seat, sleep overtaking him.

Chapter 6

Life was good in the Big House.

Now a week into their stay at her family home, Sarah and Franny found a rhythm to life here, a cadence as irresistible as the voices of children, begging them to play. Mornings were bright, dappled with sunlight, filled with the scent of muffins and minced-meat pies, of coffee and newsprint and cigarettes and white vinegar, and the cacophony of children running rampant through the house, of bright voices in old dark halls, through the kitchens and sleeping porch, in and out of Alice's bedroom, the old servant's quarters. Other than the library, which stayed closed at all times, the Big House rang with the sound of laughter.

Sarah never realized how lonely Franny had been until now, never realized how much she needed the company of other children. Franny was like some sun-loving plant put in the shade too long. Gone was the drowsy, languid child of their old home; Franny flew through the house, a jittering ball of energy with wild hair streaming behind her, yelling and chasing Lenora or Fisk. Gone was the child ready for bed at seven; she now had to be calmed for bed, her hair a dirty nest above her luminous face. Sarah felt a twinge of shame at what she'd denied her daughter all these years. Water seeks its own level, Alice would say, and Sarah would amend, love seeks its own height.

The children made lords of themselves, basking in the late glow of summer. In the morning, they gorged themselves on biscuits and honey and ham, then raced through the fields to the hen house to gather eggs with tremulous shaking fingers, shoes and socks heavy with dew. In the kitchen, with the sky lightening in the east, Franny, Lenora, and Fisk would grin at each other, proud and secret, each one keeping their happiness held close, pulling brown, still-warm eggs from a rough basket. After breakfast, when Alice reached the limits of her patience and shooed the children into the yard, they raced around the pecan grove, unharvested nuts crunching underfoot, their imaginations running wild, pistols made from index fingers, swords made from branches.

But Mimi terrified Franny. The child never overcame the idea that her grandmother was transforming into a wolf. Daily, Sarah cursed her absent husband for his insolent play on words.

"Mimi is turning into a wolf," Franny would say.

"No, baby, she's just sick. She's got lupus, honey. It makes her face dark."

"That's what I said, Mommy. Mimi's turning into a wolf."

After the first meeting, Franny absolutely refused to spend any time with her grandmother. When, driven to distraction by her daughter's obstinacy, Sarah exclaimed, "And why not? Why won't you say hello to Mimi?" Franny's face became pale, and then her lip quivered. Sarah felt ashamed, bullying her own child. Franny whispered, "Mommy, if I go up there she's gonna bite my head off."

Sarah barked a little laugh, and said, "No, baby, she won't bite—" and then stopped. Biting is what her mother would surely do, had done for years. It was her nature.

So Franny avoided her grandmother and ran wild. In the late

afternoons, the children tended the peafowl that stalked the Big House grounds like emperors, their beady eyes inscrutable and cold, their tails flaring in aggression or in love, no one could tell. The children scooped coffee cans full of feed from the barrel on the back porch of the Big House and then walked about the ground, scattering the feed into the grass or gravel, calling in high, bright voices, "Here Pea! Here Pea! Come on now, fowl! Here Pea! Here Pea!" and the birds would come, some high stepping their way through the orchard, through the grounds, from the back acres, and even the edges of the dark wood. All the fowl made haste, except for Phemus, head high and proud, taking delicate steps, tail rampant and viridescent, his dead eye lost in some long-ago fight for a hen, the other baleful eye ever moving, ever watching, his spurs long and vicious. Phemus tolerated nothing; no human nor machine could make the bird give ground. The children avoided Phemus, especially Fisk. Once, he'd moved too slow getting out of the old bird's way, and Phemus leapt up in a flurry of feathers, hissing like a cat. He landed on Fisk, gashing his thigh with a well-placed spur.

At night, they all ate dinner together, everyone except Mimi gathering round the dining room table, sharing meatloaf or hash or bologna sandwiches, drinking sweet tea and lemonade and coffee in turns. They talked about the day, the children still excited about new discoveries, words tumbling out one after another, breathless and exhausted and in pure heaven.

Sarah couldn't remember a time she'd felt more content, happier with the ebb and flow of days, the companionship of Alice and the wonder and excitement of her child, her dirty happy child.

But at night, Sarah felt lonely and her body ached for comfort.

Franny yearned too. Every bedtime, she begged and pleaded with her mother to sleep with Lenora and Fisk. It was the only point of segregation that Sarah forced on Franny.

One night, Alice overheard Franny's pleas as she brought fresh linens to Sarah's room.

"It's fine if she wants to," Alice murmured. "I know Fisk and

Lenora would be happy as clams to let that girl sleep with them. They fight over her, you know."

But what about me? Being alone here without Franny?

Instead, Sarah shook her head and said to Alice, "No, they're all tired and need their rest. This way, they'll have energy for the morning." The excuse sounded lame even to her ears. Alice nodded, and went about stacking linens in the closet.

And while the days were filled with light and laughter and activity, in the dead hours of night when the old house settled, wrapped in a wreath of darkness, the fields and dark wood pressing close all around, Sarah felt an unease creep upon her. She made a point of checking on her mother after Franny fell asleep, filling in Elizabeth on the day's events. And administering the constantly growing doses of port. Sometimes she would even take a glass herself, to her mother's great delight.

Late at night, the library drew her.

After giving her mother her port, Sarah would pad back downstairs, barefoot and silent, tray in hand, and quietly slide back the doors of the library and enter the dark room. She'd sit at the desk and smell the musky leather of the old books, and remember all those evenings so long ago when her father, uncle, and grandfather poured over these tomes, searching for something.

And now Sarah found herself doing the same almost every night, lingering in the library, running her fingers down the spines of ancient books.

It had been a long day; they'd taken the children to Old River Lake to swim. Sarah had wanted to take them to the Lonoke municipal swimming pool.

Alice grimaced and then said, "Naw, there's too many chemicals in them waters. Let's take 'em where we used to swim, the Old River Lake."

Sarah looked at Alice, puzzled.

Alice shook her head, sharply. Later when the women walked to the car to get the picnic basket, Sarah asked, "Why didn't you want to take them to the pool?"

"We ain't going to that pool cuz it's whites only, you little fool."
Sarah immediately felt ashamed. Such a stupid world they lived
in, keeping children who loved each other apart.

"It'd break all them kids' hearts—Franny's too—if Lenora and
Fisk got turned away. And I aim to keep *that* hard truth away from
them as long as I can. Look at them." Alice pointed to the three
children in the lake's green water, screeching and screaming with
delight, throwing mud at each other and dashing around the shallows, water and muck running in rivulets down their small frames.

That night Sarah woke from a strange dream. She stood at the
edge of a swimming pool in her yellow bathing suit, but it was
night with low clouds and no stars. In the pool stood children,
black children. Twenty or thirty of them, each one standing absolutely still in the water, some underneath, some chest deep, but
so still the water rippled not at all but lay smooth as glass. At first
Sarah thought the figures in the pool were Negro children, that
maybe the Lonoke city board had set aside one night this summer
for all of the black children in the county to be allowed to swim in
the municipal pool. But then, with a gasp, she realized they weren't
Negroes, they were absolutely black, silhouettes made flesh, each
one staring at her with malevolent coal eyes in jet black bodies. She
heard the wet slap of feet behind her on the swimming pool's concrete rim, then cold, clammy hands grasped her arms and shoved
her into the pool.

She woke, gasping, bed linens tangled and sweaty around her.
For a moment she couldn't recall where she was, if she was back
with Jim in Little Rock. But then the Big House settled a bit, a
fractional subsonic movement of the old timbers that even in the
dark let Sarah know she was home.

She stood up, straightened her nightgown, and moved in the
dark toward where Franny slept in the single bed by the window.
The window was open, and the sheer drapes fluttered in the hot
breeze blowing in from outside.

Jesus. She scratched at a bite on her arm. *There must be a million
mosquitoes in here.*

She shut the window as quietly as possible and turned. Half asleep, she reached out to brush Franny's hair, moving past the girl's bed, toward the fan. She felt nothing except empty sheets. She stopped.

"Franny?" She ruffled the covers of the single. "Franny?"

She raced to the door, threw it open, and bolted down the gallery, calling for her daughter in a half-whisper, half-scream.

"Franny? Baby? Franny!"

Her heart jack-hammered in her chest. She ran down the hall leading from the gallery, jerking open doors, peered into linen closets, bathrooms. An empty guest room. She paused at her mother's door. Slowly, she turned the knob and entered, her breath tight in her chest.

Her mother snored in the darkness, mouth open. Sarah turned from her mother's sleeping form and stepped quickly back to the hall. She raced down the grand stair, her feet slapping on the hardwoods.

Alice, frumpy and wrinkled with sleep, stepped into the light of the kitchen door, a plate of pecan pie in her hand. She looked at Sarah with wide eyes. "Girl, what the... what the devil are you playing at? You look like you seen a—"

"Franny's missing. She's not in her bed."

"Shit, girl, why ain't you screaming? Lemme get my shoes." With a clatter, Alice dumped her plate in the sink and dashed toward her quarters.

After a moment, she came back out of her room, smiling. She crooked at finger at Sarah, and said from the door, "Come look at this. I must not have heard her come in the room. Maybe I was having a snack."

Franny lay snuggled between Lenora and Fisk, arms wild, one leg thrown over Lenora's, a smile curling her lips. Sarah stood at the foot of the bed, tears running down her cheeks. Her shoulders shook as silent sobs wracked her body.

Alice put a warm hand on Sarah's back. "It's gone be all right, Sarah. Kids is kids, and you can't separate them. We were the same, remember?"

Sarah nodded, smiling through her tears at Alice's turn of words; so many circles within circles. Kids is kids. There's broken and there's broken. Everything is everything. She hugged Alice back, fiercely.

"You had a scare, girl. I got something to settle you down." Alice moved to the counter, pulled out a small glass, squirted raw honey into it from a bee-shaped plastic container, set a pan of water on a blue burner of the stove, and set the glass in the water. When she cut the lemon, the kitchen was filled with the bright scent of day, pushing the shadows and uncertainty away. Alice squeezed the lemon into the hot honey, stirred it with a spoon, and handed the drink to Sarah.

"Go on to the library and add a finger of whiskey, stir it up good, girl. A hot toddy'll settle anybody down. Sometimes, it's the only way I can get Fisk to sleep. Should do just fine for you. Go on." She winked, and shushed Sarah out of the kitchen, Alice's slippers whisking on the old floorboards. She yawned. "Whoo, girl, I'm tired. Big day tomorrow. Running. Playing. Cleaning. Gotta go get some sleep."

In the library, Sarah flipped on the small lamp near the desk and looked around at the shelves of books. She went to the dry bar, unstopped the bourbon decanter, splashed a good amount into the toddy, and stirred.

Sipping the drink, she walked about the library, reading titles of books. Three ornate Bibles, Episcopal and Presbyterian Hymnals, Dante's *Divine Comedy* with lithographs by Dore. *Ars Negril. The Brothers Karamazov. Quanoon al Islam. The Collected Plays of Shakespeare. A Latin to English Dictionary. Magnalia Christi Americana. A Light in August. Theographica Pneumatica. Magia Naturalis. Tom Sawyer. Unaussprechlichen Kulten. Hinzelmeier. Opusculus Noctis. The History of Freemasons. A Compendium of Vesalius Illustrations. Gone With the Wind. A Farewell to Arms. Strange Covenants. De Natura Deorum. The Life of Hermes Trismegistus. Pecheur d'Island. Occultus Esoterica. Eibon Libris. A Narrative of the Life of an American Slave.* And hundreds more.

Some of these volumes—the Twain, the Shakespeare, the Hemingway—were familiar to her. Others were utterly foreign. She pulled the big black book, *Quanoon al Islam*, and riffled the rough, crusty pages. It had a strange smell as well, one she didn't like. She slid the heavy tome back in its place.

Sarah had spent two years at Hollins College, where she'd attended classes in French and Latin, cloistered among the other young, well-to-do Southern women whose parents needed someplace to put their daughters. She remembered the interminable hours spent conjugating Latin verbs in Mrs. Cloud's class, that short dumpling of a woman walking the aisles and barking in a drill sergeant's voice, "To Love. Pluperfect. Miss Rheinhart. Latin then English. Now, please." And the girls giggling around her as she fumbled for an answer.

Sarah smiled at herself, remembering the time before Franny, before Jim, before the War.

That was '40 and '41, I think. Yes, Mom and Dad brought me home that December of '41, when we entered the war, and I never went back. Amavero. Jim was sixteen then, and just waiting to enlist, and Daddy didn't want me a thousand miles away with a war on. God, I was so young then. I Shall Have Loved… maybe. Maybe that was Future Pluperfect.

She took a drink of the toddy and shivered, the alcohol sending little tremors down her spine. The memories of school fresh in her mind, she took down a small, slim volume, a press of *Opusculus Noctis*. The tiny book was more like a pamphlet, thin and filled with what looked like verses. Sarah grabbed the Latin to English dictionary and moved to the desk, images of Mrs. Cloud running through her mind.

In the desk she found a pencil and sheaves of time-yellowed stationery. Pulling a few sheets, she placed the pamphlet in front of her and opened the dictionary. She felt the warmth of the toddy suffusing her body, spreading outward from her stomach. Like a girl, she crossed her legs and tucked her feet underneath her bottom, placed a stray strand of hair behind her ear, and bent her head to the papers in front of her.

On a piece of stationery, she wrote, *Opusculus Noctis*. She turned to the Os in the dictionary. She wrote, *little work*, then scratched that out and wrote, *little book* at the top of the piece of paper. Turning to the Ns, she looked up *Noctis*, which seemed familiar to her. She began to write in earnest now. When she was finished, she grinned again, pleased with her work. She drank the rest of the toddy in a gulp, keeping the glass to her lips, letting the dregs of honey in the bottom of the glass slide down the incline and to her mouth, and then looked back at the paper in front of her.

The Little Book of Night, it read. And underneath it she had written, *Or The Little Night Book*, which looked queer to her but charming. Calmed, she opened the pamphlet and began writing, a smile hovering around her lips.

Chapter 7

England didn't look like Ingram had pictured it from the movies.

As he drove the coupe into the little farm town, a billboard by the grain silos broke the monotony of the flat fields announcing that KENG was the "King of England, Heartbeat of the Delta." To Ingram it looked just like any of the countless farm towns he'd driven through since leaving Lonoke earlier that morning, maybe a little flatter, a little greener, the low-slung buildings passing like Indian burial mounds in the hazy, late summer air. It was Friday, and the town's main street bustled with women, young and old, shopping for the weekend; buying groceries, browsing new clothes, getting their hair and nails done.

This was the normalcy Ingram had fought for, his men died for, but he'd been left behind. So far removed from this world of bright feminine things, humdrum domestic life, from families and holidays and birthday parties and barbecues, he felt much the same way he'd felt entering the Tulagi jungles at the head of his squad, a monstrous thing skulking into the island interior like some Grendel bearing a BAR.

That morning, he'd woken in the church's parking lot not quite knowing where he was, mouth dry, sweating in his dirty, rumpled clothes. The day was hot already. In the coupe's mirror, he examined his bloody face. The long scratches going down his cheeks, away from his eyes, gave him a fierce, tribal appearance. He stopped at a filling station and washed in the bathroom, using paper towels to clean the dry, brown blood from his face.

Once in England, he found the KENG building off Main, on a side street, a very small tower a hundred yards away on the edge of a soybean field. The door jingled as he entered, and a short fat man in suspenders came out of a backroom.

"Can I help you, sir? We're about to begin our afternoon programming, but—"

"Yes, sir, maybe you can help me. My name's Ingram, and I'm looking for a man named Early Freeman, supposed to have come through here a couple of weeks ago."

"Early! I know him well, great fella. Some state troopers came through here saying he was missing, but I haven't heard anything more about that from them. I sure hope he's OK. He usually comes through, takes me to dinner, gives us some records to play, you know, colored musicians. But we don't play a lot of that stuff. Not like KQUI, out near the county line."

Ingram said, "And you are?"

The chubby man laughed and shook his head. "Sorry. I'm George White." He took a step closer to Ingram and extended his hand. They shook; Ingram was surprised at how soft the man's hands felt.

"Did Early come through here a couple of weeks ago?"

"Sure did." White turned, walked back to a desk, rummaged through it for a bit, then returned with some forty-fives. "These are the records he dropped off. We ain't played 'em, like I said. Not much call for this kinda music with the colored station broadcasting so close nearby. But Early drops 'em off anyway, just in case."

"Early say anything about where he was gonna go next?"

"No, but I imagine he'd be delivering something to Carver's outfit."

"That the station you mentioned, KQUI?"

"Yep."

"You wouldn't have their address, would you?"

"Sure." He scribbled it down on a piece of paper. "Real easy to find. Just take Highway 151 all the way out till you pass the county line, then right on 165. 165'll bring you back into this county, but you'll drive maybe fifty miles down it, and it'll stop being paved about thirty miles in. You just keep going, and after a while you'll see their tower, little thing, smaller than ours, but you'll also see one of them new fire lanes with the big electrical transformers that the WPA put across the county back in '43. One of the last projects in the state."

Ingram nodded and thanked the man. "Oh, one more question, if I could. You ever hear that pirated station? You know, the one that switches frequencies?"

White laughed again, stomach jiggling. "The Phantom Station all the field hands whisper about? No, I haven't heard it. Doubt I ever will, cause it's just a story, nothing more."

"You ever hear of a man they call Ramblin' John Hastur?"

"No. Should I have?"

Ingram stopped for lunch at the local diner before driving on to find KQUI. He surprised himself with his own hunger, wolfing down his food with a speed he hadn't had since basic training. He lingered at the counter, afterward, smoking and drinking coffee, listening to the sounds of the folk in the diner going over their daily routines, traveling down well-worn paths of conversation. He sighed, left a tip, and went back to the coupe.

Highway 151 out of England rode rough, potholed and uneven. The whir of insects grew louder, the fields giving way before trees, cypress and birch, thick and dark in the shallows of the Arkansas River. Ingram followed this road for a while, until it turned back on itself and ran parallel to the river once more. Asphalt turned to gravel, and soon Ingram saw a building through the trees and, beyond the building, a large electrical transmission tower rising above the tree line.

Ingram parked the coupe next to the other car in the lot, a older model Ford, dusted the brim of his hat, and walked into the small, shabby building with a galvanized tin roof. At the door, a small plaque read, "KQUI Arkansas' Only Negro Owned and Operated Radio Station."

Inside, the front room of the KQUI was dark, lit only by a small bulb hanging from a wire.

Ingram called, "Hello?"

Nothing.

The other radio stations he'd been to played their broadcasts in the lobby, in the waiting rooms. But not here. Ingram looked around. The front room held a desk with a big black telephone, a fabric couch threadbare at the edges, a coffee table with old newspapers and a couple of war-time posters on the wall. A door in the back led to what Ingram assumed was the recording and broadcasting booth.

Ingram rifled the desk, finding an invoice book, a telephone log, a pad of paper, and bottles of ink. Underneath the ink blotter was a piece of paper. Carefully, he pulled it out. Mimeographed on card stock and heavily folded, it held a faint, sweet odor. Blue ink. It read:

> **Saturday, Aug. 18th, 1951**
> **Ruby's on the Bayou**
>
> **J. HASTUR**
>
> **Roller Martin**
>
> **Jim Cannon and the Canonballers, etc.**
>
> **will perform for a select audience**
>
> **10 p.m.**
>
> **$1 cover**
>
> **Victuals and drinks will be served**
> **Open bottles welcome**

Ingram slid the paper into his pocket and went to the inner door. He listened for a moment, and then threw it open.

Clutter filled the low-slung room, lit by a bulb hanging from a wire. In a corner, on dark stained walls, hung two framed documents—one a radio operator's license, the other a FCC Broadcasters license. A rough-hewn worktable stood under the light, stacked with boxes and milk crates full of records. The table itself held a turntable and microphone. A morass of wires snaked across the floor and into a wall by the back door, which Ingram could only assume led to the tower. A record spun on a turntable, the needle bumping and hissing in a continual loop; untended, the record had played itself out and was now caught in its auditory death throes. The room looked empty, and Ingram stepped forward to inspect the table that held the library of records. As he moved around the table to get a better look at the collection, he noticed the leg.

From behind the makeshift table, the leg jutted into the open, foot askew. Ingram felt a sinking sensation in his gut as he moved to get a better view.

The dead man lay on the floor in a natty blue suit. An older black man—gray at the temples and through the beard—he looked as though he'd been tortured. His eyes were wide in fright, his mouth open, blood pooling around the teeth, and scratch marks ran down his cheeks, around his eyes and ears. Trails of blood came from his ears, and Ingram spotted, beside the man's body, a piece of flesh that looked like a tongue.

Ingram gingerly touched his own cheeks.

In the Pacific, Ingram had witnessed death and dead men with expressions like this, but none as bad, as gruesome. He took the man's wallet from his slacks and verified his suspicions. This was indeed George Carver, owner and operator of KQUI.

Ingram searched the room, the record on the turntable making clicks and hisses as it revolved. The record collection yielded nothing other than a few Helios records indicating Early Freeman had made some contact here.

Ingram checked the files in the bureau. He looked underneath the table. He searched the dead man again, patting him down and emptying his pockets.

He stood, looking at the turntable. It turned, hissing and clicking, the needle caught in the last spiral, diminishing toward the center. The record had no printed label, just a hand-scrawled title on a brown sticker, reading *J. Hastur*. Just watching that name turn in circles made Ingram feel tight in his shoulders, his back, like someone had a gun on him.

The record was horribly scratched, as if Carver, in a violent spasm, had knocked the needle across the face of the record trying to destroy it. Or silence it.

I've got to know.

Ingram took a deep breath and placed the needle on the record.

The music was different from what he'd heard at Helios Studio. This piece was faster, uptempo, more frenetic. The player showed obvious skill, picking the melody in an intricate counterpoint to the rhythm plucked with his thumb. The record skipped drastically, needle popping over the scratches on the vinyl, jumping forward. More guitar, but now with another instrument, an instrument Ingram couldn't place, maybe a horn, or even a human voice, but alien to his ears. The record skipped again, and there was singing.

> Come on, rise up from the sodden earth
> Come on, rise up from Death's black hearse
> That is not dead can eternal lie
> And dying know even death can die
> Have you seen the yellow sign?
> Have you seen the yellow sign?

The record skipped and cast the needle back to the first of the verse, singing it again. And once again, Ingram found his muscles clenching, his fists tightening into stones. He had a lump in his throat, and tight bands across his chest. The wounds on his face throbbed horribly in time with the music. His body took up the rhythm and beat of the record.

The record skipped back to the beginning of the verse again, but this time, Ingram heard other instruments. Even though it was the same music, the same piece of vinyl on the record, the needle trapped in an infinite loop of music, Ingram heard something different from the first two revolutions; now he heard another voice. Ingram shuddered, unable to fathom the mouth that made those sounds. Then Ingram heard a thump, and he knew exactly what made them.

The body behind him arose, its dead mouth full of coagulated black blood, repeating the words along with the record. Ingram felt a horrible chill enter the room, a darkness that froze all his nerve endings. Ingram yelled, lunging forward and knocking the turntable away, the record flying across the small room and shattering into a thousand pieces. A hand grasped Ingram's thigh. Fingers ripped into Ingram's skin.

He threw himself across the table, sending the microphone flying and knocking over boxes of records. He landed hard on the floor, on top of cracked and broken vinyl shards. When he regained his feet, the dead man had rounded the table, arms out and face contorted in pain or malice, Ingram couldn't tell.

Lumbering forward, black viscous blood drooling from his maw, the dead man reached to grab Ingram.

Ingram dropped to a crouch, fists up.

In life, the corpse had been a large man, stately even, Ingram thought, watching the blood drip from the dead man's mouth. But not now. The ghoul made strange noises in absence of the turntable's revolutions.

Tulu dundu nub sheb tulu onnu ia denu sheb tulu, the dead man rasped. It came forward.

Ingram attacked, punching with both fists, alternating blows, right and left. He struck the man's face, sending blood spattering across the wall, twisting the man's head in a queer, rubbery angle. The dead man slowly turned his face back toward Ingram, an inhuman grimace stretching the face into something beyond horrible. Ingram lashed out again with his fist, making the ghoul's head rock back.

The man who was once George Carver reached Ingram and grabbed his arm, its mouth open, black and gaping. Ingram bellowed and twisted. The corpse thrust forward its head to get closer to Ingram's face.

He wrenched free of the man's grip, his shirt tearing as he yanked himself away. He pushed the dead man back, and the thing went down, onto the piles of broken records. He grabbed its throat with his left hand, pinning the corpse's head to the floor, and pummeled the thing's face with his right. Over and over, Ingram struck the dead man, his fist falling like a blacksmith's hammer—again and again—cracking the dead man's bones, leaving the horrible face a ruined mess.

Ingram let go of the corpse and sat back, chest heaving.

All remained still, except for his labored breaths. He could make out the ticking of a clock somewhere in the building.

Then, inexorably, the dead man slumped to the side, shuddered, and began to rise. Its hands clawed the air in front of it, blind but still moving, groping.

Why won't this fucking thing die?

Ingram forced the corpse back to the floor and struck it again, driving his fist into the bloody swamp of face. Again and again he struck it, fist pounding skull. Again and again.

Still, it struggled.

Finally, Ingram grabbed the corpse's hair and slammed the head into the floor. There was a crack, and the thing's arms spasmed. He slammed the head into the floor again.

The corpse stilled, and Ingram rolled off it. Holding up his hand, he lurched across the tiny room, over to the narrow door by the filing cabinets. In the small bathroom, he fell toward the sink, grimy and streaked with rusty water. Ingram ripped off his shirt, and cranked the spigot. Water spilled weakly from the tap. He jammed his fist in the flow, feeling his hand swell and throb. Tentatively he touched it, bones grinding together.

Fuck, a boxer's break. Last thing I need.

He ripped off his shirt, doused it with water, and wiped the gore that spotted his face. Holding his dripping hand high, he walked back to the front office. The dead man stayed dead.

Ingram picked up the phone in the front office. He hit the plunger twice, and dialed.

After a moment he said, "Mr. Phelps. Yeah, I'll hold."

Then, "Mr. Phelps? Fine. I ain't found Early yet, and don't think I'm gonna to, least not alive." He nodded in the dark of the room.

"There's some strange shit going on over here. I haven't found the radio station yet, but I've got a lead on this Ramblin' John Hastur. Supposed to be playing a tonk this weekend somewhere around England."

Ingram remained silent, listening. "There's some things that'll hit the news in a few days, 'bout KQUI, black radio station outside of England. Just so you know, I didn't have nothing to do with it, just stumbled onto it, looking for Early. Yeah, he's been here. But he ain't here now. Okay. Yes, sir. No, still got plenty of dough."

Ingram hung up, looked down at the tatters of his pants, his shirt. He ground his teeth.

I'm gonna make sure Mr. Phelps never gets his hands on any Hastur tunes.

❧

He was sorely tempted to drive back to Memphis after leaving KQUI, to drive as fast and hard as he could down the small back roads until he came to the Mississippi, and from there run straight out of this deadly little backwater of a state. But his hand had swollen and turned purple, and he knew he needed to rest. He considered driving back to Lonoke in hopes of finding a doctor then discarded the idea. Instead he drove on to Stuttgart, the farm hub of the county, and checked into the Royale Hotel, an old Victorian whore of a building, down on her luck but still possessing a great figure. The desk clerk, a studious young man in bow tie and suspenders, looked at him suspiciously but took his money and told him his room number.

Ingram said, "You got a house doctor?"

The young clerk snorted and shook his head. "This isn't Memphis, sir. But I'll put in a call to Dr. Keene, who'll make his rounds in the morning. What's wrong?"

"Broke my hand." Ingram held up the mangled fist and shoved it in the clerk's face.

"Oh. Well… oh. I'll put in the call, then. That looks horrible. We don't have a doctor, but we do have an ice machine in town. We receive regular deliveries. Would you like me to bring you some?" The little man looked inordinately proud that somewhere in the building, water was in a solid state.

"Yeah. Ice." Ingram pulled his hand back toward his chest. "And get me a bottle of whiskey, would ya? There's a pal." He shoved another ten dollar bill at the man. "Oh, and I'm going to need a room with a radio."

"Sir, we don't provide radios in guest rooms. The stealing is bad enough with the towels and linens—"

Ingram put his shattered hand on the ten, took it back, and slowly pulled a twenty out of his wallet. "You got a room with a radio?"

"Yes, the presidential suite has one."

"Either let me have that suite, or bring the radio from it to my room. And bring the whiskey, and lots of ice."

Ingram took the key and limped to the staircase.

He spent the next two days drunk, swollen hand submerged in ice, waiting for the event at Ruby's on the Bayou. He drank and listened to the radio intently, slowly twisting the tuning dial backward and forward down the green lit face of the radio, filling the room with alternating bursts of song, advertisements, and static. The throbbing in his hand diminished but didn't go entirely away; the cold water soothed it a bit, as did the whiskey in his blood. Occasionally, he stopped the roaming and listened to a full song or two, Miller's "Moonlight Serenade," or Wills' "Roly Poly," and then, like a searchlight, moved on, panning the dial down the frequencies until it could go no more then reversing its course on the radio face.

The first morning, a polite rapping at the door woke Ingram from where he slept in his chair. The doctor, a rangy, stubbled man who wore a stethoscope like a badge of office, entered and hissed in sympathy when he saw Ingram's hand.

"I'm Doctor Keene," he said brusquely, and he pointed to the rumpled hotel bed with the same authority of a captain—Cap Hap even—but without the joviality. Ingram rose from the chair and turned off the radio, moving like an old man, back stiff.

He sat on the bed while Doctor Keene gently probed at his hand. He tsked a few times, then looked Ingram in the eye and said, "Idiot. You're too big to fight. If you win, nobody will think any better of you on account of your size. If you lose, no one will give you any sympathy. People love seeing a big man fall. And they don't come much bigger than you."

Ingram sat, slump shouldered, staring abjectly at the over-bright pastel painting hanging on the opposite wall as the doctor removed two sturdy wooden shims and a roll of heavy gauze and splinted his hand with quick, military proficiency. When he was through, the doctor dug in his pocket and handed Ingram a container of white pills.

"Don't drink with them," he said, nodding at the near-empty bottle of whiskey. "Or you might not wake up." He took one of Ingram's cigarettes from the bureau, lit it with a gold lighter, and smiled. "I hope you've heard something of what I've said to you." He walked to the door, opened it, and exited in a swirl of cigarette smoke. When the door shut, Ingram opened the bottle of pills, popped two, and called down for breakfast and more ice.

The day passed in a haze of cigarette smoke and bursts of static. The whiskey bottle was empty by noon, and Ingram called and ordered another.

Near dusk, when the light filtering through the threadbare drapes turned orange, someone knocked at the door. Ingram peered through the peephole then opened the door.

A small man stood in the hall, smiling, hands on his hips, looking at Ingram. He had short-cropped, kinky hair going to gray at the temples, but his complexion was smooth except for the up-ward-turned lines at the corners of his eyes. Blue eyes. Notable for a black man. Those same eyes roved up and down Ingram's frame, taking in all the details, lingering on his wounded hand and the scratches down his cheeks.

He wore a tan maintenance uniform, immaculate and pressed, with an almost military air. The pants were creased, and the black patent leather shoes polished to a high sheen. A large ring of keys hung from his gleaming belt. His name tag read Randall.

"You wanted a driver?" the man asked.

"You ever been to Ruby's before?"

The man whistled. "Might be yes and might be no, depending on why you asking. Mabel didn't send you, did she?"

"No. I don't know any Mabel. I'm looking for someone other than you."

"Of course you is. But I ain't never seen anybody that looks like they's looking for somebody as bad as you is looking for somebody. Just wanted to be sure you ain't looking for me."

"No. Not you. You been to Ruby's? Know how to get there?"

"Course I do. I know every place where people congregate from here to Little Rock. I've been in every tonk and every dive and every saloon with or without a pool table that accepts Negroes and some that don't. I can take you where you need to go."

"OK. How long's it gonna take us to get to Ruby's?"

"Not long, an hour, hour and a half tops. We'll get there for the show."

"You know about it? This Ramblin' John Hastur fella? You ever seen him before?"

Randall looked left and right down the hall, then said, "Think maybe we can talk 'bout this inside your room? Just so folks don't think we're crazy?"

Ingram retreated and waved the smaller man in. He freshened his own drink, then made another for his guest without asking, and handed it to him silently. Randall sat on the edge of Ingram's bed, his bright blue eyes following the bigger man. He took the drink in a small hand—even delicate, for a maintenance man—and rolled the cold glass of whiskey in pink palms, then brought it to his lips and drank. He smiled.

"They call me Rabbit, might as well tell you that now. You welcome to call me that, or Randall, or whatever else you want to, but never call me boy. I ain't your boy, and you ain't my master."

"Don't want to be. Can't even master myself. You got a license?"

"Course."

Ingram took a drink of whiskey, set down the glass. In a drawer of the hotel room bureau, he found pen and paper. "Let me see it." He copied down Rabbit's name and license number. Then he looked at Rabbit and said, "I'm gonna deal it to you straight. I've been in this state for going on three days now, and I must've looked like a babe in the woods when I got here cause there's... some—" Ingram paused, the word *things* on his tongue, and reconsidered. "There's some folks that don't want me poking around. Did a few things to me that weren't so nice. I think they're friends of this Hastur character. I mean to find out who."

"You ain't looking quite as fresh as a daisy, that's for sure."

"More like a Black-Eyed Susan, I'd say." Both men laughed. "They call you Rabbit? My name's Ingram, but they call me Bull."

"The Rabbit and the Bull. I think we might have something there."

Rabbit threw back his head and laughed. Ingram saw gold fillings in the back of his mouth, and smiled with the little man. He found himself enjoying Rabbit's company. He couldn't trust Rabbit as far as he could throw him, but he could probably throw him a good ways, if he wanted to.

"So, what can you tell me about Hastur?"

"Lots of things. None of 'em make much sense."

"You ever seen him play?" Ingram asked, raising his eyebrows. "Heard his music?"

"Hell naw. I like the boogie-woogie—it's like when they make the blues rock and roll like a man and woman in a bed, you know? But blues men without a band ain't my thing. Can't dance to it, and the ladies like to dance."

"What have you heard 'bout him?"

"Shit. Everything. Like he's the Devil in the flesh, that he just the opposite, a saint sent here to save... well, to save the black folks from the oppression of the white man." Having said it, Rabbit looked at Ingram with a defiant glare. "Some ignorant black folks say he's gonna bring round the end of the world with his voice, and carry us over the river Jordan into the promised land. But them country black folk say that 'bout every preacher from here to Memphis." Ingram sat thinking. He raised his swaddled hand to ease the swelling, and groaned. "I can believe some of that. See, I've heard his music."

Rabbit said nothing, but his smile faded and he grew still.

"Don't know why I'm telling you this. I guess I like you or maybe you got an honest face."

"Shit," Rabbit said. "That ain't so. A hundred ladies know it from Des Arc to Dumas."

"Well, it doesn't matter. What matters is that a man in Memphis played me a recording of a radio station coming out of Arkansas, a pirated radio station, changing frequencies. You heard of that?"

"Yeah, I heard of it. I ain't heard it."

"He'd found the station and recorded part of a Hastur song. I haven't heard nothing like that ever in my life, and I don't mean that in a good way. I started getting worked up, like I wanted to kill somebody, like I was going crazy, like the bottom had dropped out of the well. Do you know what I mean?"

Rabbit nodded, face serious. "Like everything you ever known has died. Like it's all over, 'cept for the crying."

Ingram nodded. "Yes. Felt just like that. But I took the job anyway, to find a man. He's got a family and I... I don't have nothing really 'cept scars and time. This man, a white man, he'd been looking for Hastur. Now he's missing. So I'm looking for two men now, Early Freeman—the white fella—and Ramblin' John Hastur. But people and... things... keep getting in my way."

He poured himself another glass, offered more to Rabbit.

"Naw. No more for me."

Ingram sipped his drink, then shivered. "So, this is where we stand. Tomorrow, I'm going to Ruby's, where Hastur is supposed to play." Ingram took the rumpled mimeograph out of his shirt pocket and tossed it to Rabbit, who snatched it out of the air with deft fingers. "One man has gone missing looking for this fella and other... other... fucked up things have happened. I need a driver. I know I told that clerk downstairs five dollars, but I'll pay you ten, cause it could be dangerous. But I need you to help me, get me to where I need to go. Without someone like you—" Ingram smiled, recognizing the strangeness of what he was saying. "Without a local, I don't think I'll have a chance here, I'll meet another accident."

Ingram sipped his drink again and watched Rabbit. Rabbit took a pack of Pall Malls out of his perfectly creased pants, shook a cigarette out of the pack, tamped the cigarette on his wrist, then lit the tip with a match, all done with slow, deliberate motions as Ingram looked on, waiting for his answer.

Then he smiled. "I'll do it for twenty. Half up front."

Ingram motioned to Rabbit for a smoke. Rabbit packed another one on his wrist, then, with a little flourish, twisted the end to keep the loose tobacco in. He handed it to Ingram, who lit it with a match. The larger man coughed.

"Okay. Ten up front. Ten when you get me back here. I'll buy your drinks."

"Deal." The smaller man grinned. "I guess I will take another drink. And that ten up front." Rabbit grinned even larger, gold flashing in his mouth.

The two men sat for a while, smoking Rabbit's cigarettes, drinking Ingram's whiskey. It was night now; Ingram reached out and flipped on the radio, began searching through the frequencies, static hissing. After a while, Rabbit stood, straightened his pants legs, and said, "Well, I best be on my way home. Dark already, and I need to lay out some clothes for tomorrow night. Been a long time since I've been to Ruby's so I need to look tight."

Ingram dug out his keys, tossed them to the smaller man. "Take the coupe, green, parked out front. Make sure you can drive her. Gas comes out of your end—you're getting paid enough. If you've got a gun, I'd take a little time and make friends with her again, if you haven't held her for a while. Just in case."

"I guess you're paying me enough. But we'll have to settle up if I actually have to shoot some fool."

"Understood. Be here in time to get me there before the main act starts. Hastur."

"Mr. Ingram, I'm your man, tomorrow at least. Be here, bells on, five o'clock."

When the door shut, Ingram poured another drink and turned back to the radio, searching.

Chapter 8

After the night Franny went missing, Sarah relented on the child's sleeping arrangements. Some nights, she would allow Franny to sleep with Lenora and Fisk. But the nights when she kept Franny with her, they slept together. Those nights, she curled against her daughter in a quiet, desperate half-circle, her body curled around the sleeping form of her child, her arm laid over Franny, her nose in the child's hair, breathing her scent, watching her chest rise and fall. Watching her eyes move underneath her eyelids.

Sarah, as she bathed Franny, treated the luminous child like some object of worship, silently ministering to the girl as Franny talked through her day.

"Then Fisk said he saw a snake in the woods and Lenora said he didn't and I was scared, a little. But Fisk is brave and he told me to stand behind him when we went into the woods, and we walked for a while, Fisk was going to show us the snake. He called it a fat snake. That's funny, don't you think, Mommy? A fat snake."

Sarah lathered up Franny's hair with baby shampoo. She loved the smell and feel of the soap, so soothing to her. "That does sound funny, baby. Did you see one? Did Fisk show you a fat snake?"

"We walked to the river, not too far from here, through that wood." Franny pointed to the window, out over the fallow field, toward the dark wood. Sarah leaned over the claw-footed tub and dipped a ladle full of water, then gently poured it over Franny's head, rinsing soap away from her hair in rivulets.

"You all go there? Into the woods?" She frowned. "I don't know if you should be going in there without an adult."

"*Mommy.*" Franny was irritated and frightened all at once. "Mommy, it's fine. I'm with Fisk and Lenora. Fisk is eight and Lenora is ten. And I'm not scared. It's *not* scary. It's just dark but the sun comes through the leaves some too."

"That's not what I'm worried about, honey. I need to know exactly where you are at all times. It can be dangerous in the country. Okay?"

"Okay. I'll tell you."

Sarah placed her hands on Franny's shoulders and turned her gently toward her. "Really? Promise me you won't wander off and not tell me where you're going."

"I promise, Mommy. Really. I will."

Sarah took a deep breath, sighed, and chewed her lip. "Okay."

Sarah thought about her endless summer afternoons exploring the fields and forests around the Big House as a girl; with Alice there had been adventures, a wonderful sprawling childhood, field upon field and day after day, wide open and unrestrained.

She smiled and tweaked Franny under her arm, tickling her rib-cage. Franny squealed, splashing in the murky water.

The laughing felt good. She wished there was more times like this with her daughter, more time spent together, happy. Fisk and Lenora filled Franny's world right now, and Sarah was just a touch-stone to visit while the children tested the boundaries of their bodies, their minds, and the land around them.

"So, did you see a snake?"

Franny nodded. Then giggled. "He was fat! And black all over, lying on a log right by the water. Fisk threw a rock at it, and it slithered into the river." Franny held out her hands to indicated something large. Water splashed Sarah's leg. "And the *river*... it was huge. Have you ever been to the river, Mommy? We could barely see across it. Fisk said it was the Arkansas River, and Lenora said that's right and then I saw a man across the river standing in the trees. He was a black man."

She held up her hand to her eye, the index and thumb barely separated. "And he was only this big. That's how big the river is. And he was looking at me, I could tell. Fisk and Lenora didn't see him, but I did. They were looking at the big boat that was coming up the river. Fisk said its name was the *Hellion*, said it was painted on the side. What's a hellion?"

Sarah smiled and said, "I don't know, baby. I'd have to see the boat. Was it big?"

Franny looked puzzled, then nodded again. "But it was kinda hard to tell how big it was because the river is so much bigger. Mommy, do you think someone could swim across the river?"

Sarah poured more bath water on the girl's pale shoulders. "No, honey, I don't think there's any way a person could swim across the river."

Franny looked slightly relieved. Sarah asked, "Did Fisk say that he was going to swim across the river?"

Franny didn't answer, just looked at the wall and shook her head again.

"Well, if he ever tries to, you run and tell Alice or me, because the river is very dangerous. It's not like swimming in Old River Lake. The river has currents that can carry you off, or suck you under water. Promise me you'll never swim in the river."

"I don't want the black man to swim across the river." Franny turned in the bath, and said earnestly, "I will never swim in the river, Mommy, because there are snakes in the river. It's scary."

Sarah leaned forward, kissed her daughter on the nose. "Good, punkin. But we'll go to Old River Lake real soon, and you and Fisk and Lenora can swim again. How's that sound? Good?"

I hope to God she doesn't find out that Old River has snakes too.

The girl nodded. "Can I sleep with Lenora and Fisk tonight?"

"I wanted you to be my snuggle buddy."

"Please?" She drew out the word into multiple syllables. "Please, can I?"

Sarah brushed a loose strand of hair back from her face, and tucked it behind her ear. "If you get dried off, comb your hair, and brush your teeth, then we'll go down and ask Alice."

Franny squealed, sloshing gray water in the tub. "You're the bestest Mommy in the whole world." She splashed Sarah with water again as she held out her arms to encompass everything.

"I hope so, baby. I hope so."

Alice was puttering around in the kitchen when Franny and Sarah entered. She took one look at Franny, glanced at Sarah's despondent face, and smiled ruefully. "Franny, I think they're still up. You go tee-tee and then get in bed, child."

Franny scampered off, disappearing into Alice's quarters. Alice turned to Sarah, said, "Don't look at me like somebody shot your dog, girl. Looks to me like Fisk and Lenora are her first friends, and living here under the same roof, they're gonna want to be together." Alice turned around to the sink, started washing the dishes.

"I feel like I'm losing my baby to you. This place."

Alice stiffened. "You done some stupid things in your time, girl—and that Jim was the *most*—but that's the dumbest thing you *ever* said."

It was surprising that she could feel such anger toward her oldest friend, but there it was, burning bright. It felt like a hot ember smoldering in her stomach. Blood rushed to her cheeks.

"And Calvin was—"

Alice slammed a plate down into the sink. There was a sharp crack. She turned, her eyes pained and weathered at the edges.

"We ain't talking bout *me*, Sarah. We talking about *you*."

Her hands were clutched into fists, Sarah saw, and dripping water onto the floor.

"Something wrong, Alice? Mommy?" Franny stood, jammied and frizzy, in the door to Alice's rooms.

Sarah made her body unclench, loosened her shoulders. This was *Alice*. If there was anyone she should listen to, to trust, it was her. "No, baby. We were just talking."

"Girl, you go brush them teeth. Now," Alice said, and Sarah marveled at how brusque she could be yet still put love in her voice.

Franny stuck out her tongue at Alice, turned, and disappeared.

And suddenly, Sarah couldn't find any reason to be angry with Alice anymore. It was as if anger in her had been snuffed out, like a candle.

Alice eased, opened her dripping hands, and then turned back to the sink.

"Your momma asked for you this afternoon, wants you to bring her sip. She's a little cranky, to be honest." Alice paused here, slumped her shoulders and leaned into the counter. "Or she was earlier. Might be better now, but I doubt it. I'll make sure the kids get to sleep real soon. You go on and talk to your momma. Don't let nothing she's got to say bother you." Alice winked at her. A peace offering. "Oh, there's another bottle of Wellings in the Library. Saw you been working in there. You getting ready to go back to school?"

Sarah shook her head, laughed a little at the idea. "No, of course not. That night I couldn't sleep, I just started remembering the two years I spent at Hollins before the war, and Latin class." Sarah almost said translating the little book kept her mind off things, but stopped when she realized she didn't want to say what.

"Always knew you were happy when you were at college, though I missed you something fierce. After you see your momma, I'll have a toddy waiting for you down in the library, if you want. You can do a little more reading, or whatever, and drink it there. After talking to you momma, you might need it."

"That sounds wonderful, Alice. What would I do without you?"

"Don't have to flatter me, none, Sarah. I'm here. You know that.

I'll always be here."

Alice stopped her dishwashing, looked down into the water.

❧

Sarah went to the library, glanced at the open book on the green ink blotter of the oak desk, then retrieved the port from the dry bar nestled amongst the volumes.

The gallery was dark as Sarah walked up to the second floor where her room, the bathroom she'd just bathed Franny in, and her mother's room were located. Around the other side of the gallery were two more rooms, one a ladies' den and the other an unused guest room. At her mother's door, she knocked.

There was no answer. Sarah rapped again, louder. Again no answer.

Sarah pushed her way in to the room, totally black except for the blue light coming from a big open bay window, ruffling the sheer drapes in the breeze. Sarah's mind went briefly back to the night that Franny went missing. Sometimes, the sensation of her fright and pure terror of that night came back to her unwillingly and unwanted, catching in her chest and making her breath come in hard gasps.

She moved to her mother's bed, realized it was empty, and looked around. In the shadow by the window, her mother sat on a padded bench, pulled from her vanity. She stared out the window, looking at something in the yard, or the field beyond it. Sarah came closer, walking up behind her mother. The old woman's hair shone whitish blue from the moonlight streaming in through the window. Her shoulders slumped a little, but otherwise she looked at ease. As Sarah drew near, she could make out black shapes moving in the yard.

"Momma?" Sarah whispered.

Sarah's mother muttered something she couldn't make out, words in a low tone that hovered just beyond understanding. Sarah turned away, placed the tray of Wellings down on the bedside table, and returned to her mother.

"Momma? Are you okay?"

Sarah walked as softly as she could, rolling on each foot ball to toe, ball to toe. She paused, squatting, trying to hear the mutterings her mother made. But they were nonsense, breathy and unintelligible, like the Pentecostals speaking in tongues that she'd seen at a tent revival as a child. She tried to read her mother's lips, but the older woman's wild white hair covered her mouth. Sarah reached out and softly touched her mother's hand, white with age, thin as parchment.

The moment Sarah's hand came into contact with her mother's, the old woman whipped her head around, snarling. Sarah, startled, fell backward, onto her haunches, sitting down heavily.

For an instant—a fleeting moment like the after image of a photographer's flash—her mother's face had been vicious, enraged. Her eyes appeared totally black, her cheeks mottled, her lips pulled back like those of a feral, savage dog, showing yellow teeth in black gums.

But then the image passed and Sarah wasn't sure what had happened, what she had seen. She rose up from her seat on the floor.

"Sarah, don't sneak up on your mother like that, goddammit. At least Alice has got the sense to just leave when I'm in my reverie." The old woman smoothed the empty bust of her dress. "I'm sorry, honey. I'm not feeling too well, so I'm gonna be a little short. And sneaking up on me like that! I was lost in my own thoughts, staring out at the moon in the yard."

"Momma, I knocked twice. Then I called your name a couple of times too. You didn't answer. What were you saying?"

Sarah's mother looked at her with narrowed eyes. "That's none of your business, missy. You ought to let an old lady have her secrets. Anywho, I was just sitting here—"

"In the dark."

"That's right, in the dark, watching the peafowl out in the yard. If I turn on the light, they can see my silhouette and they know I'm watching them, which won't do at all. Not at all."

She turned toward Sarah, white hair a tangled spray in the blue light. Her dark eyes brightened. "Did you bring my sip?"

Sarah nodded and retrieved the tray by the bed.

"No, come help me get back in bed and then pour one."

Sarah started back across the room, and her mother hissed, "Turn on the damned light, you ninny, so I can see." Sarah turned once more, switched on the beside lamp, and then returned to her mother. She helped the old woman rise, and led her back to bed. Once her mother was comfortable, tucked under a goose down comforter, she poured a glass of the port. Her mother downed it immediately and held out the glass for another. She downed that one as well, and then sipped the third.

"Tell me, daughter. Why hasn't that miscreant child of yours come to see me more often since she's been here? I can hear her and Alice's brood tromping up and down the halls—"

"Have they been bothering you, Momma? If they've been bothering you, we'll stop them from coming up on this floor."

"It's not that, girl. Why hasn't my granddaughter come to see me more?" Her mother stuck out a gnarled finger and jabbed it at Sarah. "More to the point, why haven't you brought her to me? Hmm?"

Sarah remembered the years growing up in this house, her mother's fierce interrogations, her rants, her rages. Elizabeth Rheinhart Werner had neither respect nor tolerance for timidity or shyness.

"She's scared of you, mother. Franny thinks you're turning into a wolf, to gobble her up. A stupid play on words that Jim made planted that idea in her head."

Sarah's mother gave a thick, wheezing laugh that quickly turned into a cough. When the coughs died, the old woman smiled, tears streaming down the sides of her withered, discolored face.

She laughed again, and said, "Whoo-ee, I'm starting to like that girl. I watch her from my window, you know. She's a wild thing, not like you or your father. She's like me." Sarah's mother tapped her ribcage with a gnarled finger. "Tell that little dumpling that I was born a wolf, and after many years, I'm finally becoming human."

At that, Elizabeth settled into her cushions and asked Sarah to read to her from the volume of Dickens at her bedside table.

"I've been trying to finish *Bleak House* for months, my eyes are becoming so bad. And it's not really a good book for right now, now that the big house isn't so bleak anymore, eh? How bout young master Copperfield, or *Great Expectations?*"

Sarah poured her mother another port, leaned back in the chair beside the bed, and picked up *Great Expectations*.

After the first page, her mother asked for more port, which Sarah gave her, then started to snore, making a light chuffing sound. Sarah remained still, looking at her mother, hands in her lap, lightly holding the big book. Finally, she rubbed away the tears at the corners of her eyes and stood. Sarah carefully maneuvered the bookmark to the right page and quietly crept from her mother's room.

On the gallery, it was darker than earlier, and a hush had fallen over the old house. The quiet made Sarah uneasy. In some ways coming home had been the most natural thing she'd done in years, but in other ways she felt dislocated, separated from her life and world and daughter.

I can't compete for her affections against other children. They fill her world now, I only constrain it. If I try and supplant those kids, she'll never forgive me... and she'd be right not to. But what do I do with— for—myself? Drinking gallons of coffee with Alice every morning and sneaking cigarettes on the sleeping porch... well, it just ain't cutting it, as Jim would say.

She thought about Jim then, playing with the idea of going home to visit, just her, just to see how he was. He hadn't called or written in the weeks they'd been here, and every one of her phone calls went unanswered. None of her letters had been returned, though. So he was still receiving the mail.

She lightly touched her breast, shivering in the dark of the gallery, goose bumps rippling over her skin.

Then she noticed the black figure standing in a spill of shadow at the foot of the stairs. A silhouette, jet black, looked up at her, head cocked and staring intently, silent, eyes like flecks of obsidian.

Sarah's breath caught in her chest, and the goose bumps of plea-
sure quickly turned to those of fear. She dropped her arms to her
sides, not knowing what to do. A clock ticked somewhere and the
old timbers of the house settled around her. The black thing below
stared, its eyes fierce and black.

Then Alice passed in the doorway of the kitchen, beneath Sarah,
blocking the spray of light slanting into the atrium below, changing the configuration of shadows.

And the thing was gone, if it had ever really been there at all.

Sarah exhaled suddenly. She hadn't realized she'd been holding
her breath.

She went downstairs and into the kitchen.

Alice turned to look at her, then said, "*Humph*. She must've
been real bad. I've got the water hot. You go on into the library,
I'll bring your toddy in to you." Alice pointed to a bowl in a far
corner of the counter. "I'm gonna be up for a bit, got some dough
rising. I'll come check on you in a bit. Go on, girl. I know you
been waiting."

In the library, *Opusculus Noctis* was open on the desk, and as she
sat down in front of it, Sarah took a deep breath, placed a hand on
the yellowed sheet, and turned over her page of translation from
the night before. It read:

> the little book of shadows
> or the little night book
> a ~~glance~~ look into the shadows
> ~~demands~~ requires many things
> if one ~~wishes~~ would like to ~~converse~~ bargain
> with the ~~animals~~ creatures kept locked
> beyond ~~the stars or~~ the vorago?
> admonitio admonition? warning
> a warning
> do not call up that which you haven't ~~pulli~~
> ~~sent away~~
> don't call up

> *what you cannot put down*
> *all ~~sermons~~ converse with the prodigious*
> *must begin start with a payment ~~tithe~~ of*
> *inculpatis innocent? blood*
> *~~in addition to~~ also*
> *the ~~will~~ intention to bargain, the caller*
> *is ~~helped~~ assisted by the*
> *intention to do ~~necessity~~ the necessary things?*

Sarah had managed the translation with great effort, flipping backward and forward in the Latin English dictionary. The fact it made no sense depressed her, but she felt, for the first time in years, a desire to *know*, to understand. What was the meaning behind the words? They blended together on each line of the pamphlet, having no spaces between letters to indicate the beginning or end of a thought or phrase. There were certain words, like *vorago* and *prodigium*, that were not provided for in the library's poor dictionary. She couldn't tell if it was some religious manual or an ancient recipe book. She knew she'd committed mistakes in the translation, but hoped the gist of it was right. She couldn't be sure without consulting someone who knew better.

Sarah frowned and nibbled on the eraser of her pencil. When she looked up, she noticed that Alice had entered the library, placed the toddy in front of her, and left with her none the wiser.

Sarah picked up the glass and felt the warmth of the golden drink, took a swallow, and shivered. Alice had made this one strong.

Sarah smiled and turned back to her translation.

Chapter 9

Rabbit came to the Royale Hotel to pick up Ingram at five in the afternoon, dressed in dark blue slacks and a silky white shirt. A gold chain gleamed in the V of his open collar, and his hair was smoothed back.

Rabbit walked into Ingram's hotel room, filling the small space with the scent of pomade. Ingram raised his eyebrows and said, "Well, you sure are sparkly. You fall into a vat of perfume?"

Rabbit cocked an eyebrow at Ingram. His hair was darker now that the pomade kept it tight against his head. "Naw, I ain't fell into no vat o' perfume. Yet. Maybe later. Maybe it ain't something you can appreciate but the ladies will be ready for me, and the smell-good is just part of the program."

Ingram thought for a moment. "Turn around."

Rabbit hesitated, then smiled, turning around, rotating slowly. "Nice, ain't they? Got 'em in Little Rock. That's real imported silk."

"Nice. Real nice. So where's your gun?"

Rabbit's smile vanished. "It's in the coupe, under the driver's seat."

"Caliber?"

".25."

Ingram smiled. "It is Saturday night."

"Ain't no Saturday night pistol. It's a good piece, chrome plated, real sweet."

"Semi or revolver?"

"Semi."

"It's a Saturday Night Pistol, but that's okay. We're gonna be in a bar. You gotta shoot somebody, stick it in his stomach or his face and pull the trigger. It should probably do the trick."

Ingram went to his suitcase, picked up a rumpled jacket, put it on. He followed that with a Morley .38 and slipped it into the jacket pocket. He rummaged around in his suitcase a little more, then threw a small leather holster at Rabbit, who snatched it out of the air.

"If it looks rough, just stay in the coupe, Rabbit. You don't have to deal with any trouble."

"Wait in the car? Not with all the ladies waiting inside. What's this?"

"Ankle holster. For your not-a-Saturday-Night-pistol."

"All right then, I'm your man. Let's get on."

Ingram stretched in the hall, reached up and touched the ceiling, then bent over to touch his toes. Rabbit watched him with a puzzled look on his face.

"What're you doing, Bull?"

"Working out the kinks."

His hand throbbed horribly, and he held it above his head to ease the swelling as they went downstairs, out of the lobby, and into the parking lot.

❦

It was hot in the coupe, rumbling over asphalt and potholes, motor humming.

Rabbit cranked down the driver's side window all the way and hung his silk-clad arm out the side. Ingram popped the smoker's window and angled it inward, so that the breeze blew directly on him. He was breaking out in cold sweats and feverish heats alternately; two days of whiskey and pills had taken its toll.

They passed through deep delta, low country interspersed with fields and farms that gave way to forests and scrub-brush. They trundled down dusty roads, rolling in an out of cane breaks, past amber fields, through the late sunny haze of afternoon.

Rabbit told Ingram about the layout of Ruby's.

"Big long building, it is, lemme tell you. Got a stage in the back. When you come in the front door, you got an aisle going between tables, got your bar—a real long one—on your right with stools. They's an office at the back, back of the kitchen, I think but can't be sure." Rabbit took his hands off the coupe's wheel and adjusted the rear view mirror. "There's a hallway to the right of the stage, just beyond the bar, that leads back to a back door where they take deliveries from the pier. Got some storerooms and closets and a pisser back there too."

"Pier? So it's on a wharf?"

Rabbit gave a sharp look to Ingram, then nodded. "Sure. Named Ruby's on the Bayou, ain't it? When I was a youngun, working in the cotton fields, after harvest we'd put them cotton bales on barges—shallow rafts back then—and pole the barges down the bayou until we'd hit Ruby's. It was called McFeely's Wharf back then. We'd load the bales on the pier, and after a little bit a steamer or one of the new diesel freighters would come pick it up, float it down the Arkansas to the Mississippi. To Helena or Natchez or New Orleans." He sighed and looked off into the tree line. "That was some hard work."

After another pause, he said, "I remember Ruby made good etoufee. Heard that ole girl died a while back, so we'll find out about the grub."

Ingram snorted. "Last thing on my mind is food."

"Better eat. A body wants food, and your mind ain't gone work right if you don't. If bad things happen, you'll need to have ate. That's a fact."

"Yeah. Okay."

They drove on in silence. It was nearing dark when they rejoined pavement. Rabbit steered for ten or twenty miles down the unmarked highway, then took a left toward a large wood with smoke rising behind the trees. Oily-leafed magnolia trees lined the gravel road, their white blossoms filling the coupe with a sweet, cloying scent. Well graveled, the road was twice as wide as the highway, and the rocks crunched heavily under the coupe's tires.

Once they passed the tree line, Ingram smelled the bayou and the river beyond, a thick muddy scent, wet and filled with life. He bummed another smoke from Rabbit, and blew billows out the window. The wind whisked the smoke away behind them. Through the trees, Ingram noticed thin yellow light from a building, and heard the slamming of car doors. The sun had extinguished itself in the waters of the bayou and sent up pink and purple streamers into the night air.

Rabbit steered the coupe into a large gravel area next to a dark brown building on the edge of a muddy expanse of water. The trees didn't crowd so close here. Ingram judged there to be twenty or thirty cars clustered around the building. He watched as two couples walked to the front doors of the building, noticed another couple sitting in a darkened car, either smoking or drinking. Or something else.

The building itself was wooden with brick work around what Ingram assumed was the kitchen area. On a wrap-around porch, kerosene lanterns cast guttering pools of yellow light, except for the far side of the building, where a pier stretched a good thirty or forty yards into the waters of Bayou Bartholomew.

Rabbit parked the coupe, wheels crunching on the gravel, and the men exited. Ingram checked his gun and put on his rumpled jacket. He motioned Rabbit to follow and walked around to the side of the building to the pier. A couple of big flat john-boats with outboard motors were moored there, along with a skiff that looked unstable and carious as a rotten tooth. At the very end of the pier sat a large river tug, heavy in the water, painted black and silhouetted against the last vestiges of the dying sun, stars salting the sky around its stacks. It was a big boat, made for pushing heavy barges up and down the Mississippi and Arkansas rivers, barges filled with coal, or granite, or other dense materials. The boat had three decks, the main, a second deck, and then the pilot's roost, with a big smokestack sprouting behind it. Antennae poked skyward from along the main stack, giving the tug a jagged, insectile appearance.

Ingram walked up the access stairs to the pier. Drowsy waves washed onto the muddy shore with low, gurgling sounds. The moored boats knocked and bumped against the pilings. Ingram's feet echoed loudly on the tarred planks. The air was filled with the smell of burning kerosene and dead fish.

As he drew closer to the end of the pier, the word *Hellion* painted in white on the hull of the boat became clear. He could make out the word *Natchez* a little further down the gunwale. Ingram scratched his head.

He had forgotten Rabbit until he heard him say, "This here's Bayou Bartholomew. Runs from where we stand down to the river if you go that way." A long, well-manicured finger pointed north.

Arm out, Rabbit swung around and pointed south. "But it also runs that way, for a country mile. You could probably float all the way down into Louisiana on that bayou. It's the only water transportation for a lot of counties, and it was pretty important for us coming up, right after the war. Not that European one." Rabbit looked sharply at Ingram. "Or your war, Bull. But the one between the states. Spent a lot of time on it when I was younger, floating cotton right to this pier we're standing on." He waved his hand toward the dark. "Used to be good fishing out there."

Rabbit stared out into the bayou, a half smile shadowing his face, lost in his own thoughts. Ingram looked at him, noticing for the first time the ineffable tracery of time and experience etched into his skin.

Ingram asked, "How old are you, Rabbit? I can't tell."

Rabbit barked a laugh. "White folk never can, can they?" Then he smiled, a little rueful. "Do it matter? You're all right, Bull, I ain't got no call to give you any grief. I was born in '88. Makes me sixty-three, which is old, by just about anybody's reckoning. I've seen just about everything there is to see, at least when you talking 'bout your fellow man."

Rabbit walked back up the pier, around to the front of the building. Ingram followed. A gigantic man took their cover inside the front door, giving Ingram a suspicious glance.

It was hot inside. The building was as Rabbit described, long and narrow with the stage in the back. Somewhere around a fifty or sixty people sat or milled about, drinking and smoking. He scanned the tables.

People held bottles in brown bags, pouring liquor into cheap blue chipped glasses provided by the house. Each table had candles and no tablecloths. Where the bar stood, two smiling men took dinner and drink orders, greeted friends and patrons.

Ingram whispered to Rabbit, "Are white people allowed in here?"

"White people allowed wherever the hell they want, Bull, especially when they're as big and ugly looking as you."

Ingram glanced at Rabbit. "Ugly? Hey—"

Rabbit held up his hands. "All white folk is ugly until you get to know them. Then they usually get uglier. But I wouldn't worry none. You're a big—I mean *big*—fella. Ain't nobody here gonna mess with you."

A jukebox pushed the faint strains of blues into the air, its lit face crowded with men and women, smiling and talking.

"Let's see if we can get a table, Rabbit. Close to the stage."

The two men elbowed their way to the front of the room. Dim lights barely lit the stage. There were two amplifiers, a drum set, and a microphone stand. Cables snaked across the stage and disappeared into the PA system.

"What time is it?"

"Nine. We got least an hour to wait. There's a table right there."

Ingram pointed at the bar and said, "Get me a whiskey, willya?"

Rabbit raised an eyebrow, said, "I look like a waiter to you?"

Ingram held his bandaged hand in front of Rabbit's face. "No, you don't. Do I?" Ingram pulled a bill out of his jacket's inner pocket, crumpled it in his fist, and threw it at Rabbit. "I think maybe a one-armed white man might stand out in this crowd. Keep the ten I gave you, take this. Get us some drinks. And listen. Tell what folks are talking about. I wouldn't be able to get that info."

Rabbit cocked his head, considering. "Well, there is the ladies to consider. What you want to drink again?" He winked at Ingram then turned and moved through the crowd to the bar.

Ingram found a table close to the stage, occupied by one man, an overweight fellow with blunt features. He stood over the table, hand held close to his chest, and fumbled at his wallet with his left. He gave the man a dollar to get up, and took the man's seat. There was a low red candle burning in the middle of the table. With his good hand, Ingram pulled the candle toward him, and idly played with the wax dripping down its sides.

The lights came up on the stage. A man dressed in an expensively cut suit, slicked hair, and tightly groomed facial hair came onto the elevated platform from the hallway behind the stage. Guitars and drums glinted in the light behind him. He approached center microphone. A smattering of applause came from the audience.

"Hello," he said, squelching the microphone. He looked toward the servers at the bar. One of the men ducked down underneath the counter, adjusting something, and gave the man on stage thumbs up.

"Good evening, ladies and gentlemen." He had a smooth voice, deep and rich.

I've heard this guy's voice before.

"I'd like to welcome y'all to Ruby's. We've got a real exciting evening planned for you. First up, we got Helena's own Jim Cannon, a great bluesman who's gonna go places with his new sound. After that, we got Roller Winslow, straight from Memphis, on a Southern tour of Arkansas, Louisiana, and Texas. We're real excited about hearing his new single, 'Miss You When You're Gone.'" A few women hooted and whistled.

The well spoken man cleared his throat, then dabbed at his forehead with a white handkerchief. A sheen of sweat beaded on the man's forehead, glistening on his oiled mustache. With the kitchen, the press of human flesh, the room had become stifling; the fans that hung from the ceiling did very little to move the air in the building.

"My name is Grover Johnson, and I'm honored to be your emcee tonight. But of course, all you fine and beautiful people didn't come to hear me. You came to hear the last guest of the night. Curiosity might've brought you, rumor might have led you, or you might even be here by chance. But the man you've really come to see is at the end of the night, the Tattered Man, the Rambler—" He raised his voice a bit and said louder, "Ramblin' John! Here tonight. That's right. So whatever brought you, sit back, listen, dance and drink and enjoy yourselves, because all of your questions are going to be answered. But for now, I'd like to invite you all to put your hands together for Jim Cannon and the Cannonballers!"

Clapping, the people in the crowd moved forward to the stage, some with drinks in hand, others hopping excitedly. Men came from the hallway by the performance area, joined it, taking up their instruments, some grinning, some serious. Couples pressed the stage, men and women dressed in their finest, holding hands. But there were a few single women going toward the stage as well.

Once some of the throng moved away from the tables, more of the audience became visible, the observers. There were people here, like him, who weren't interested in having a good time; they were interested in Ramblin' John. Ingram didn't need a degree or a telescope to tell him that, he could see it written clearly on their faces. Maybe they were preachers, maybe they were folk who had brushed up against the same mystery he had.

Across the room he spied a man sitting alone, watching the stage intently.

He felt a small jolt.

The man sat in the far, shadowed corner. The man's skin was so pale Ingram began to question whether he was white or a black man afflicted with the albinism he occasionally saw on the streets of Memphis, alabaster skin with black or pink eyes.

The band began to play, guitar, bass, and drums washing like waves into the shore of the audience, thumping and buzzing. Ingram turned away from scrutinizing the pale man across the dark room to watch the group of people between him and the band. The faces of the women seemed ecstatic, the men's intense. Their bodies rubbed against each other rhythmically, clothes shimmying and swishing, dress hems swaying.

Rabbit sat down heavily in the chair opposite from Ingram, cigarette dangling from his lip. He was smiling. He shoved blue glass tumblers toward Ingram, each with two fingers of amber liquid swirling in the bottom. He kept two more glasses in front of himself.

"Bar's busy tonight, there's a press for drinks. Got us extra. They're out of gumbo, but gonna bring round some bread."

Ingram looked at Rabbit, raised his eyebrows, and waited.

Rabbit took a long drag of his smoke, blew the smoke at Ingram, and belted back one of the blue glasses of liquor.

"So?"

"So, what? There's a lot of fools come to hear what Ramblin' John got to offer. There's one fool in particular who thinks all the ladies are gonna drop their britches and let him get on down with them, right on the dance floor. Might happen. Maybe yes, maybe no. You can't never tell, really."

The band moved into another number, this one upbeat, a shuffle. Rabbit patted his hand along with the music. "There's women here sure need me to dance with, Lord help them. Guess I better stay with you, though, so you ain't scared? Rabbit's gonna take care of you." He winked at Ingram.

Ingram snorted. "Remember what I'm here for." He picked up one of the glasses and tossed back the liquor. His throat burned, and he hitched his face in pain. After a moment, he said, "Get up. Go dance. Don't look right now, but I want you to move over by that fellow over there, ask him something, if his seat is taken. But do it inconspicuously."

Rabbit languidly turned in his seat, as if surveying the crowd. "Which fella, Bull? The room's full of 'em."

"The white one."

It was Rabbit's turn to raise his eyebrows. "Shit. Nother white man in here?" He shook his head. "Oh, no. That means trouble. One white man is passing tolerable. Two is trouble. And *you* two is sure to get along like a house on fire."

"That's to say not at all?" Ingram asked.

"Exactly."

"Right. Go on anyway. This band'll be finished in a minute, and the crowd will start moving. You can overhear him, or see who he's with."

"All right, then. But I ain't figured out what kinda hazard pay this'll cost you."

Rabbit stood and sauntered away from Ingram's table. Ingram briefly regretted bringing the man along with him; Ingram had put him in danger. And judging by his jovial behavior, Rabbit wasn't prepared for what might happen.

Ingram waited. Surrounded by revelers, he played with the burning candle, dripping red wax onto the table in front of him with his free hand, making small pools and then rolling the still warm wax puddles into balls. Nobody bothered him, though some stared.

The first band struck set and left the stage to a smattering of applause. The dancers evaporated. Rabbit was conversing with a woman easily twenty years his junior, speaking to her earnestly, holding her slim, well-formed arm, and Ingram wished he could hear the lines, at least for his own edification. The second band, Roller Winslow and the Debonnaires, quickly set up their instruments and, with only a brief word from Grover Johnson, started to play. The first outfit had played light frothy tunes that bounced and floated. But this new band was something different; the band pumped out music with a heavy beat, steady and powerful. The instruments were rooted, percussive and rotund, the bass coming through and filling out the sound to something that seemed to pull at his insides. Ingram found himself wishing he was here for something other than business, other than self-preservation.

Each song became more percussive and driving than the last. When the singer announced their new single, "Miss You When You're Gone," there was raucous clapping, and more people from behind Ingram rushed the stage so that he was left looking at a clothed wall of backs. Once again he was alone in a mass of people. He finished his drink and dripped wax onto the table, pushing at the warm red stuff with his fingertips.

The band worked through two more numbers, and men and women sweated freely now, clutching each other tight as they moved their bodies in time with the thumping music. Ingram, unmoving except to sip his drink or to take small glances at the Pale Man in the corner, watched the musicians. He lost Rabbit in the crowd.

The band stopped, and the emcee came onstage. Despite the loudness of the PA system, Ingram ignored him as he thanked the band and introduced the members; he scanned the far side of the venue for Rabbit.

People moved away from the stage, toward the bar, and Ingram saw Rabbit. He stood stock still in front of the Pale Man's table, arms rigid at his sides.

Something's not right here.

The Pale Man turned his head glacially, at first toward Rabbit, then onward. His gaze fastened on Ingram.

Ingram felt a small electric thrum and realized he couldn't make out the man's eyes. From across the room, the intervening space hazy with smoke, the Pale Man's face seemed mottled with darkness, like he'd been bruised in a heavy fistfight. His eyes were lost in the paleness of his face, like shadows, except for tiny pinpricks of white, maybe the reflection of the halogen stage lights. Looking at the man transfixed Ingram; his good hand paused in raising the glass to his lips, his body went slack.

This isn't any good. Something bad's gonna happen.

Grover Johnson jumped up on stage and bellowed into the microphone.

"This is it, ya'll! The man you been waiting for! The rambler, the gambler, the Tattered Man himself, John Hastur!"

As the crowd erupted in applause, pressing tighter toward the stage, Rabbit bent over in a labored, jerky manner and reached for his ankle.

Ingram stood. He kicked his chair away. Rabbit raised a small chrome-plated pistol—the Saturday Night Special. He brought it over his head as if to fire a warning shot, then lowered it to point toward the Pale Man. The Pale Man continued to stare at Ingram. The Pale Man's mouth made strange shapes.

Eyes fixed on the Pale Man, Ingram didn't notice the figure walking onto the stage until he was near the microphone. Finally, Ingram wrenched his gaze away from the Pale Man's glare.

He had found who he'd been looking for.

Early Freeman took the stage.

Early looked gray, desiccated, the open sores on his arms and face oozing viscous black fluid. People in the crowd started muttering, shifting uncomfortably.

One man yelled, "What is this? Some damn hoedown?"

Other people muttered profanities. One man yelled, "What's wrong with him? Where's Ramblin' John?"

"Didn't come to see no peckerwood!"

People turned to look at Ingram, as if he had something to do with another white man taking the stage.

Ingram looked back at Rabbit and the Pale Man. He could see the man's lips moving slowly, forming unintelligible words. Rabbit shook, and his head rolled back.

Rabbit slowly pivoted, arm holding the pistol extended, and sighted Ingram's chest.

Early reached the microphone. He stood there motionless, arms dangling at his sides. Dark fluid dripped from his mouth, and his white, vacant eyes remained open, unblinking.

That ain't Early anymore.

Hastur opened his mouth.

And sang.

There were landscapes contained in the noise, landscapes and strange, foreign harmonies that no human ear was meant to hear. It was music, but screaming too, black tri-tones blasting forward. Early didn't move his lips; he kept his mouth motionless like the bell of a horn signaling the end of the world. The sound moved away from the stage like a wave, pushing the crowd before it, each person taking a step back as if warding off a blow. Ingram brought his hands up to the sides of his head, placed his splinted hand up to his ear.

A woman jittered as if electrocuted. She turned and slapped the man next to her, raking her nails across his face. The man, seemingly unsurprised, leaned forward and bit off her nose.

Ingram's body tightened. His arms were like steel bands. He felt like a Jap Betty was strafing in over the Pacific waters, or there was invisible and silent gunfire streaming around him. His temples throbbed, and the blood rushed to his face. He felt happy and enraged all at once. He was surprised to find he had an erection. Desperately, he reached forward and grabbed at the table-top with his good hand. He stuffed the still-warm wax into his ears and the feeling subsided. Subsided, but didn't disappear.

He turned back to Rabbit. The man looked at Ingram with a face so sorrowful it seemed distorted. He screamed in agony, tears streaking his face. His arm shook, holding the gun.

As Ingram rose from the table, Rabbit fired. Ingram's body twisted, expecting the bullet to hit his chest; instead, Rabbit's hand disappeared in a smoky red mist. The Saturday Night Special was gone, and it had taken Rabbit's hand with it.

Understanding washed across Rabbit's face, and his eyes went wide. Then a shadow passed over him, and Ingram shivered, feeling an impalpable coldness from across the room. When the shadow passed, Rabbit glared at Ingram with pure hatred. His eyes rolled back. He took a step forward. From the right, a man and woman, working in tandem, grabbed Rabbit, clawing at his face, his arms, and dragged him to the floor.

Ingram screamed, "Rabbit! No!" He lunged forward, throwing

his body toward his fallen companion. A grinning man moved between them, blocking his way. It was the doorman who'd taken their cover.

Other people looked at Ingram now too. Men and women turned toward him with teeth bared, snarling. He jerked up the nearest chair and held it easily in his hand. The door man lunged for him, hands extended like claws, and Ingram smashed his face with the chair, breaking it into pieces and dropping the man to the floor.

All across the room, people tore into one another with grinning, mad faces. Ingram saw one woman jab a shard of glass into the eye of a man Ingram could have sworn she was dancing with earlier. Another pair began to fuck on the dance floor, the man driving his cock into the woman powerfully from behind, hand full of her hair, roughly shoving her into a submissive position.

Ingram snatched up another chair and started swinging it in wide arcs.

A pretty woman in a calico dress lunged at him with an open straight razor. Her eyes bled, and blood dripped from her mouth. Her dress was ripped wide and one breast swung free, giving her an aspect like a demented Amazon. She whisked the razor through the air in front of Ingram's face. He brought the chair across her head, knocking her sideways. The chair splintered into pieces, leaving a short, lightweight leg in Ingram's hand. The woman scrambled up, hissing like a cat. He jabbed the chair leg into her eye, filling the cavity, and she fell.

He felt an exploding pain and screamed. A slight, thin man had worked around his bad side and sunk his teeth into Ingram's bicep. He shoved the man away, his greater weight pushing the would-be cannibal back, knocking down other combatants and giving Ingram a small clearing free of attackers. Ingram pulled out the Morley, cocked the hammer, and waited.

Everything moved as though in a nightmare, the wax in his ears making the violence play out around him like a silent movie. All over the room, people were falling. Man turned on man, woman on woman. Of the couple that had been having sex earlier, only the man was still alive, now bloodier and thrusting into the woman's corpse. Even as Ingram watched, someone come up from behind and opened up the man's throat with a pocket knife, then laughed and turned to look for another victim.

Beyond it all, Ingram saw the Pale Man sitting. He mouthed words, and instantly Ingram knew that this man was responsible for the carnage. He glanced at Hastur, still singing onstage. Like the cadaver at KQUI, he was just a reanimated corpse, a puppet, and the puppet-master sat across the room from him.

A man lurched toward Ingram, a shard of glass in his fist, jabbing, swaying. Blood poured from his clenched fist, dripping down the bright edge of the piece of glass. Ingram shot him in the face. The back of his skull exploded, spattering the people behind him. He fell backward, slipping on the ever-darkening floor. The sound of the pistol fire was a small pop through the wax stuffing of his ears. Ingram pushed his way across the room, swinging his splinted hand like a club. A woman crouched on all fours, snarling. When she leapt, he smashed her face with the revolver and felt bones crunch.

He vaulted over the bar, putting the counter between him and the lunatics on the other side. He shoved open the door that he assumed led to the kitchen. Before he could react, one of the bartenders leapt toward him from the opening. The knife sank into Ingram's chest, the meaty part of his pectoral muscle. He twisted away, ripping the knife from his attacker's grip.

Ingram screamed silently, tears and blood filling his vision. He pulled the knife from his chest, threw it away. His body moved forward of its own volition, the old habits and instincts of a life of violence reasserting themselves. His senses filled with blurry impressions and sensations caught in the half-light of the bar and the overpowering desire to maim, to kill these people—*these things*—all around him. He shoved the revolver in the bartender's face, putting the snub nosed barrel into the man's eye socket, and pulled the trigger. He whirled and pistol-whipped a woman climbing over the bar, grinning at him with bloody teeth, knocking her to the floor behind the bar. He stomped on her neck, felt something crack and give. She didn't get up. Another man pushed his way through the hinged door at the end of the bar, part of his cheek ripped away to expose teeth, swinging what looked like a three-foot metal rod taken from some part of the musical equipment.

He whipped the rod at Ingram's head, and Ingram raised his arm to block it. It twanged off his splint, and bright metallic pain shot through his whole frame. He reached forward, placed his splinted hand on the man's chest, and clubbed him with his left hand, using the revolver as a bludgeon. The first blow crushed the man's nose, the second collapsed his face in to a bloody, burbling mess.

Then, for a moment, everything was still. Ingram panted in the low light of the club, sequestered in his own little island behind the bar, bodies strewn around him. He wanted someone else to kill. He looked to where the Pale Man had been sitting, trying to find Rabbit, but he could only see the dead and the near-dead. A fat man, grinning eerily, was struggling to rise from the floor, his legs jutting sideways from his body, nerve-dead. His eyes were vacant. As was his mouth. It appeared he'd bitten off his own tongue.

Rabbit was gone, if he survived. The floor was covered with gore and the bodies of the people who had only moments before been audience; even now the injured clawed at one another, biting and tearing. As Ingram watched, a woman missing half of her face throttled a man whose guts hung outside his body, spooling around where he sat, blue, brown, and bloody.

Ingram jumped over the bar door, slipped, and went down on one knee. His ruined right hand throbbed horribly, and he knew it would never be the same. If it had not been shattered before, surely it was now.

He looked at the stage. Hastur remained standing at the microphone, but now he looked into the smoke in the room, at the ceiling, staring abjectly, unknowing, staring with dead eyes, milky-white. Beside the stage, the Pale Man stood too, looking at Ingram, face still half in shadow, half-obscured by what looked like bruises. But now the white glints were angry, burning with a malevolence that hit Ingram like a blow, rocking him back on the heels of his feet.

Ingram realized his revolver was still in his bloody left fist. He raised it, pointed at the Pale Man, and pulled the trigger. It clicked. Empty.

The Pale Man opened his mouth, and Ingram saw the interior was black like oil. He reached his good hand to his ear, feeling. He'd lost one of his wax earplugs. The pale man's voice was soft when he spoke.

"Turn around, human, and leave this place. You cannot hope to survive any more."

"Human?" Ingram asked. There was no posturing with this man, this thing. There was only the truth and questions, and Ingram meant to have them answered.

Ingram raised his bloody, splinted hand and said, "I seem to be doing just fine. All these poor folk are dead, and I'm still standing."

The Pale Man raised a bone-white hand, mirroring Ingram, and pointed it at Hastur. The movement, so still yet menacing, made Ingram shiver.

"He is coming. I prepare the way. There is nothing you can do to stop us. There will be other reckonings, human." The Pale Man slowly turned his back to Ingram and walked down the hall away from the carnage and what was once a dance floor, down the back hall toward the pier.

The *Hellion*!

Ingram pushed forward, following.

Hastur opened his mouth again, eyes on Ingram, and sang. Ingram fell, the force of the sound pummeling him, beating at his face, his ears. The obscene harmonies were softer now, pleading, wooing. The force of the music, if it could be called music, had waned. In the war, the sirens on Ingram's transport ships could render strong, grown men helpless, the sound waves traveling through the men's bodies, almost liquefying bowels and "rattling the chassis," they'd joke. But this was worse and easier all at once. While the ship's sirens had a physical affect, this song—for it was a song, speaking of far-away dark shores—affected not so much his body, but his mind. Ingram felt as though there was some fierce raptorial bird beating at his consciousness, trying to get in, clawing and crying out in anger. He understood now the strange words coming from the revenant's mouth.

> Rise up from the sodden earth
> Rise up from Death's black hearse
> That is not dead can eternal lie
> And dying know even death can die
> Have you seen the yellow sign?
> Have you found the yellow sign?

The song from the radio station!

Ingram threw his body forward, toward the thing that once had been Early Freeman. He slipped again in blood and viscera, but scrambled to the stage and pulled himself over the lip of the platform and onto his knees. The undead thing kept singing, without breath or life, a siren of madness and despair.

Ingram rose. He stood in front of the dead man and grabbed the microphone stand. Before he'd felt rage when he had been stabbed, a berserk madness that consumed him; now he felt only sadness and exhaustion. He knew this man's wife, his boss, his friends. Somewhere behind Ingram, Rabbit's body lay, abandoned and faceless. Another soldier Ingram had led to his death. The infernal song had to stop now, before it was too late.

With both hands, Ingram raised the microphone stand above his head and brought it down on Hastur, the thing that had once been Early Freeman. The revenant's skull collapsed like an overripe melon. The corpse fell to the stage.

Ingram fell to his knees and wept. Hot tears spilled out on his cheeks, his chest wracked with sobs. He cried for himself, for Rabbit, for Early Freeman and his orphaned son; he wept for his hand, now ruined, a living thing of blood and pain. He wept with exhaustion.

A whisper, the slap of wet flesh on floor made Ingram turn, his sobs stopping abruptly.

The dead rose.

They rose in bloody tatters, missing limbs, arms, eyes; the rich integuments of flesh that made them human were gone, but they rose. And they looked at Ingram with hateful eyes.

Ingram scrambled to his feet. He threw himself off the stage and moved into the dim hallway to the pier, following where the Pale Man had gone before. He pushed open doors as he searched for an exit, a weapon, anything to arm himself against the dead that followed. A storage room littered with cleaning agents and crates, a maintenance closet with tins and tanks and mops. A restroom.

At the end of the dark hall, arms outstretched in front of him, he found double doors, and pushed hard. He burst through to the pier, the cool night air washing over him and making him shiver.

Limbs heavy from drink and exertion, he felt like a sponge with all the moisture wrung from it. His mouth was tacky and dry, and he wished he could just fall forward into the bayou and drink, but the dark waters didn't smell wholesome and the dead followed behind.

He looked down the pier and saw the black tug pulling away from its mooring, moving glacially away from the tarred pilings, smoke billowing from its stack.

Behind him the door opened.

A dead man, his throat open, wet and red in the low light, lurched out of the building, arms outstretched to grab Ingram, knocking the door wide as he came through. More dead shambled forward into the light.

God, I'm tired.

Ingram kicked the corpse in the chest, knocking it back into the building and toppling the nearest dead behind it. His limbs felt leaden, and looking down at himself he realized he'd lost quite a bit of blood in the last few days.

The corpse slowly rose again, arms and legs moving in an ungainly, awkward manner. A shard of glass protruded from its eye, and its hair rose away from his skull in a flap. Half-way scalped.

Glancing around, Ingram spotted the guttering light of a kerosene lantern. He lumbered toward it. Snatching it down by the wire handle, he unscrewed the cap to the fuel reservoir, then pitched the lantern through the doors, into the crowd of undead, and nearly screamed in frustration when the lantern hit the front man's chest, shattering, but didn't catch fire. A dead woman, the skin stripped from her lower jaw, kicked the lantern and it spun in a circle, rattling and spreading kerosene in a widening pool.

The corpses moved through the door, walking in strange, stiff gaits, and Ingram backed away, down the pier, toward the remaining boats. He couldn't recall dropping his Morley in the fray, everything was becoming blurred. He looked over his shoulder, spotting an oar in the closest flat-bottom, and turned toward it.

For an instant, the shambling dead were backlit by a yellow light, each ghoul traced in brilliant relief, and then the yellow turned white and expanded to fill all of Ingram's senses, blossoming and thunderous. The building exploded, expanding outward, pieces of wood and glass and tile rocketing past, pushing him forward so that he lost his feet and found himself in the air, flying away from the heat, away from the new sun that had come to life in the night.

There are tanks in there!

Something hard and silver flashed in his eyes, whanged off his skull, sending him spinning. He landed in a twisted heap on the hull of a flat-bottom.

He felt the boat rock, heard the water lap at its sides. Using the last of his strength, Ingram twisted his body to look back at the pier. The first dead man now loomed above him, silhouetted by fire, his hair a burning halo, and then another explosion rocked the night, and the dead man's corpse pitched over as streamers and dark objects—shrapnel—whizzed by it, and suddenly the boat was loose and floating away from the burning ruin of the nightclub and the pier, its mooring severed.

Ingram struggled to rise, but his limbs felt like lead, and, giving up the fight, he slumped back to the bottom of the boat. His breath whooshed out of him, and he passed out of consciousness, borne away from the burning dead on the waters of the bayou. To the river.

human struggled in vain, but his limbs held like lead, and, giving up the fight, he slumped back to the bottom of the boat. His breath whooshed out of him, and he passed out of consciousness. As he was floating lifeless, the water rose of the bayou to the river.

Chapter 10

"**M**omma! Momma! There's a dead man at the river!" Lenora raced up the back porch steps, panting heavily with Fisk and Franny quick behind her.

Alice and Sarah were in the middle of their morning ritual; Sarah staring lazily out the window, Alice slowly reading the paper and sipping black coffee.

In the mornings, Sarah usually revisited her translation work of the night before. The work had progressed quite nicely, at least to Sarah's uneducated eyes, until some very strange and unknown words came up in a passage. If only she knew what the subject of the book was, she might be able to figure out some of the more pesky lines through context. Unfortunately, the little town of Gethsemane didn't have a Catholic church, where she could drop by and quiz the priest as to the accuracy of her Latin, and she was worried she'd have to go all the way to Little Rock to the teacher's college or seminary there to find out what *Opsculus Noctis* had to say for itself. Part of her didn't want to find out;

sheltered in the library, late at night, she felt at once alone and part of something larger, a communion with other minds, other hearts, even if through the pages of the old, dry volumes on the shelves. She felt like she'd joined some higher calling, been initiated into some select group, but she couldn't explain this feeling; it pervaded her nights and crept into her days as well. Some of the passages were on her lips, faintly tugging at her, at the strangest of times, like now, with Lenora shouting and Franny wild-eyed with excitement.

Alice half rose from her chair and said, "What's this, a dead man? What you talking bout, Nora?"

Lenora stood in the kitchen doorway with Franny and Fisk behind her, her breath coming heavy in her chest. She swallowed exaggeratedly.

"After breakfast we went walking in the dark wood, looking for Indian arrowheads. Couldn't find none but we walked down to the river to see if we could get some driftwood to make a fort—"

"Driftwood makes the best fort cause it's smooth from the water," Fisk volunteered.

Lenora turned to glare at him for interrupting her story, then, after a suitable length, turned back to the adults.

"When we came to the river, Franny saw a little boat snagged in the branches of a tree, bumping up against the shore. First we thought folks might be fishing or hunting till we looked in it. There's a man. Dead and dried blood all over him. We ran all the way back here to get you."

Alice pushed away from the table. "All right, then. Let's go see this dead man."

Lenora looked down at her mother's slippers and said, "You ain't gonna get very far in them."

Alice frowned, looking over her matronly bust at her nightgown and slippers. Sarah laughed, and Alice turned her frown toward the other woman. Sarah stood and said, "Alice, why don't you get dressed and then go get some of Reuben's boys to meet us at the river. I'll go with the children."

Alice looked at Sarah, as if surprised by her words. Usually Alice made the decisions.

Sarah grinned. "At least I've got on real shoes."

There was a moment when she thought Alice would argue. But, reluctantly, Alice nodded.

Sarah's shoes were heavy with mud a few minutes later as they trudged through the wood behind the house. The sky was overcast, turning the light hazy and casting the wood into a sepia scene of browns and blacks and whites. The day was cool and moist and rich odors burst up as each footstep marred the ground. The children chirped away like earthbound birds, happy with the new adventure.

Sarah smelled the river before she saw it. It smelled like dirt and fish and... *yes*... dead things.

"Lenora, show me where the man is. Franny, you stay with Fisk, please."

Sarah maneuvered herself over the driftwood logs and down the mud slope toward the bank behind Lenora. She could see a small craft, its rope tangled in submerged branches, its outboard motor caught in the bank's brush. The hull knocked against a log mired in the muddy shore. Climbing to the top of the log, Sarah looked inside the flat-bottom.

There was a giant in the boat. The man streaked with blood and grime lay on the wooden hull. His hand was wrapped with a bandage, and black blood caked the side of his head and spotted his chest and arm. His skin was pale.

Sarah called back to the other children. "Franny, Fisk! Run tell Alice we're gonna need extra men to move him. Jesus, he's massive."

She managed to get herself from the top of the log into the boat, and once it stopped rocking, she perched herself to one side of the giant and tentatively reached out to touch his cheek.

Sarah gasped. "Lenora, run as fast as you can and tell them that he's alive and we need to get Dr. Polk. Hurry!"

In his pocket, Sarah found his wallet and a bottle of pills. The

Tennessee license revealed his name to be Lewis Patrick Ingram. A veteran Marine. From Memphis.

Sarah brushed his hair out of his face. She wet her hand in the river and, lacking a towel or bandana, used her wet fingers to wipe some of the grime from his face and forehead.

He moaned and shifted slightly.

"It's all right. Sssh. It's okay. We're gonna get you to a doctor."

With his face clean, he looked somewhat boyish, his face strangely unlined except for small crow's feet at the corners of his eyes. His straight, well-formed features were marred only by the fierce, strange scratches streaking away from his eyes.

Even unconscious, he looked earnest and uncomplicated. Squatting next to him in the unsure balance of the boat, Sarah felt intense compassion for this man, wounded and lost on waters carrying him where he knew not.

"Why are you crying, Mommy?" Franny asked from the shore.

Sarah jumped. She turned, looked at Franny, and wiped her eyes. "What? Oh, honey, you startled me! I thought you went with Fisk."

"I couldn't keep up with Fisk. He runs too fast. So I came back to stay with you. Sometimes the dark woods scare me."

Sarah put a hand on the man's chest, feeling his heart beat.

"This man has wounds all over him. I can't understand how he got them."

"But why are you crying?"

"Oh, honey... I feel sorry for this man. He's lost and hurt, and I don't know if there's anything sadder than that."

She looked at Franny. The girl's luminous face was framed by a bright halo of wild hair.

Franny said, "Oh. That is sad. But what if he's a bad man?"

Sarah looked back at the man's face. *That's the question, isn't it? With all men. But he doesn't look bad, he just looks... lost.*

Sarah heard field-hands approaching through the wood, their calls muffled by the forest, obscured by the soft gurgle of the river, the knocking of the boat against the driftwood.

Franny turned, looking into the wood.

"Go get them, honey, and lead them back here," Sarah said.

It took six men in all to raise the giant. In the end, two of them had to go back to the farm and get a plank of wood to carry the injured man back to the Big House. They dropped him once, in the wood, when a branch scratched at one of the bearer's faces and he released his corner of the plank, spilling the giant to the ground with a thump. Sarah nearly screeched at the men. They ducked their heads and looked chagrined. The giant was half-mired in mud and leafy debris from the tumble. Sarah worried for the state of the man's injuries, fearing infection.

Alice met them on the steps, waving frantically.

"Dr. Polk's coming! I got the bed ready in the front guest room. You put him there, hear?"

The porters nodded, and among themselves decided it would be better going through the front door, so they carried the man around the house, through the front entryway, and up the grand stairway with Sarah, Franny, Fisk, and Lenora following like acolytes in a procession.

The men rolled the giant into the double bed of the guest room, smearing the covers with dirt. Alice bustled in, bearing towels and a steaming pot of water. Briskly, she took charge of the scene, barking orders at the field-hands.

"Festus, take off his shoe! Mike, start unbuttoning his shirt and mind the covers! Don't get more dirt on them than already there, hear? Sarah, go down and wait for Dr. Polk, should be getting here sometime soon. And take these children with you! Go on, Fisk. Git!"

Sarah, the children, and all the porters except for Festus and Mike fled the guest room. On the way back downstairs, Sarah heard her mother yelling for her.

Sarah poked her head in her mother's door. "Are you alright, Momma?"

Her mother sat upright in bed, her face mottled and angry. "What in the goddamned world is going on out there? What is going on in my house?"

"Momma, I don't have a lot of time to explain but I'll tell you everything later when I bring your sip. The children found a badly injured man by the river, and Dr. Polk is coming to tend to him."

"Do we know this man, Sarah?"

"No. He's a stranger, Momma. And hurt too."

"If we don't know him, why the hell is he in my house? Why didn't you just leave him?"

Sarah looked at her mother and shook her head.

Elizabeth's gaze remained fixed on her daughter, the silence between them lengthening, until finally she turned away and muttered, "You always were a weakling, girl. If it wasn't for Alice you'd never have survived." She placed her withered hands in her lap and shook her head, looking at the light from the window. "When Polk is done with the man, send him in here to see me."

੶

Dr. Polk arrived nearly an hour later.

Good thing no one was choking to death or we would already have had the funeral by now.

Doddering and ancient, Dr. Polk had treated Sarah as girl. She remembered him with more hair. He carried a black physician's bag and wore a dark gray suit with a somber blue tie and glasses, which he continually pushed back on his nose. A small man, he took dainty steps, Sarah noticed, as she escorted him up to the guest room.

With the help of her two porters, Alice had managed to undress, wash, and get the injured giant under the covers. Dr. Polk examined him and undressed the giant's injured right hand. As he unwound the black bandages, a rotten smell filled the room, making Sarah gag.

"Well, this hand was professionally bandaged," Dr. Polk said. "But it's obviously in need of a change. We'll keep the plaster splint. Ah, Sarah, take this. Can you clean it up for me?"

He handed her a hard piece of yellowed plaster in the shape of a crooked shovel. Alice moved forward, and began to wash the man's injured right hand.

"Just use some rubbing alcohol and try and clean it up. I've got gauze and bandages here. His hand is broken but this injury is older than this one here." He pointed at the man's skull. "And here." He pointed at his heart. "Strange thing is, he's got a pretty vicious bite wound on his arm, too, that looks like it might be getting infected. Hmm."

Dr. Polk stared at the large man, rubbing his chin and thinking.

"A bite wound?" Sarah asked. "From a dog?"

"No, not a dog. It looks like a bite wound from a human mouth, which would explain the infection. The wound in his chest appears to be a very shallow knife wound. And his hand appears to be what we call a 'boxer's break,' an injury common to fist-fighters and brawlers. The wound on his scalp—which looks like it might've concussed him—it was made by something sharp and metal, at least that's what the wound is telling me. Clean edges, not ragged."

Alice harumphed but continued to clean the man's injured hand.

"Strange." Dr. Polk lifted the coverlet shrouding the giant's legs. "He's various abrasions and contusions, the kind of scratches and bruises you'd get in fights. Multiple fights." He shook his head. "One thing's for sure, this man has done major violence to someone, and more recently, had major violence done to him. I wouldn't much like to live in his world."

The doctor unpacked a large roll of gauze and some cotton pads and medical tape and went to work alongside Alice, cleaning and bandaging the giant.

"Whatever happened to him, Sarah, you'd be well advised to call Sheriff Wocziak and let him know who you've found. I heard on the radio this morning that a lot of people died in a fire two counties over, and they don't know if it was an accident or arson. Ruby's on the Bayou, I believe they said. How did the children find this man?"

Sarah was reluctant to answer. She looked at the man in the bed, his brown hair and boyish features.

She didn't have to answer, Alice did it for her. "They found him in a boat that got itself tangled in the rushes. Must've been floating downriver away from the scene of the crime."

"Crime?" Sarah asked. "We don't know where he comes from, or why he was hurt. Why don't we let him tell us that before we make plans to hang him."

Alice stopped washing the man's hand, and turned to Sarah. She raised an eyebrow as if to say, "What're you doing, girl?"

Dr. Polk tore a piece of white tape off a roll and said, "It's up to you. It's quite possible he'll never come out of this coma, but he appears to be breathing well. Once we get his wounds cleaned, I'll set you up with a saline drip and some pain killers should he wake up. Penicillin for the infection. And I'll make sure to drop by in a couple of days." He looked at Sarah, eyebrows raised.

"Of course, doctor. We'll take care of the bill, at least until we figure out who he is. He's got some cash in his wallet, if all else fails, and he—"

Dr. Polk cleared his throat. "Well, there's always that possibility. But I doubt it. If he was going to die, he would have done so. This man could have endured any of these wounds taken individually. Easily." The doctor laughed then, a dry chuckle. "But look at him. He's gigantic. He has to have the constitution of a bull to survive all of these wounds. Indeed, I've never seen a more impressive collection of injuries in my career as a doctor." He smiled, pleased to have seen something new. "Anyway, please be careful around him, Sarah. He'll be weak for a long time, but by the looks of him, he could be dangerous."

Sarah remained in the room, watching as Alice and the doctor ministered to the injured man. After they were finished, Dr. Polk winked at Alice and said, "Alice, good work. Should you ever want a position as my assistant—"

Alice laughed, bright and embarrassed. "Dr. Polk, you is sweet. But you know the Rheinharts are my people. If I wasn't here to watch over them, they'd all be like this here fella, bedridden. Hungry. Mangy too, probably."

Sarah grinned then. "Oh, yes, doctor, that reminds me. Momma asked to see you before you go."

Dr. Polk's smile curdled. "I guess that makes sense. It's been what, four weeks since my last visit?"

Alice snorted. "No. 'Bout six months, Doc. April, I think it was, or early May."

"Well, yes. Of course, I'll see her."

Once he was gone, Alice and Sarah burst into peals of laughter, familiar with his reluctance to see Sarah's mother, happy it was not them. The strain of the morning slowly drained from Sarah as the giggles subsided. She hadn't realized how tense she'd been throughout the doctor's visit.

That evening, after taking her mother her sip and enduring a long harangue about getting the man out of the house, Sarah went to the guest room and sat in the wing-backed chair nearest the bed and watched the giant. He hadn't moved much since earlier, but his skin looked less pale in the thin light of the lamp.

As she watched, his face occasionally hitched in pain. In those moments, he seemed older, tired and weary. Then his face would relax again, regaining the appearance of a boy. Sarah felt herself attracted and repulsed by the man in turns. And she found herself fantasizing about what he might be like, concocting explanations for his wounds and imaging the story of his life.

In the dim room, she smiled at her own foolishness. Standing, she walked over to his bed and placed her hand on his forehead, feeling for the fever Dr. Polk warned about before leaving. The man's skin was cool to the touch. He moaned and turned his body in the bed.

"*No*," he whispered, unknowing. "*No*. Rabbit… don't sing… the dead—"

"Hush," Sarah murmured to the man. *Lewis. His name is Lewis.*

Later, after Alice made her an extra strong toddy and she seated herself in the library, she pulled the telephone close to her on the desk and picked up the receiver. After a moment, the operator came on the line.

"This is Phyllis," said a voice, high and tinny.

"This is me… um, Sarah Williams. Sarah Rheinhart, I used to be."

"Sarah! How are you? Your mother and Alice tell me that Franny is precious. My lands, I can't wait to see her, but come to think of it, I haven't seen you since you were in pigtails. Why don't you come by the Central?"

Sarah smiled and tucked her feet underneath her in the office chair, fiddled with a pencil.

"We'll try to get by next week. But I need to ask you a question."

There was a loud click. Phyllis said, "Hold on, sweetie. Caller, this is Phyllis at the Central, how can I help you?"

A man's voice came on the line. "I need to make a phone call to my niece in Little Rock, Mohawk two, one, one—"

"I'm sorry sir, there's already a call on this line. I will ring you when the connection is complete."

The man said, "Phyllis, it's me, Ray. That's fine, let me know."

Another click sounded as he rang off. Phyllis chuckled. "Ray's niece is having trouble with her help, and Ray keeps calling her with ideas on how to get them in line."

"I don't…" Sarah stammered. "Um… that's not really my—"

"That's OK, honey. I hear things, you know. I'm always listening. It's my job."

Not really. Your job is to complete calls, not eavesdrop, you old biddy. But she said, "Phyllis, I need to contact the nearest Catholic church if I can. Do you know what that would be?"

"Probably St. Thomas' in Stuttgart. Father Andrez might could help you. You converting, honey? I thought you were Episcopalian like your mother and father."

"No, not converting. I need help translating a… well… translating something. I don't have anyone to turn to so I thought—"

"That's right," Phyllis said. "You're a college girl. I forgot that your momma and daddy sent you off east. What're you translating?"

Sarah felt her back tighten. She couldn't remember what Phyllis looked like now, so Sarah pictured her as an enormous spider, black and foul, spinning its web, spinning lies, its fat carapace beading with condensation. She saw the spider reclining, one long digit curled around a receiver and holding it up to a head crowded with a multitude of eyes. But not really a spider, some bizarre hybrid between woman and arachnid; a black shell with flabby human breasts, insect eyes perched over a wicked red over-ripe mouth—

Sarah shook her head. *What's happening to me?*

Phyllis said, "Honey? You all right? You still on the line?"

"Yes... uh, yes." Sarah wiped her face, clearing the imaginary cobwebs. "I'm still here. I dropped my pencil."

"Oh, that's OK. Oh, I almost forgot. I heard you've got a house guest. What's his name? Was he hurt bad? Everyone is saying he was badly hurt—"

Sarah's blood went cold. *She knows, the old harridan!*

"No... no, he's not hurt badly. Um... can you connect me to St. Thomas'? Father Andrez is his name?"

"Yes. But about the man—"

"Phyllis, I'm a little tired right now, and I need to make this call. Can we talk about it when Franny and I come to see you at the Central?"

Phyllis paused. Sarah worried for a moment that she might have offended the operator, but then Phyllis came back on the line.

"That'd be wonderful, sugar! I can't wait to see your little one. You can tell me all about it then."

Fat chance.

"Will do, Phyllis. It's been so nice talking to you again."

"Same here. Now let me connect you, and I'll stay on the line so I can let Ray know when you're done."

The phone rang four times before someone answered. The man's voice sounded hoarse and cracked, but cheerful enough. "Hello. This is Andrez." He had a heavy accent, but spoke the words clear and slow.

"Father? My name is Sarah Williams, and I recently came home to Gethsemane—"

"Yes? How can I help you? It is nearing Compline but I have a bit of time, so if you would—"

"Of course. Well," Sarah chewed her lip, then blurted, "I need help translating a book. And I thought you might be able to help me?"

The man on the other end of the line was silent for a moment, but when he came back on the line, he could hear the smile in his voice. "This is good, though it depends on the book. And the language, of course."

"It's Latin. I assumed that all priests—"

He chuckled, the sound dry and brittle across the line. "Well, in the best of all possible worlds, my," he paused, as though embarrassed, "brothers of the cloth would be able to read Latin, but unfortunately many of the clergy just memorize the Liturgy and… hem… get by."

"Oh," Sarah said, letting the disappointment in her voice show through. "Well, maybe the seminary in Little Rock will have someone."

He chuckled again, then exhaled. He was smoking. "So easily discouraged, eh? Ye of little faith? You are in luck, Mrs. Williams, but it has been awhile since I've translated anything other than the Vulgate. What work is it that you'd like translated?"

"Well, I'm not looking for you to translate it for me," Sarah said. "I'd like for you to help me with my translation."

"Ah! You are translating! A veritable Margaret More, you are. Your father and mother must be proud."

Sarah couldn't tell, but she felt that this man, this priest, was making fun of her. She could feel a blush coming on.

"Yes, well. I took Latin in college and recently picked up *Opusculus Noctis* in my family library…"

He was silent for a long while. "Hmm. *Opusculus Noctis* you say?"

"So can you help me?" Sarah asked.

"Yes, Mrs. Williams. I would be happy to. However small my parish is, I must still tend to my flock. Which means you'll have to come from the garden, Gethsemane, and bring the work and manuscript to me here. I have some time tomorrow afternoon, if you would like? After four?"

"Yes, that would be wonderful. Thank you so much."

"It is not a difficulty. I have translated nothing yet. But I look forward to seeing you and the manuscript. I prefer chicken. Chicken salads are good, or fried if you can manage, but chicken is truly my favorite."

"Um ... what? Chicken?"

"Yes. Correct. Chicken is my favorite. But you can bring ham if you have to. Or cake. I like cake. Pies are... ehh... so so. It is up to you, of course."

What a funny, strange man.

"All right," Sarah said. "I will see you at four."

"*Do Widzenia*, Mrs. Williams. Goodbye."

After he rang off, Phyllis came back on. "I guess you better get cooking."

Sarah hung up and went to find Alice.

Chapter 11

They landed on Tulagi in the Solomons in the dark of early morning. After hours of bombing from the Jap Bettys, each one streaking in screaming, wreathed in flak like bolls of black cotton, the deep foliage of the jungle was quiet and still. Deathly still. The heat enveloped his troops, causing their fatigues to dampen and cling to them, each face white and wide-eyed, each hand white knuckled on a rifle and sweating, sweating through the morning gloom, sweating into the Solomon heat. Through the fetid green wall they went, pack-heavy mules moving forward to the enemy.

Ingram paused to check his BAR, popping the magazine and inspecting the rounds. The men moved past him, swallowed by green, disappearing into the brush and palms and dark, their passing marked by faint clinks of weapons and the soft whisking of damp fabric. Ingram peered into the dark, looking to the sides and to the rear, making sure nothing was flanking or a beam. The dark had textures, rich fabrics and patterns. The sounds from the carriers and transport ships, the dull thrum of the ship's diesel dynamos pushing the enormous screws, the .30 and .50 cals answering the screaming of the Bettys strafing in, Ingram felt lost without those sounds at his back. He turned in the dark, trying to find the direction of the landing, of the shore, and could hear and see nothing. He turned back to where his men had disappeared and moved into the dark green, deathly lush interior of Tulagi.

The bullets came then, making spluttering sounds as they perforated the thick, oily leaves. Ingram heard distant reports. Nearer he could hear his men, screaming into the dark, screaming into the green, firing.

Ingram ran.

His body felt slow, suspended in oil, the air around him thick with smoke and screams and sharp, hard trajectories of rifle fire, each bullets *fitthing* by, clipping tree and leaf and branch.

Ingram ran.

His body heavy, moving into the fire and the dark, screaming now for his men like Cap Hap, gone but not forgotten, Ingram moved further into Tulagi, further into the dark edges of stygian Guadalcanal darkness. Through the trees and brush and lush undergrowth, he ran. He heard his men shrieking in pain, men calling for their brothers, men calling for mothers, men calling for Ingram.

This isn't how it happened.

Ingram ran and something snapped, the heaviness lifted. He moved forward with ease and burst through the undergrowth into a clearing. No more bullets whizzed past, no more screams or reports from weapons. Everything was still, and the smell of gunpowder floated upon the air, clouds of it obscuring the far side of the clearing, obscuring the ground.

Then came a breeze, and the thick fragrant smoke moved past him like a gigantic albino creature wrought of gauze and the evil of men. It moved past and through him, back into the green.

He saw the dead bodies of his men.

This isn't how it happened! We took the airfield!

All around him were bodies. They were ravaged, chewed up by the fusillade, missing faces, missing limbs, guts pooling into the loam. The men lay face down, or in tangled heaps that obscured their faces. Ingram stood panting among the dead. Off, in the green, he could feel something there, something immense and malevolent and waiting.

It grew lighter in the east. For a moment Ingram thought the sun rose, then he smelled smoke, the gunpowder creature's cousin, bigger and noxious and coming for him, through the green, consuming the green, coming for him. He could see the fire now, to the east, like a wall, a cliff of fire stretching up into the heavens and behind it blackness, the blackness coming on.

Ingram twisted in place, hands sweaty on the BAR's stock, and raised the gun as if to fire into the inferno. He barked a short laugh.

Oun tulu dundu nub sheb tulu onnu ia denu fin de nulu sheb lar stir rub neb, a voice came.

Ingram looked down and saw his men—empty faces, bloody eyes, tongueless mouths, riddled with gunshot—turning toward him, each face a study in blood and hatred and hunger; each one, eyeless or not, peering at him through the shroud of smoke, each one moving his mouth in time with the strange utterances.

Again, the dead rose. Ingram had been pushed to his limits in the bar, in Ruby's. *Ruby's! The dead had risen, they had risen!*

The Pale Man had stripped them all of their masks of humanity and revealed them as they truly were, abject creatures of hate and spite and lust and hunger.

Ingram shook his head in the green dark of Guadalcanal. *This isn't how it happened!* His dead men clawed at the earth now, some rising to their haunches, some crawling, some levering themselves up, looking at Ingram with horrible blood-rimmed eyes.

The weird sounds took new shapes and forms in Ingram's ear. Wet and guttural the words came, for they truly were words, forgotten or forbidden but words spilling out from the bloody tongues and hateful mouths of his men.

Oun tulu! Dennu tulu! Re'nub shelub tulu ia dennu! Tulu!

Ingram hesitated. At Ruby's, he'd fought them, shooting and snapping necks. But now the fire was coming and these dead, these things that were once men, rose against him. And he knew nothing except fear and shame because he couldn't raise his hand against those who once were his brothers.

You can't kill the dead!

Something broke in him then. The pain and suffering of the war, his violent past, his work and the life he lived with his fists all calcified in him. He looked upon the rising Marines, each one gory and grotesque and filled with hate toward him but each one still wearing a mask—the mask of a friend. In every revenant Ingram saw the familiar: Sid's tattoo, Vic's pockmarked face, Jerry's slight gut, now blood-smeared and gory. Ingram's hard, brittle core shattered, and he lowered his head in the clearing, tears streaming down his face.

The fire neared him now, roaring into the clearing, pushing forward a thin layer of superheated air. He raised his massive head, his horns snapping the low-hanging fronds of a palm. His nostrils flared, and he washed a rough tongue over his nose, wetting it. Clawed hands fell on his side, gripping the hair there, ripping gashes in his hide. He twisted again, whipping his massive body around, the splayed hooves of his forelegs tearing great gouges in the loamy earth, his hindquarters trampling the dead that surrounded him, and he lowed and bellowed for the horrible damage he caused them.

Fire overtook him, and he knew darkness and the sensation of countless teeth ripping into his flesh.

Chapter 12

Stuttgart was indistinguishable from any other town in Arkansas; like an island in a green sea, its outlying shores were washed in rice, beans, cotton. In the fields, harvest progressed. Lumbering combines walked down the green aisles and a flurry of tractors followed, waiting at the field edges, waiting for the harvesters to dump their heavy loads into the tractor bins. As Sarah drove, smoking and drinking the coffee that Alice had provided her in a thermos, she remembered the exchange between them earlier.

"You know what the best invention in the world is?" Alice asked.

Sarah smiled. "Nope. What is it?"

"Thermos."

She laughed at the incongruity of it all. "Why's that?"

Alice looked at her very seriously and said, "It keeps the hot hot, and the cold cold. But how do it know?"

Sarah looked at her quizzically, then laughed again. *Circles in words, so many circles in words.*

The car smelled of fried chicken. Alice had left the Big House in the gray of morning, carrying a hatchet, ignoring the drizzle that fogged the air. She walked behind the peafowl pens, and, a few minutes later, came back with a headless chicken swinging from her fist.

Of course, Sarah always knew that the Big House was just one cog in the larger machinery of a working farm, but until the still warm carcass of a hen was plopped down in front of her, it hadn't really occurred to her that one of her whims might influence the farm so that something had to die.

"Go pluck that, girl. You remember how to clean a chicken."

And, honestly, Sarah didn't. She recalled, as a child, wanting to be with her friend Alice whatever that entailed, but she had no recollection of plucking chickens.

Sarah said, "No, I don't remember. I'm going to go up and check on Momma and look over my translation before I go. Can you please take care of it?"

Alice looked at her, brow furrowing.

"Alice." Sarah tilted her head to the side and smiled. "Please?"

Alice sighed, then smiled, flashing white teeth in a brown face.

Sarah found she was less willing to submit to Alice's will than when she was younger. Life for her had been one submission after another, and now she wasn't going to do it anymore.

Alice had fried the chicken, and now it rode happily next to Sarah in a small basket, swathed in cloth napkins like some fragrant deep-fried infant.

The Chrysler rolled past the green shores of England, past the silos and grain bins and hoppers, into town. She stopped and asked directions from a gas station attendant who cheerfully filled her tank. She drove on to the church.

St. Thomas of Aquinas' church was small, wooden, and empty. A humble building, with scaling paint and small steeple, it reminded her of the Big House, though the Big House dwarfed this small building.

She parked the car in the gravel lot adjacent to the church and approached the double front doors. The church was in a nice little neighborhood of Stuttgart; tiny gingerbread houses lined the street, along with hoary, old oaks, while new cars sat in driveways and children played in yards, or rode bikes down the pavement. People were happy here, and in a different life, Sarah could see herself here, spending her days in an apron, watching Fran grow up—tame and beautiful and desperate, not wild haired and tawny and dirty like she was now.

Sarah shook her head, smiling sadly. *No, I like the wild Franny better. At least she's happy. The Franny who lives on this street might be happy, but the wild Franny is happy now.*

The church doors were unlocked, and Sarah entered, the basket of fried chicken in the crook of her arm.

The church consisted of narthex and nave and almost nothing else. A forlorn confessional sat at the rear of the church.

"Hello?" Sarah called. "Hello? Father Andrez?"

Sarah looked at her watch. It was a little past four. Right on time.

At the far end of the nave, past the altar, was a small door. It opened to the outside, a small concrete walkway leading to a very small house.

She knocked on the door of the house, and after a moment, a man dressed in black came to the door.

"Father Andrez?" she asked as he cracked the door. "I'm Sarah Williams."

"Sarah! Please, come in, come in." *Sorrah. Plis, kammin kammin.* The sound of his voice and the lilt of his accent put her at ease.

Inside, she could see Andrez a little better. If the church could be considered small, this house would be tiny, and the man minuscule. White haired and wrinkled, he was no larger than a boy. But lean as a tightrope.

Andrez grinned at her, looking up slightly.

"Eh... most people are surprised when they first meet me. Growing up in Montenegro, I learned at an early age to defend myself. Of course, mostly from my brothers." Andrez winked at her, and raised his arm to make a muscle.

"Oh!" she exclaimed. "I was only—"

"Sarah, it is no matter. I might be small in body. Not in spirit, not in heart, and that is all that matters."

"Father, I—"

His eyes fastened on the basket. "Is that—"

It was Sarah's turn to smile. "Yes. Fried chicken."

The man clapped his hands together, looked to the ceiling, and said, "Bless you, child. You would be better named Providence than Sarah." He winked again and looked at her more closely. "But Sarah suits you well. Yes, I see the Sarah in you."

Andrez took the basket of chicken from her like he was lifting a chalice. Sarah sat her purse down on a small linoleum table near a window and brought out the copy of *Opusculus Noctis* and the pages of her translation.

"Would you like some ice tea? I dearly love the tea in this country. A neighbor taught me to make it the correct way, and I cannot get enough."

"Yes, please. Is it sweet?"

"Yes, Sarah. Very sweet. Very good. Yes?"

The house resembled the church itself, small and composed of just two rooms: a living room with a kitchenette and, through the door in the back wall, a bedroom. Sarah peeked through the door into the bedroom.

Andrez bustled in the kitchenette, pulling chipped floral glasses from the cabinets.

"Father Andrez? Um… is there a… um, restroom I might be able to use? I've been in the car for a while."

"Oh! My apologies, Sarah. The sight and smell of the chicken has made me lose all my wits. Go out the front door, to the right, and you will find the outhouse right by the tall hedge. A privy by the privet, so to speak."

Sarah raised her eyebrows. She remembered the days before plumbing in the Big House. Chamber pots and outhouses were the course of her early years. It seemed that in this age of technology some people still lived like their parents and grandparents, stretching back into antiquity.

Andrez smiled and raised his shoulders. "I am sorry, Sarah. We are a small parish, and I did take a vow of poverty."

Sarah laughed and said, "I used an outhouse until I was near eighteen and went to college. I can handle it."

"I'm sure it was a... eh... how do they say? A two-holer. I will wait until you get back."

The outhouse had a moon on the door, and true to form, a Sears-Roebuck catalogue as well. Luckily, it also had toilet paper.

When Sarah returned to the little house, she found Andrez sitting at the linoleum table, looking at the *Opusculus Noctis* pamphlet and frowning. He looked up when she came in through the door.

"Ah, Sarah." He was smoking now, and sipping tea. "I am puzzled. How did you come by this piece?" *How deed you cam by thees peeze?*

"It came from my family library."

"Family?"

"Yes. Is there something wrong?"

"I know this work, the *Opusculus Noctis*. From first glance it seems quite ordinary, but just glancing over it you'll notice it is not printed, though it looks like it, the hand that wrought this was so sure. Also, the paper is thick and handmade, not milled, which means... well... it's more than likely three, maybe four, hundred years old." Andrez smiled.

He put down the pamphlet gingerly, as if it was spun glass. Or a gun.

"You have been translating this?"

"Well... yes. To the best of my ability, which isn't much. And I've only gone through a little bit. I have trouble with the lack of separation between the words."

Andrez smiled again and took a sip of his tea. "Let's have some of this wonderful-smelling chicken and we will talk all about it. Afterward. It has been a tradition of my family dating back, eh, at least a century to reserve meals for talk of good things, happiness and art and current events."

Andrez brought a head of lettuce out from a cold box under the counter and quickly mixed a cold salad of greens, olive oil, and vinegar. With deft, delicate fingers, Andrez prepared Sarah's plate, giving her a small wing, poured her a glass of tea, and then, as an afterthought, set the table with place settings.

On his plate, he placed the two thighs, a leg, a breast, and the bony back piece, followed by the greasy giblets that Alice had included. When Andrez saw them, he clucked in his throat strangely, obviously happy, but Sarah had never heard nor seen any man act as oddly before.

He noticed her watching him, and flushed.

"Sarah, I am a poor priest. This is a German town, but founded by Northern German immigrants who favored the Luther's Church over the church in Rome. I have been here, hmm... let me see now... ten years now, and my congregation has gone from fifty families to thirty people. This country is not suitable to Rome and the Church. I often find myself hungry. My parishioners provide me what they can, however, it can be paltry for," he smiled again, winking at her, "a man of my stature."

Indeed, he was a strange man. His features were delicate and childlike, possessed of some innocence that even Sarah did not have. But his skin was heavily wrinkled and his hands had liver spots, making Sarah think he had to be in his sixties at least.

"It's all right. I brought the chicken for you. I'm not really hungry."

"Oh? Well, then. I shall start."

As he ate, between bites, they spoke.

"So what made you interested in translating this pamphlet?"

"I found it in my family library, and it seemed the most inviting, really. The text was clear, compared to some of the other volumes in the library, and it was smaller than many of the other books. And it sort of drew me in, so to speak. Once I had figured out the title." Sarah laughed. "Even though I'm still not sure I got the title right. Is it *The Little Night Book?* Or the *Little Book of Night?*"

Andrez put down the breast he was devouring, wiping his chin with a napkin. "Either. Both. Neither. Hard to say. We can't know really. The author of *Opusculus* did not tell us, did he? But the *Little Book of Night* sounds right to me. Misleading though."

Sarah nodded. "I'd taken Latin in college and recently…"

Andrez looked at her with clear eyes, nodding and watching her closely.

"I've gone through some problems with my… the man I used to be married to."

"This is a strange way of saying husband."

Sarah scoffed. "Marriages are a contract. He broke his side of the bargain." She resisted raising her hand to her cheek. It had stopped hurting weeks ago, but the memory of pain remained.

Andrez eyes grew wide. "You are right. Many forms of interaction and communication become contractual, though most people do not believe that."

They were quiet for a while. Andrez ate steadily, with small exclamations of joy and delight of the meal. Sarah sat contemplating the man.

"So you're from Montenegro? I'm afraid I don't know very much about that country."

"I am Montenegran, but my father was English. I had many brothers, though quite a few of them are dead. My youngest brother has made quite a name for himself in New York. The Lupa family has many ambitious men, Nero not being the least."

"Lupa? I thought your name was Andrez."

"Yes. Andrez Lupa, at your service." The man raised his chin and cocked his head at her like some black-clad little king until she laughed.

He laughed too.

"So, how long have you been here? I mean in America?"

He picked up a napkin and wiped his mouth and fingers. "Eh… twenty years now, I think. I am just recently beginning to dream in English. And you? You mentioned your family library. Do you have a large family?"

Sarah paused and sipped her tea. It was very sweet.

"No, just my mother and my daughter. It was a bigger family years ago, but my brother was killed in the war, and my father died... well, during the war as well. Heartsick, I guess."

"Ah... this is not good. Will you take back your family name, since your... eh... divorce?"

"Rheinhart? I haven't thought about it—"

Andrez's face turned white, and he dropped the thigh he had been eating. He stood up and carried his plate to the counter. He rinsed his hands in the sink, then dried them on a towel, silent but clearly thinking. From his black shirt pocket he took a cigarette and lit it, hands shaking.

"What's wrong?" Sarah asked.

Andrez stared into space, unconsciously bringing the cigarette to his lips.

"Eh? Oh, you just startled me. I know of a Gregor Rheinhart. I must think on this."

Sarah stood. "My uncle? Gregor? I don't know what could be—"

Andrez shook his head and waved her to sit back down. "Eh... this makes things different. You are a Rheinhart, yes? Then there are things I must speak to you of. But first, let us look at this. This *Opusculus Noctis*. Then we will speak of Gregor."

Puzzled, she brought forth the translation from her purse and set it down on the table in front of Andrez.

He read *Opusculus Noctis* in silence, smoking, holding his cigarette away from the pamphlet so as not to get ash on the paper. His expression grew dark at times. Finally, after he had read quite a bit, he looked at Sarah and gave her a pained smile.

"Sarah? What do you know of this piece? What do you think it is about?"

"I don't know. Sometimes it seems like a legal document, sometimes it seems like poetry, sometime like recipes. I can't figure it out."

"Have you read it aloud?" Andrez face became very serious. He leaned closer, eyes wide. "Have you spoken the Latin aloud?"

His intensity startled Sarah.

She shook her head. "No. I'm doing the best I can to just understand the words."

Andrez exhaled, relief washing through him. His shoulders slumped.

"This is good. This is a good thing."

"What is going on here? This whole conversation is starting to get me worried."

He sighed again and got up, went into the kitchenette. From a cabinet he retrieved a bottle of claret and two short glasses.

"In Montenegro, we do not use wine glasses. We use these," he said placing the smaller glasses on the table. "No stems." With precise movements, he popped the cork, placed the glasses on the table, and poured each a full measure.

They both sipped at their wine. It was good. Sarah had become used to the sharp, sweet tang of the toddies that Alice made for her. The wine had a body and depth to it that reminded Sarah of meat, smoke, and spices.

"Sarah, this book is not what it seems to be. Its title is misleading, and it misleads on purpose. To all prying eyes, this pamphlet looks like a religious document from the Quattrocento... eh, the fifteenth century. And it *is* a religious document from the fifteenth century, though it is not Christian. It is written in Ecclesiastical Latin for... how do you say this... protective coloration. Eh, what do the hunters call it? Camouflage. That is what this is. It seems harmless; the title indicates it is a 'little book.' It is not.

"Here is what the first page says: '*The Little Book of Night*, a labor of... or the work of... Beleth, wrought by his great hand with instruction from the Prodigium beyond the cold silences. If one would like to make covenant with the entities locked beyond the stars, in the abyss, you must be willing to enter shadow. A warning to all: Do not call up what you cannot put down.'"

As he spoke, Sarah grew puzzled. "But what does that mean? I don't understand."

Andrez nodded and placed a finger on his temple, looking at

her seriously. "I will read a little more, so that you might come to understand more fully, then you can ask questions."

He cleared his throat and took another sip of wine. "'Any summoning or compact with the... here the author uses the word *prodigium* again, which we've changed over the centuries to become 'prodigy' but what it really means is 'vastness' or 'omen' and even 'monster' but... really something huge and unknowable. So the sentence reads, 'Any summoning or compact with the Prodigium must be first consecrated with blood and a willingness to sacrifice the innocent as sign of one's intent.'"

He shut the pamphlet and sniffed, showing a hint of his own revulsion to the text. "This text is mentioned in some ancient tracts and at least two Papal missives. When you mentioned it on the phone, I didn't... how is it said? I thought I had heard you wrong."

Andrez held up the pamphlet with an unsteady hand. "Earlier this century, it was stolen from the protected vault in the Vatican where it was stored. And that brings us to your uncle. Of course, all of this was unknown to me before you came here. The fact that you have come here, the blood of the man I've been looking for... I don't know what to think. Did someone send you? Can I be so fortunate?"

"Andrez, please tell me what you're talking about. I don't understand."

He reached forward and grasped Sarah hands in his own. They were warm, soft.

"I know you don't. This will be hard to understand. I need you to try to keep your mind open. Things are not as they seem. They never were. This *Opusculus Noctis*, it is a very evil book. It outlines, for someone with the knowledge to read it, ways to summon and make bargains with... other things."

"You can't be telling me that... that you believe this? You're a priest!"

He looked pained for a moment, embarrassed, the wrinkles at the edges of his eyes deepening. He looked out the kitchen window, and he sighed. Then he turned back to her. His eyes searched her face.

Sarah felt a building urge to release his hands and leave, just grab the pamphlet and her translations and run, run back to her car and haul ass back to the Big House. Andrez looked at her as though trying to detect something that might be hidden in her composure, her features.

She began to draw away, but he held her hands firm, his fingers clasping like stone traps, not hard, not rough, but immovable.

"I wear the garb of a priest. I was a priest once. But I have eaten of the fruit of knowledge. I have learned things I'd rather forget—"

Sarah shook her head. "It's," she hesitated. "It's... *absurd!*"

She laughed, and watched as Andrez's face grew somber.

He bowed his head. He remained that way for a long while.

He took a large breath; his shoulders rose and fell, and raised his head to look at Sarah with pained eyes.

"I need you to believe what I'm about to say. It will go against everything you've ever known or believed." He looked at her, thinking, an interior dialogue that she couldn't fathom going on inside his head. "The Catholic Church, Gods forgive me for what I'm about to say, has waged a war that has been going on for centuries. This war is not with Satan, or the Devil."

Sarah remained silent.

"It is a war against the other gods."

He's crazy! Unbalanced. Or a drunk. Something.

"Other gods?"

"Yes, the other gods. Baal. Cybele. Mithras. Hastur. Chernobog. Rakshasa. Ahriman. More names that, I can see from the look on your face, you have never heard before. And why should you? This is secret knowledge, handed down through the years by scholars. The war waged by law and aided by the ascendancy of the Church.

"In the Church we call them devils because it makes them easier to understand the story that the Church—that *we*—created. But they are gods. They are petty and small-minded, these gods. They are... what is the word? Capricious. Yes. It's easy to mistake them for devils."

He stopped and bowed his head in thought.

"They can enter you, if you're weak, or invite them by mistake. People do invite them. Believe it." *Beleef hit.* "They can shatter your mind and inhabit your flesh. It's how they move through the world. But even killing the body doesn't kill the god. They can travel without flesh. They've always been here. And there are new gods, new entities. They can die, and they can be born. From the ones that came before them, their parents, the Old Ones. The Prodigium.

"The church needed to protect itself! And out of all of these gods, never was there evidence of the only God that we are desperate to exist. Yahweh.

"But the Church has its own weight, its own momentum, its own plan, and an absence of proof that the entity that it worships does not exists is ignored, suppressed. Even with a multitude of real gods to choose from. The Church protects itself, first and foremost. And like anyone, or any nation under attack, we did our best to destroy those that threatened us. Strange things possessed our brethren, members of the church. We killed them... We did it through the destruction of knowledge. By destroying the liturgy of these gods, by destroying what we could of their books, their scrolls and tablets, by gaining ascendancy in the Roman Empire so that the full force of law could be brought to bear on their followers, the Christian Church effectively eradicated their worship, and so, to a certain extent, eradicated the gods themselves. Some. Not all. There are entities that do not depend on believers to exist. That is why this 'little book' does its best to seem like something harmless. To hide itself. But it is not harmless."

"You're pulling my leg, right?" Sarah laughed. When his expression didn't change, she said, "You should be in a padded cell. This is insane." She pulled at her hands, trying to release them from his grip.

"Sarah, listen. *Opusculus Noctis* was written not to summon the gods that the Christian church has warred against for centuries, but it was written to call up the... the Prodigium. The Old Ones. The parents of these gods. And if that should happen, there's really no—"

"You can't be serious." Sarah yanked her hands from Andrez grip, startling even herself. It couldn't be true. She snatched *Opusculus Noctis* from the table and shoved it roughly into her purse, and pushed away from the table. "It's 1951, for crying out loud, and this mumbo jumbo—"

"Sarah, please listen to me. *Opusculus* is very, very dangerous. You can't just—"

She stood. Andrez stood as well, holding up his hands. "Sarah, I didn't want to frighten you. I know it might seem crazy, but—"

"No," she said. "No. It's all right. I'm sorry I wasted your time. Thank you for the tea."

She slowly backed to the door, not willing to turn her back to him. Andrez wrung his hands.

"*Sarah, do not translate any more of it!*"

When her hand touched the doorknob, she whirled and pulled the door open. Stiffly, she walked around the dilapidated church to the Plymouth. She kept her back straight, fearing any moment to feel his hand on her arm, jerking her around. She fumbled with her keys at the car.

Later, sun in the west, Sarah drove with the windows down, smoking and thinking. *The Prodigium! Gods and devils. He must be off his rocker.*

Only when she turned the Plymouth into the graveled, pecan-lined drive of the Big House did she realize that she had left the priest before learning what he knew about Uncle Gregor. Gregor Rheinhart, whom she'd loved. Gregor, who brought her presents, Russian dolls and dresses, from Paris. Fat Gregor. Itchy Gregor, all beard and belly. Always smelling of cherry tobacco and wine.

Darkness had fallen by the time she pulled up at the Big House. A police car waited in the drive.

Chapter 13

S he sat in the car, gripping the wheel, looking at the Big House. For a moment, blood filled her vision like a shroud.

It was horribly clear—the giant had risen while she'd been gone and painted the walls of the Big House in her family's blood. In her mind's eye, Alice lay bleeding in the kitchen, her head nearly severed. Fisk and Lenora lay beside her, bathed in sticky, blackening blood. And on the kitchen table...

On the kitchen table was Franny, splayed open like the carcass of some animal.

She shook her head, trying to clear the horrible vision. It clung, as sticky as blood, and flashed behind her eyes every time she blinked.

She left the car and approached the Big House on trembling legs. She paused at the door, terrified at what she might find beyond.

Wouldn't there be more police cars? Wouldn't there be ambulances?

She turned the knob and swung open the door.

Sheriff Jay Wocziak stood in the atrium of the Big House, hat in hand, speaking with Alice in hushed tones. They both turned as the front door opened.

Sarah shivered.

"Is everything…"

Alice came to her.

"Is everyone all right? I thought that—"

"You thought what?"

"Everyone was dead. That the man had woken up and…"

Alice stayed silent, but her eyes softened and she drew Sarah into a tight, fierce hug.

"I thought—"

"I know what you thought. But know this—I woulda laid that man flat, busted his ass with your momma's shotgun, before he'd ever lay a finger on Fisk or Franny. Or Lenora. Believe that."

They were in the orchard again and Alice's eyes blazed, holding the cudgel she came so close to braining the Alexander boy with.

Finally, Sarah nodded.

"Now, get yourself together, Miss Thing. Beansy is here," Alice said. And again Sarah was amazed that she could be so imperious yet infuse her words with love. It was almost as though she'd become the daughter Sarah should have been. Strong. Fierce. Unafraid.

Sarah shivered again, almost ashamed of the feeling. That she'd been weak and so full of doubt and bloody thoughts.

What kind of mother thinks those things?

But she nodded.

"Sarah." Beansy nodded to her, his Adam's apple bobbing dramatically. "It's good to see you, girl. Let me look at you." Sheriff Wocziak been a friend of Sarah's as a child, and now he smiled at her in a way so familiar, she thought of Gethsemane Elementary playground, where she had first kissed a boy. Beans, they had called him affectionately.

"Hey, Beansy. God, it's been—"

"A long time, that's for sure. Dang sure. I'd heard you'd come back, and I've been meaning to get on by, check in with Alice and," he looked up, toward the hall by the gallery and Sarah's mother's room, "your mother. But I've been so danged busy with, you know, sheriffing I haven't had a chance."

Sarah came forward and hugged him, smiling at his discomfort with her body's closeness. He felt like a lumpy board underneath the fabric, all bones and skin. "It's good to see you too, Beansy. You still married to Louise?"

He shuffled his feet and turned his hat in his hands. "Yup. Kids are getting up there too. Lil Jerry just bout to hit ten. Of course, Louise and me got started a tad earlier than you did."

Sarah nodded. "Have you been waiting for me long?"

"Naw. I'm waiting for... Alice was just going upstairs to... well... the reason I'm here is—"

"You're here to see the man. Ingram."

"That his name? He got identification?"

"Yes." She frowned. "How did you learn about him?"

"Let me just run upstairs and check on him," said Alice.

He grinned. "Phyllis. She overheard Dr. Polk calling around to hospitals, asking if they'd admitted any folks with obvious battery or gunshot wounds. How'dya think I found out?"

"Have you seen him?"

"Not yet."

From above, Alice's voice came. "He's still out. Moaning." She looked down, over the railing, at Sarah and Wocziak and winked. "Why don't y'all come on up, take a peek at him."

Sarah and Wocziak mounted the stair to the gallery. As they climbed, he shoved his hat onto his head fiercely, as if preparing himself for some confrontation.

They followed Alice down the long gallery, through the hall to the guest room, the rich Persian rugs and cypress walls absorbing the sounds of their footfalls. Alice had lit the hallway lamp, which threw long shadows behind them.

"So, I called Doc Polk," Wocziak said. "And he told me this guy's been torn up something fierce. I mean multiple wounds."

"That's right. He looks like he was in the wrong place at the wrong time."

He glanced sidelong at her as they came to the door. He raised a thin eyebrow and squinted. "That right? A broken fist, a knife wound, a bite mark too? Sounds to me like he was in the wrong place a few too many times. Like maybe he *is* the wrong place, his ownself."

Alice looked over her shoulder at them. In a lowered voice, she said, "Here we is. Y'all keep your voices down." She opened the door and moved into the room.

Inside the room, Wocziak whistled. "Damnation. A regular hoss, he is." He took off his hat.

Ingram lay sprawled on the bed, the thin bed linens covering his privates like an oversized loin-cloth. His pale skin blended with the white bandages littering the landscape of his body. Head, chest, arm, and hand—all were covered in stark white gauze.

Wocziak whistled again. "I wouldn't want to tangle with this one. Look at his hands."

"Dr. Polk said he's got a fracture."

"Naw. Not that one. The good one. He could pick up a watermelon with that hand. Criminy. Look at his knuckles. The brute's got scars on his scars. Seen his fair share of fighting, that's for sure. That's for dang sure."

Wocziak turned to Sarah and rested his hand on the butt of his gun.

"Listen, Sarah. This fella's no dang good. All you have to do is look at him. He's a brute and a bruiser. Looks like he makes his living by using his fists." He gulped, his Adam's apple working underneath his skin. "I don't usually say things like this, especially to folk who ain't deputized, but... I order you to call me the minute he wakes up. You hear? The exact minute. I don't want to hear anything out of your mouth other than yes sir. You got kids here, remember?"

Sarah looked at him closely. "Yessir," she said, wrinkling her nose, "Sheriff Beansy."

He rolled his eyes. "Dang it, Sarah. This is serious."

She thought of the bloody kitchen and her smiled died. She nodded.

Wocziak dug at his belt and handed over a pair of handcuffs. He took a small key from his pocket.

"I ain't supposed to do this, but here. I got another set in the car. I suggest you handcuff him to the bed."

Alice held her hand out for Sarah to give her the handcuffs.

"No, Alice. I'll keep them."

There was a spark of anger on Alice's face but she said nothing. She wasn't going to let this pass.

Later, after Wocziak drove off into the night in his cruiser, Sarah took her purse and went into the library, placing *Opusculus Noctis* face up on the livid green blotter of the desk. She followed it with the yellow paper of her own poor translation.

For a while, she sat at the desk, holding the handcuffs in her hands, turning them over and over and making the metal teeth click through the latches. *Why can't I control my feelings? I just bolted out of Andrez's house. My head's filled with bloody images. I'm out of control. I've never felt like this before.*

But that wasn't true. She's felt as lost and uncontrolled once before.

❧

It was 1944 and Christmas was coming while her father lay abed, dying. The stroke that felled him in the field rendered half of his body useless. He slurred his speech horribly, lips dead on his left side, spittle flying when he tried to talk. He slammed a balled fist on his leg in frustration and railed at the use of his wheelchair, such anger at his traitorous body that Sarah felt he'd hurt himself if he could. But his lopsided body, once so strong and proud, denied him even that. Sarah told herself to try to remember him as he was before the stroke, gray eyed, gray haired, and hard of jaw. A lord, truly, as far as anyone here in these United States could be considered a lord.

As a young man, before the first Great War, he'd left the dim grains and moist dirt of the Arkansas fields and traveled East, across the sea to Europe, and found his way to Heidelberg to study there. Sarah thought of that time in his life like some splendid, roseate myth in which he wandered Europe seeking wisdom, tutored by wise men. And Gregor had gone with him, the rake, the jester, owning nothing and caring for nothing except laughter and love and revelry. And his brother.

He returned, the Southern son, educated in Germany and home prodigal and strong to take up the burden and honor of responsibility: the family farm. She imagined his train trip back, the darkened fields passing her father's window like faint dirges sung in the dark, each one a threat and a promise, a trunk of books riding with him, while Gregor drank and cursed, sometimes in French, sometimes in German. And coming home, her father found a woman who matched his force of will in equal measure; she matched his fortune with her own.

Miles upon miles of farmland he owned, more than any landowner in the state other *than* the state. And as his influence and wisdom and money grew, he acquired other things, the Gethsemane Mercantile, the John Deere tractor dealership, the Kerr-McGehee service station at the corner of Pulaski and Main. He held controlling interest in the First Bank of Gethsemane, and held outright and in toto the Grain Exchange on the outskirts of town. If you lived and breathed, ate or drank, drove or rode, at some point, you came before a representative of James Ware Rheinhart or one of his minions. And Gregor remained always at his side, his red hair like a fire-brand blazing, his booming laugh a challenge and a promise as well.

Love and pride brought James Ware Rheinhart low.

Baird, Sarah's brother, took a round in the gut at Bastogne, and came home in a pine box, draped in a flag. But it was her father who never recovered. He took to walking his land, his fields, face dark and eyes startling in their aspect. He frightened Sarah, and made her cry. Sometimes she wanted to scream at him, *"But I'm still here!*" But she couldn't, the words died on her lips when she saw his wounded eyes and fierce expression.

They found him insensible in a field of wheat, the stalks like spears rising around him. When Gregor came home and discovered what had happened, he tore at his hair, ripped his clothes, drank whiskey furiously, and wept. His grief was as big as Gregor himself.

The strokes kept coming. Micro-strokes, Dr. Polk called them, each one passing unseen through her father's body like ghosts fleeting through flesh. Then he was gone, come from the earth to labor on it and then return to it. They buried him in the family graveyard among the pecan trees.

Through it all, Gregor was there. He ushered his brother into the ground, face red from crying and stinking of whiskey. Sarah remembered. She'd felt lost and desperate, like a tiny boat on a storm-tossed sea, infinitesimal on the massive bosom of ocean. Her emotions careened out of control—she wanted to weep for her father, she wanted to kill him for dying without ever truly having *seen* her.

It rained the night before the funeral and the sky was still moist from the downpour, the earth sodden and loose, eager to receive James Rheinhart's body. In the Big House atrium before the service, Gregor raged that he couldn't be one of the pallbearers.

"*Goddamn it!* You're drunk," her mother had yelled at Gregor. Sarah winced at her mother's language. She stood in the dining room, looking into the atrium where Elizabeth Rheinhart and Gregor argued.

"You're his brother, why don't you act like it?"

"That's right, Elizabeth. I'm his damned brother! I should help carry him, just like—just like I did all through his life!"

"Carry him? *Pfah.* He carried you, the profligate fool. Drunk and maudlin and useless except for your arcane family studies. You and James, always closeting yourself in the library, going on book buying trips—as if that was what you were really doing. I wouldn't be surprised if you weren't pouring over pornographic Grecian urns when you left, or whoring in Memphis." She paused, smoothing her dress. Sarah blinked, eyes raw from a night of crying. Her mother seemed indomitable and unafraid. If anything, she seemed enraged by her husband's death.

"Why can't you act like a man?" Elizabeth spat. "Go drink some coffee, take a shower, get ready for the funeral."

"I'm going to speak."

"So speak."

"Not now, you damned Xanthippe. At the service."

Her slap echoed in the vaulted atrium. "I'll remind you that he was my husband. And here, you blubber like a child. I won't have you doing it at the service."

Gregor touched his cheek. The red of his skin showed through even the red of his beard. He smiled.

"Gods, you're a trial. It's a wonder Ware didn't throttle you to keep you silent." He took out a silver flask, twisted off the cap, making small *eek eek* sounds, and drank deeply. "I'll speak, and there's nothing you can do about it, woman."

She swung at him again, but this time, even drunk, he snatched her hand out of the air. From where she watched, Sarah saw her mother tense as Gregor squeezed her hand, his knuckles turning white with the pressure.

"Let me go," Elizabeth said, her voice low.

Gregor stared at her, whiskey fumes pouring off him. They stood that way for a long time, her mother's back taut with outrage and indignation. Gregor looked at Elizabeth, a lazy smile spreading across his florid face. As Sarah watched, she felt like Gregor and her mother were just actors conjured from her heart, acting out the war going on inside of her. Her warring feeling for her father.

It hurt so damned bad. Never having been loved.

With a great wrench, Elizabeth Werner Rheinhart yanked her hand from Gregor's, turned in place like a soldier pivoting in parade, and marched away, up the great stairs, and through the gallery.

Gregor slumped, sitting down on the atrium's banquet bench.

He sighed and passed a hand over his eyes, rubbing fiercely as if to dislodge the alcohol and grief.

He looked up and saw Sarah peering into the atrium from the dining room. His eyes softened, and he motioned her to join him.

"Hey, Sar-baby." She sat by him and he patted her knee, squeezing a little. "It's... it's a bad deal here, isn't it?"

Sarah nodded, her eyes raw. They thought the same way. "*Geeg*, I... I wish she wouldn't... be like that. Sometimes I hate her."

Gregor took her hand in his. It was warm and scaly with calluses. "That makes two of us. But she's hurting too. She might not show it, but she is."

Sarah turned her head to look at him, surprised. He pulled his flask from his pocket again and twisted off the cap. In the low light of the atrium, she could see engraved upon the silver of his flask the stylized face of Bacchus, grinning and strewn with grapes.

Gregor looked at her, squinting. "How old are you now, Sar-baby?"

"Twenty last month." She jabbed his belly with a finger. "You gave me an orchid and the frilly pink dress."

"Oh." He looked lost. Tilting the flask to his mouth, he said, "You like it?"

"It died."

"The dress died?"

"The orchid. I'm not good with plants."

He nodded. "Me neither. But the dress, Sar. You like it?"

She smiled. "I love it." It had been two sizes too big and childish in its cut. Maybe some freakishly large eleven year old could wear it, but Sarah never would.

"Good." He tweaked her knee again then rested his head in one large paw, the other loosely gripping the flask.

"Here you've lost your father," he muttered, "and all I can think about is myself." He turned to Sarah and squeezed her hand, looking into her eyes. "Your father and I were the closest of all our family. But Papa had another family before James and me. Did you know that? That we're... we're Papa's second try?"

Sarah shook her head, puzzled. "How is that possible? I mean…
Paw-paw never mentioned ever having—"

"Another family? No, Papa wouldn't. He was like James. Here."
He handed her the flask. It felt warm and smooth in her hands.
"You're old enough to try whiskey, if you haven't already.
It's gonna sting and taste awful. *Ein Geschmack der Hölle, ein
Geschmack des Himmels.*"

She lifted the flask to her lips and drank. It tasted like a field of
corn on fire. She coughed. But her stomach grew warm and her
eyes stopped hurting.

Gregor took back the flask. His eyes looked sad and a little
frightened.

"His first wife was named Graine Masters Rheinhart. They had
two sons together. One named Karl and the other named Wilhelm.
Papa had gone to Little Rock, to tend to business there, when he
used to keep an office." He stopped, eyes focusing on the far wall.
"When he came home he found everyone dead. Blood everywhere,
trailing all over the Big House."

He held her hand up and looked at it, tracing the tendons and
veins.

"I've questioned the servants myself about what they found.
Graine was at the piano, struck through the heart. She hemor-
rhaged out in less than a minute. Before she knew what even happened. In the kitchen, a serving woman was near decapitated. And
on the table, Karl Rheinhart—your uncle—was split open like
someone breasting a duck. The doctor who collected the body—
there wasn't any coroner or medical examiner back in the 1800s—
his report says that Karl's heart was missing. And on the floor was
Papa's sword. The one issued him in the Civil War. Funny thing
about that sword, it wasn't a saber, like you see in all the paintings."

He drew up his flask again and shook it. Sarah heard the high
pitched slosh of the liquor in the silver container.

"Here. I don't need it anymore." He handed it to her. She took
another swallow.

"What was it?"

"What?"

"The sword."

He scratched the back of his hand and then let his hands fall limply on his knees.

"A gladius. Jefferson Davis was a fiend for the glory of Rome, the goddamned prat. Anyway, for the first few months of the war, he had foundries in Atlanta pumping out these flat, short Roman gladii. Larger than the largest dagger, but not as long as a saber. These were made for chopping and stabbing. Clunky and heavier than shit. First thing the Rebs threw away on any extended march. It's stored away in the library somewhere."

Sarah shifted on the bench. The spirits from the flask had warmed her but she found herself getting more discomfited with the story.

"They found the sword on the kitchen floor covered in blood. Bloody bare footprints all over the house leading from there—" He pointed to the kitchen. "And coming to right here." Gregor jabbed his finger at the front door. "And Wilhelm was missing."

"Wilhelm?"

"The other brother. *My* brother, who I'll never know." He shook his head. "They didn't find his body. The hand prints on the sword and the footprints on the floor were small. A boy's."

Confused, Sarah asked, "What does that mean? I don't understand."

"Wilhelm Rheinhart, by all accounts, was dying of tuberculosis. He couldn't even get out of bed without coughing up a lungful of blood. However, it looks like he got out of his death-bed, murdered his mother and brother and a serving woman, removed his brother's heart, and walked out of the house, never to be heard from again."

"Jesus. That's horrible."

"Yes. Horrible. And now James is gone. I always tried to be the best brother I could be to him. I never wanted to be like… like Wilhelm." He barked a short, bitter laugh. "Or Karl for that matter."

Sarah patted his hand, not knowing what else to do. She smiled at him.

"You were a good brother, Geeg. Of course you were. Daddy loved you."

He bowed his head, and Sarah saw tears streaming down his face, disappearing in his beard. He balled his fists, and Sarah remembered her father doing the same thing, in frustration at the wheelchair. Gregor sniffed—a snort really—and wiped his face with his sleeve in that awkward, halting way men had of dealing with tears.

"We tried to find him. James and I. We tried to find Wilhelm. Of course this was forty years later, but we searched. We had field-hands hunting through all of the woods with poles, jabbing at the ground, looking for a boy's remains. We searched the town records of every burg in Arkansas, looking for the tubercular deaths of children, or orphans. He couldn't have lived much longer. We found nothing; or the leads we did find turned out to be worthless. Wilhelm Rheinhart disappeared." He held his hand and flared his fingers, like holding a feather to the wind and letting go.

"He probably died in the woods and no one found his body before it rotted or was eaten by animals," Sarah offered.

Gregor nodded, eyes red. "There was always that possibility. But how did the boy get the strength to slaughter three people? Why did he do it? Where did he go? Sar-baby... I couldn't just let it lie. Wilhelm is—or was—*my brother*! I needed to know what happened to him. So we searched until we both were accepted and went to Heidelberg, to the University. And we forgot about Wilhelm."

He raised the flask again, bringing it to his lips. Finding it empty, he shook the flask as if pouring the contents on the floor, then smiled ruefully.

"Ah. It's probably better I'm not stinking drunk."

He stood uneasily, and staggered a few steps away.

"You're pretty drunk. Let me help you, Geeg."

"No, I'm fine." He shooed her away. Frowning, he said, "We had forgotten all about our half brother during the years in Heidelberg, until I got my hands on an old book of German lore. We were crazy for the stuff then; James and I dreamt of being the new Brothers Grimm, or at least Aarne and Thompson. This particular tome was written in the sixteenth century by a syphilitic goliard slowly going crazy."

He wiped his lips and looked around. "I need something to drink."

"I can get you some... I don't know, port, I think. Mama has a bottle somewhere."

"No, I need water and coffee. And a shower."

"Yes. You're right," Sarah said, then paused. "But what about the book?"

"Eh? Oh. One of the tales told a story about a dying girl, sick with the plague. As she lies on her death bed, surrounded by her dying family, she's approached by an elf. Not the nice, girly elves that ladies like to believe traipse around the English countryside. We're talking about an Old World spirit, a *vaettir*, a creature of blood and stone and hate. She begs him to heal her, and her family. He refuses. She pleads, tearing her hair. He refuses. Finally, throwing herself at his feet, she makes one last request for healing. He tells her he can heal her, but *only* her. She cries, of course, because she loves her parents and her sister. But as a payment, he demands her sister's heart. She refuses, horrified. He tells the girl she will die anyway, so why not? She refuses, once again, hoping against hope that her sister will recover. But the girl's sister is listening from her bed and offers up her heart to save the girl. The elf laughs and cuts out the sister's heart. Holding the still-warm thing in front of the girl, he says that she must eat it, take the strength of it into herself, if she wants to be cured. The girl refuses, and the elf disappears with the heart. The girl dies of grief, alongside the body of her sister."

"How sad. Surely people didn't tell these stories, did they? They're... they're hideous."

"They ate them up like hotcakes. Loved them." He walked back toward the kitchen, at first unsteady but getting more sure-footed as he went.

"But what does this have to do with Wilhelm?"

"You won't believe me."

"Uh..."

He stopped, turned to her. "In our studies, James and I found this story repeated in every culture known to man. Sometimes the heart gets eaten, sometimes it doesn't. The further we looked into it, we found more books, ones that take this myth seriously, books that tell of making bargains with... with... things you'd rather not know about."

Confused and not a little frightened by Gregor's tone and the strange look on his face, Sarah asked, "But what about Wilhelm?"

He cleared his throat, hocking up phlegm. He looked around helplessly for somewhere to spit. He stood there for a little while, as if making up his mind about telling her. Then he swallowed, and Sarah, despite herself, shuddered.

He said, "You should know this, because when I'm gone... well... you'll be the last Rheinhart. The last with any of my blood, at least, except for Wilhelm, if he's still out there. So remember and don't think of me as a lunatic."

She smiled and turned her head coyly, as if she was five again, begging for candy. "I've always thought of you as a lunatic, Geeg. Whatever you tell me won't change that."

He laughed, the sound a big rumble like casks of ale being rolled across a hardwood floor.

"Okay. I warned you, Sar-baby. I think something came to Wilhelm on *his* deathbed." He waved his hands at the old timbers of the Big House. "I think something old—something very old—walked out of the swamps, or the river, or the woods and tempted Wilhelm with life in exchange for his family's death. Unlike the story, he accepted. I think Wilhelm ate his brother's heart. Now I've got to get ready to put *my* brother in the earth."

He turned and walked into the kitchen.

Sarah *remembered*.

These memories, unbidden and frightening, had remained deep underneath the still pool of her experience, only to come to the surface now. It had been seven years since that conversation. And now, seven years later, she was as scared and confused as she was then and surprised at the memories, memories she'd put into the ground with her father's body.

Once James Ware Rheinhart was in the ground, Gregor took his share of the farm and money, sold everything he could, and moved to Munich for further study. At fifty, Gregor started a new life. For the first time in his life—old or new—he married, a woman named Brigitte who baked him cakes and made him stop drinking, everything except wine. He lost weight and shaved his beard and rolled his own cigarettes. He wrote Sarah regularly, long discursive letters slipping into and out of German and French that—quite honestly—Sarah had not paid much attention to. She'd been heavily pregnant with Franny, and Jim had already begun to drink himself into insensibility every night. Letters from Gregor seemed unreal and arcane. And he had left. Sarah tried as hard as she could to ignore the fact that Gregor—her Gregor, her Geeg—had left her to deal with life without him.

She sent Gregor a letter telling him of Franny's birth, but he never responded. She discovered he had been walking in the fields by the Neckar River when the stroke hit him, dropping him in his tracks. He was the same age as his brother when James had died. Gregor lived on, though, as an invalid, without movement or voice. His wife hired a translator and sent Sarah a telegram saying Gregor was comfortable, sitting in the sun every day, and was able to take soup and drink wine, if she helped him. He couldn't write, his body was too damaged by the stroke for that.

Sarah rubbed her eyes, sitting cramped at the desk, and pushed *Opusculis Noctis* away from her.

Standing, she moved around the desk, toward the bookcases.

"Wait a second…"

Bending down, she rapped on the wooden foot panels of the bookcases, listening. She went around the room knocking each wooden rectangle. She couldn't tell any difference between the sound of one panel to the other. She stood, rolled up her sleeves, and turned to the bar. There she pulled each bottle out of the enclosed space and put them on the green blotter of the desk. Scotch, gin, whiskey. Mimi's port. The virulent green bottle of Creme de Menthe. Le Roi's Peppermint Schnapps.

Jesus. Who drinks this stuff?

The dry-bar mirror glared at her, mocking. She went to the kitchen, and, surprised to find Alice gone, dug through the junk drawer, returning to the library with a flat-head screwdriver. Carefully, Sarah popped the mirror off the back of the bar, its silvered hide coming away with a ripping sound. The adhesive that fixed it left an ugly curlicue on the wall. She propped it against the paneling by the door.

Sarah put her hands on her hips and huffed in exasperation, riffling her bangs. Even though the air in the Big House was cool, her forehead beaded with sweat. Going to the far left wall, closest to the window, she pulled the stepladder to the bookcase.

Very carefully, she removed each volume, turning each book over and fanning the pages so that any paper, string, or thread fell from the book. Soon, a confetti of bookmarks, playing cards, ribbons, and flakes of old parchment littered the library floor. She made individual stacks of books around the room's baseboards, each stack a small tower of arcane knowledge.

On the shelf that held the massive volume titled *Quanoon-e-Islam* she found the sword, wrapped in a chamois and twine and stored in the empty space behind the row of books, out of sight but not exactly hidden.

What had Andrez said? Hiding in plain sight?

She knew she had found it the moment her hands touched the covering, fingers rapping on the steel even through the chamois. She brought it down and untied the twine, holding the bundle to the light. As the chamois fell away, Sarah looked at the sharp metal leaf of steel jutting from the darker, leather-wrapped hilt. The base of the blade, where the thin cross guard met sharp edges and center ridge, was covered with a black grime. *Old blood.*

A sense of dread washed over her. She carefully put the sword on the desk, full of reverence and loathing for such a deadly thing. All weapons hold the possibility of violence but this one had a history of it, and Sarah found herself uncomfortable and wary of its potential.

Standing on back on the stool, she groped behind the books remaining on the shelf, afraid of what more she might find. And then she felt it—tucked away in the corner, a small packet of papers wrapped with a strip of leather. The letters crackled in her hands as she lifted them, filling her nose with a scent of tobacco and vinegar.

She brought them to the desk and gingerly untied the leather strip. She turned the small stack over in her hand.

Gregor's script, she'd know it anywhere. Taking off a sheet and unfolding it, she read the letter.

1923 - Salzburg, Austria

Brother Ware,

I'm writing you now from the courtyard of an inn outside Salzburg where Beethoven reputedly wrote one of his symphonies. They serve rich wine here, and as I write this, I sit in a sun-dappled nook of the tabled courtyard, the trellis above me covered in ripening grapes and leaves. Truly, an idyllic little spot. I plan on getting drunk, drunk as sin, drunk as a lord, drunk as Cooter Brown sitting on the fence. I have found the item that we have often spoken of, lusted after, and dreaded finding. The mad Arab's treatise, Quanoon-e-Islam.

I've spent the last month combing through the estate of one Frau Kuester, who responded to our ad in the Kronen Zeitung regarding books. Her husband, who disappeared walking in the Tyrolean foothills—very mysteriously, Adala assures me—seemed to have a fondness for the blacker arts. I've found various books from that boorish English "magician" and sodomite which are pure bullshit, as they say back in Arkansas. In the Kuester shelves I've found a very early version of the Key of Solomon—a proto-version maybe, I haven't finished the translation and the manuscript is in very poor condition so a comparative read is impossible currently.

Yes, I know of your opinion of the Lemegeton. But I went ahead and acquired the volume just in case.

That was the first week.

The enormous amount of books to sort through and the private papers of Herr Kuester—a very successful engraver—have occupied my time almost constantly. I spent two weeks more rifling through them until I found the volume. Strangely, it's not titled Necronomicon. The content is not the Arabic but a Greek translation so the Quanoon-e-Islam is somewhat of a misnomer. And slanderous to the noble Bedouin tribes. That old argument between us.

It's hand-lettered and illuminated, if you can call it that, illumination. It is a good stroke of fortune to have found a Greek translation of that vile treatise; I've arranged for an expatriated Macedonian scholar in Vienna to take a look at it and give me a quote for translation. I don't know what I would have done if it had been in Arabic.

I'm uncomfortable with the Quanoon in my room. I sleep poorly and have bad dreams. Last night, after beginning my translation of the Lemegeton, I fancied something was at the window, peering in at me. Of course, this was silly; I've taken rooms on the second floor. But the feeling persisted, all because of the book. The illustrations alone are like windows into the worst hells imaginable. Tomorrow I will take it to the Austrian National Bank and place it in a safety box there and maybe I can get some rest.

I placed an advert in the Venice paper regarding the acquisition of old tomes of historical and occult bent, and I hope we can make some headway though I fear it might be expensive. I've found no other volumes, pamphlets, scrolls that might help us determine what happened to, or became of, our unknown murderous kin.

I need more money, brother. Adverts don't grow on trees, and everything here in Austria is getting more expensive now that the League of Nations have set up shop in Vienna. Send the funds to the Salzburg branch of the Austrian National Bank, where I'll be storing the Quanoon. Five hundred dollars should suffice.

I've been contacted by a priest, recently, who says he has some volumes of interest. I must travel to Florence next week to meet him. I

have high hopes for the meeting. He tells me the work is called Opus-
culis Noctis. And another called the Book Eibon. I've never heard of
either of these works before, so I am excited. Maybe it will hold a clue
as to what happened to Wilhelm.

I will write again soon. I should be home by the end of the summer,
gods willing, just in time for harvest. Kiss young Baird and little Sar
for me and tell them I'll be bringing presents.

Gregor

Sarah put down the letter and walked over to the stack that held
the *Quanoon.* She picked up the dense book, weighing it in her
hand. A wisp of her hair crept into her mouth, and she began to
chew.

She opened the book to a random page, and her breath caught
in her throat.

She lurched over to the desk and set the book down, pages open
to the illustration, a picture rendered in simple brush-strokes with
the faintest of coloration: black outlines, red gore, brown background. The illustration depicted a woman or a girl—her age was
indeterminate—lying spread eagle on a poorly drawn table while
two men assaulted her, one ramming a disproportionate horned
phallus in her mouth and the other ejaculating onto—no, into—
the bloody expanse of what once might have been stomach but was
now, in the rough yet expressive way the illustrator had with line,
a mass of guts. They'd split the girl open like gutting a fish, splayed
her across the table, spilling roughly drawn entrails and innards
outward from her torso. The men possessed faces—illustrated in
the same rudimentary yet detailed fashion—resembling wolves.
And in the gaping wound of the woman's stomach and chest, a
demonic face and hands appeared. The hands held a scepter and a
crown. Blocks of Greek text surrounded the picture.

As she looked at the illustration she felt herself becoming di-
vorced from the person she had been only moments before. The
person she had been when she took down the sword.

She shook her head. *I don't understand,* she thought madly. *I thought it was all just crazy people, crazy talk.*

I don't even have to be able to read the Greek to understand what's going on here. The knowledge of the image suffused her, possessed her.

What other ways are there of making bargains? Opusculus Noctis said innocence and the will to do what was necessary was all you need to deal with ...with... the Prodigium. *If I took Fisk or Lenora and the sword down to the river...*

She shuddered, horrified at what she'd been thinking. She walked to the phone and picked it up.

"Phyllis?" She clicked the receiver twice. "Phyllis?"

"Yeah, honey? That you, Sarah?"

"Yes. Please connect me to Father Andrez in Stuttgart."

"Oh? You two hit it off? I guess you just got back."

Sarah looked down at the *Quanoon,* staring at the hideous illustration.

Has it only been a few hours since I left Andrez?

She ground her teeth and could feel the muscles in her cheek tightening, her jaw locking down. She growled, "Whatever I've done or said is none of your business. I would like to remind you that my father was a major shareholder in the Bell Corporation, who I believe is your employer. If I look around here hard enough, I might be able to find the schedule for the next shareholders meeting. From there it will be an easy matter to make sure you never pick up a call again. Do you understand, Phyllis? From this moment on, you will neither listen in, nor repeat anything that I say, or any other person on this circuit."

"Well, Sarah, I just can't see why—"

"Do you understand? I will make sure that you lose your job if I ever hear that you've repeated anything said on this party line."

"Sarah... I—"

"All you need to say is, 'I understand.' And then connect me to Father Andrez."

"I... I understand."

Sarah breathed into the phone, staring at the gruesome rendering. She turned the page. And gasped again. Another illustration, this time of two toddlers, each one gouging out the eyes of the other. Men and women watched the gory combat, their faces like gargoyles. Blood ran from the children's eyes, down their bodies, pooling on the floor. One gargoyle-faced man used the blood to draw an enormous picture of a clawed hand with thirty coins in the palm. Sarah turned another page. A woman standing at a bench, a knife in her fist and her own severed hand lying on the floor. A horrible silent O for a mouth, as if she was singing. Through the door, a field. On the field, a black figure, watching. Sarah turned the page. A gigantic face with a dog in its gaping mouth. The dog's maw held a serpent, and the serpent's tail punched a hole in the back of the face, curved around underneath and became a gigantic phallus with a miniature face at the tip. In the face's mouth stood a dog. Sarah turned the page. A monstrous octopus-like creature looking up from the bottom of a well, eyes black and liquid. Around the rim of the well, tiny people hurled children into the abyss, to plummet to their deaths.

Sarah felt uneasy on her feet, and the room began to distort and skew perspective. Her stomach tightened and her limbs ached as if she had a fever.

The phone clicked twice and in the receiver, she could hear the buzzing to indicate a ring. After a long time, he came on the line.

"Yes? This is Father Andrez."

Sarah remained silent, breathing heavy. Trembling, she reached forward—her limbs like lead—and slowly shut the book. She took a deep breath.

"Sarah?" Andrez's worried voice came through the receiver.

She swallowed and pushed the book away from her.

"Sarah? Are you all right? Please tell me you haven't been translating any more of the *Opusculis*."

She nodded. Her body shook as if a tremor passed through it, and she gasped one last time.

"Andrez. Andrez... I—" Sarah's voice sounded raw, even to herself.

"Sarah! Are you all right? What is the matter?"

"I... I need your help. You were right... I believe you now. You must come—"

"Sarah, listen to me. I don't know what has happened, but I will come—somehow. One of my parishioners will give me a ride. But where are you?"

"Gethsemane. Just get to Gethsemane and ask for me, or the Big House. Everybody knows where we are."

"Yes, I will. Don't read or translate any more. Promise me."

She nodded again, then gave a rueful smile, realizing he couldn't see her gestures through the telephone line.

"I just... I looked into the *Quanoon*."

"What? What was the name?"

"*Quanoon-e-Islam*. I looked into it and... I... *What's happening to me?*"

"*Bodanstvo*," Andrez whispered under his breath. "Where in the world did you get that foul book? No. I am coming. Now. I will be there as soon as I can. Do not touch either of the books."

"What is happening? I don't understand. I feel like I'm going crazy."

"Sarah, how you could possess two evil books in one place, it amazes me. But evil calls to itself. And it can change you, just by knowing it exists. Believe me."

She nodded involuntarily, then said, "Yes." She took another deep breath.

"I will be there as soon as possible, but it might not be until morning. Stay put and don't think too much on the things you might have seen or read in the books. Keep your mind away from those subjects."

"Okay. I'll try."

"*Dovidenja*, Sarah. I will see you soon." He hung up, and Sarah replaced the receiver on its cradle.

She moved to the chair by the desk and slumped down in it, pulling open the drawer. From inside, she withdrew a pack of Pall Malls and lit one from a match. She took a huge draught from the cigarette and kept the smoke deep in her lungs, holding it in, then exhaled violently, blowing smoke toward the paneled ceiling. *Opusculis Noctis* and the *Quanoon* kept drawing her eyes back. When she shut her eyes, her mind painted lurid pictures of eviscerated girls and strange gargoyle-faced men. When she looked up, Alice was at the door showing the whites of her eyes. If Sarah had known any better, she'd think Alice was afraid. But that was just silly. Alice feared nothing.

"He's awake. The giant," she said, and turned to go back upstairs.

Chapter 14

He didn't bother to cover up as she entered the room. His heavy body, thick with muscles and scar tissue, lay in an easy repose that she'd only seen in children. He watched her intently as she walked in the room, eyes flicking over her hips, breasts, hands, face. He smiled when he saw the handcuffs.

"You gonna lock me up?"

Well, he doesn't look lost anymore.

"Hi, Lewis. I'm Sarah Rheinhart." Alice looked at her sharply. "And that's Alice. We found you at the river, in a boat."

"Bull," he said.

"We did… we found you by—"

"No, that's what everyone calls me." He motioned down to his body as if to say, *this.* "Since I was a kid."

He opened his mouth as if to say more, then shut it.

"Bull, you been messed up real bad," Alice said, moving near the bedside table. "Been out for a coupla days now. We been taking

179

care of you." A pitcher sat on the bedside table near a glass. Alice
picked up the pitcher and filled the glass with water.

There was a long silence.

"What're you gonna do with those handcuffs?"

Sarah tossed them into his lap.

"I want you to lock yourself to the bed."

He raised an eyebrow. "Why?"

"Everyone tells me you're dangerous. I haven't seen anything to
disprove that."

"What if I say no?"

"We'll call the sheriff, and he'll be here in minutes." Sarah
glanced at Alice. "Alice here will get the shotgun and blow your
head off before you can get to the door."

His expression didn't change. There was no anger, no surprise,
no shame. He snapped the handcuff on one of his thick wrists,
lifted his arm over his head, and tried to snap the other cuff around
one of the wooden struts of the headboard. His mangled, gauze-
wrapped hand couldn't work them shut.

"I'm gonna need help."

Sarah approached him, slowly.

"Sarah, don't," Alice said. Her voice was tense. "Wait till I can
get the shotgun."

Sarah ignored her and approached the bed. She paused when she
was in his arm reach. He remained still.

She snapped the cuff shut, locking him to the bed.

Alice sighed, explosively.

"Damnation, girl. Get away from him."

Sarah ignored her.

"What happened?" Sarah said. "What happened to you?" She
pointed to his bandaged hand.

He smiled, a painful thing for Sarah to watch. She could see the
lost boy again.

"I'm much obliged to you both for fixing me up but I don't
know what to tell you ladies. I don't want you to call the police or
carry me off to the nuthouse."

Sarah and Alice looked at each other.

"Bull, the police have already been here, not long ago. We're supposed to call them the moment you wake up."

He blinked. Sarah saw his jaw tighten.

"You got me locked up already. Go ahead and call them."

"They said it was related to that fire at Ruby's. They want to question you."

He nodded and took a sip of water. Then his eyes went to the door.

Both women turned to find Franny and Lenora standing there, eyes wide. Fisk peeked around the door jamb.

Franny said, "Mommy? Is the dead man better now?"

Alice drew in a sharp breath, and Sarah said, "Yes, baby. It looks like it."

Franny took two steps into the room, Fisk and Lenora behind her. She looked at Ingram. "It took six men to carry you. On a board. They dropped you once."

He laughed, a big rumble coming from deep in his chest. The sound filled the room, reminding Sarah of her Uncle Gregor. He was always tickled by the absurd.

Ingram smiled at the little girl. "It sure feels like I got dropped. I think they might've bumped my head."

Franny beamed.

"Naw. You was already all ripped up before they dropped you," Fisk said. "Anyways, you hit the leaves and mud—hey! Why are you handcuffed to the—"

"Fisk!" Alice barked. "Get yourself downstairs! I'll be down in a second to put you to bed. You girls go too. Go on!"

Ingram looked at his gauzed hand, then raised it to paw at his temple. He closed his eyes. "Wait." He rubbed the sides of his head. "Did you say Fisk?"

He pointed his wounded hand at Lenora like a club. "Is your name Lenora?"

Her jaw dropped. She took a step back. "Momma, how'd he know that?"

Alice turned to Ingram, anger filling her face. "Mister, you best not be messing around with my children. You ain't never gonna walk out that door."

Franny moved closer to the bed. "What's my name, mister? Do you know my name?"

He shook his head, a sad smile touching his eyes. "I'm sorry, sugar. I don't. Just these two."

"How the hell do you know my children's names, and why shouldn't we call the police right now?"

Sarah put a hand on Alice's arm. But the man only stared at her with the same cool gaze as before, eyebrows raised as if to say, *Okay, what are you going to do?*

Alice blanched. No one reacted to her like this.

"Maggie Washington," Ingram said slowly. "Call her and ask about me."

"You... you telling me you know my momma?"

He nodded.

Alice walked to the door. "Kids, come with me." She marched out, whisking down the hall in her slippers. With one glance back, Franny followed Fisk and Lenora. She waved at Ingram, and he waved back, his mittened hand awkward in the air.

"How do you know Maggie?"

"She's the housekeeper where I keep a room. Boarding house."

Sarah took that in. There were gunshot wounds on the hard ridges of his stomach, on the left side. Old wounds, silver. For a moment, the images in the *Quanoon* flashed behind her eyes. And she remembered the person she had been before gaining that knowledge. Sarah retrieved the sheets wadded at his feet and threw them over him. She walked to the corner of the room, grabbed a chair, and returned to his bedside. She sat facing him, eyes serious.

"Give me one reason we shouldn't call the cops right now."

He blinked again. "I didn't do anything wrong. I'm trying... I was trying to find a man."

"You found him?"

He was silent for a moment. "Yes."

"Did you kill him?"

He shook his head, eyes narrowing. "No. Hell no. He was already dead."

"You have anything to do with the fire at Ruby's?"

He didn't say anything.

"So you did. Sixty people died there, you know." She stood, smoothing her dress. "I can't have you in this house if you're dangerous."

Alice bustled into the room.

"Momma said you're okay, I guess. She got upset that you were hurt. Said you were a good boy. But messy. Told me to make sure you get better."

He nodded, expecting it.

Alice moved behind Sarah, placing her big hands on Sarah's shoulders. They both looked at Ingram expectantly.

He sighed, his chest rising and falling.

"I'll tell you everything, but you have to listen to me fairly. And even if you don't believe me… well… at least get me something to eat before you call the police."

Sarah smiled thinly, not letting it touch her eyes.

"Spill it. Everything. And we'll decide if we call the cops right away. Whatever you say, we're gonna have to call eventually."

He raised his eyebrow in an arch look that didn't go well with his blunt features. He closed his eyes for a long time.

When he opened them, he began speaking in a low tone, as if repeating by rote what he'd done.

"I was hired by a man named Sam Phelps to find someone," he began.

His tone frightened Sarah a little; here was a man who could divorce himself from himself so easily as to become an automaton.

When he was through, he shifted in the bed, sitting higher. "But there's more to my story. This pirate station broadcasts music—Phelps played me a snippet of a song—by a musician named Ramblin' John Hastur. Either of you ever heard of him?"

Sarah looked puzzled, shaking her head. Alice narrowed her eyes and peered at Ingram.

"What you wanna know about Ramblin' John?" she asked.

He looked at Alice. "You heard of him?"

"Yes," she offered reluctantly.

"What've you heard?"

"He a blues man. Sold his soul to the Devil, like they say about every blues man."

"You heard anything else?"

"His music is crazy. Makes you wanna drink and—" She paused. "Make love."

He continued to look at her, weighing her response.

"My man... my children's daddy—" Her eyes blazed as if defying him. "He was a blues man too. He could sing... well, he could sing a girl right outta her clothes, he could." She blushed. Sarah felt Alice's hands squeeze her shoulders.

"He came home from *giggin'*—that's what he called playing music, *giggin'*—and said he heard about a blues man over Desha County way, who could the change the weather and all sorts of other things with his music. Some good and some not so good. And Calvin—my man—he believed, and maybe I did too. A little at least. My momma always told me that the most powerful spells were sung, not spoken. And Calvin himself had a little of that, the magic in his voice. I mean, he was a damned fool, but he sure sung his way into my heart. And I *knew* he weren't any good. But he got in anyway. So Calvin decided he was gonna find this blues man, who went by the name of Ramblin' John Hastur. He left two, maybe three, years ago now and never came back. I thought he took up with another woman. That's all I know."

Ingram looked thoughtful as she spoke. His expression never changed, except once. When she mentioned Ramblin' John Hastur, he winced.

He said, "Well, you're partly right."

He continued with his story.

Alice looked surprised when he mentioned KQUI. "It's been off the air for a week or so. But that happens from time to time, after storms and such. We didn't think nothing of it."

Ingram nodded. "When I got to KQUI, there was no one there, and I got a bad feeling about the place. So I poked around a little. I found the owner lying dead on the floor right behind his microphones and records and turntable. He looked like he clawed his own face to shreds and his heart exploded. Can you guess what record was on the player?"

"Ramblin' John," Sarah said.

He nodded again. "It was rolling around at the end of the record, like when you put a phono on and let it play and don't take it off at the end. You know?"

"Yes."

"So I moved the needle back a little bit, just to hear it for a second, and the record got caught in a loop, between scratches. The music was… I don't have words for it really. It touched me, and I don't mean in a good way. I felt like I could murder somebody when I heard that music. But it caught me up in its web too, and it was hard for me to move. And even though the record was caught in a loop, the music grew. Got more… horrible. Till I couldn't take it anymore. But it was too late by then, because the dead man on the floor started to get up and come after me."

He held up his hands.

"Now, I know you're thinking now that I'm insane or that I just didn't realize that the man was asleep on the floor. No. I checked his pulse. He was dead. But once that music started playing, he got up and came for me."

It was Ingram who looked defiant now. He looked at the women as if challenging them to argue.

"I don't care if you believe me or not, it's true. I'd searched the station and found a slip of paper saying that Ramblin' John was gonna play at Ruby's, so after that I checked into the Royale in Stuttgart to wait. I spent my time listening to the radio, searching for the signal coming from the station. I didn't ever want to hear that sound again, but, what was I gonna do? If something like that can exist out there—"

He paused, shifted in the bed, trying to make himself comfortable with his arm above his head. He looked like the boy again, and Sarah wanted to take his hand or brush the hair out of his eyes.

She said, "How can you know you'll ever be safe? That anyone will? Is that what you were thinking?"

"Yes," he said, sounding relieved that she understood. He looked at her quizzically. "Yes. How can folks have families, fall in love—anything—if that music is out there, waiting to be played? It's like any minute can be the last minute. The end of the world. How can someone find happiness like that?"

"I guess everybody lives like that, I mean... you never know. They always say you can get run over by a bus. But damned if I'll just accept it. Or allow it to happen, if I can stop it. Nobody deserves that—for their life to end just because they heard a song. And then, to get back up, after they're dead. To dance to somebody else's... something else's... tune." He shuddered.

Ingram finished the story, telling them in a dead voice of the events at Ruby's, of finding Early's reanimated corpse and realizing it was Hastur.

The women were quiet, each looking at him with wide eyes.

Alice sniffed. "It's pretty hard to stomach, to tell the truth. But there are some things in this world that just can't be explained away." She looked over at Sarah. "I always talked about my doodle-bugs, and you never believed." She looked down, smiled sadly, and then looked back up. "Rightly so, I guess. I ain't got no doodle-bugs. But my momma do, and my grandmame even more before her. Being born in Africa and brought over here as a slave, the magic was strong in her. I remember. She could heal the sick with her hands and find things that no one else could. I saw it with my own eyes. So I guess there ain't any reason not to consider what this man said, even though it might not have happened exactly as he said."

Tension seemed to flow from Ingram's shoulders, and it looked to Sarah, for a moment, like he might cry.

"There's something else," Sarah said, lowering her voice. "What brought you here?"

"What do you mean? The river did."

She shook her head, hair swinging. "No. How did the river know to bring you here?"

He looked dumbfounded. "It didn't. It was just chance. A coincidence."

"It's just too much for coincidence. I want to know what brought you here because... if there is a... Pale Man out there and he has this song or sound of madness, then someone or something is working against him, through us. And I want to know what and who it is."

She hesitated, not knowing how to go on. She sighed, squared her shoulders, then said, "There's even more. I've found some books in the library, here, that have something to do with this."

Alice drew a sharp breath. "What? In the library?" She looked as though she'd found a snake under her pillow.

Sarah nodded. "The book I've been translating. I took it, just today, to a priest."

She told them about Andrez, about the *Opusculus Noctis* and the Prodigium.

"The thing is, I found another book in the library... a horrible, evil book. The illustrations are so... so... ghastly that once you've seen them, it's like something changes in your mind. Like how you described Ramblin' John's song. Hearing it, or seeing these illustrations, unlocks something in you, an awareness like a door opening. These drawings are so simple and... *hideous*... you don't have to know the language to know what it's saying. About how to... I don't know... raise up the dead. Bargain with devils."

"In our library? Here? At the Big House?" Alice was incredulous. Sarah nodded slowly. She pulled the key out of her pocket, walked forward and unlocked the handcuffs.

He lowered his arm, slowly, wincing.

"I'm sorry, Bull. We had to be sure."

"What? This isn't a face you can trust?"

Sarah was quiet, taking his question seriously. Actually, it *was* a face she could trust. But she wasn't going to tell him that. Her heart gave a lurch in her chest, and her cheeks burned.

"What about that goddamned book," asked Alice. "You got to put that thing somewhere safe. What if Fisk got a hold of it?"

"It's still there, on the desk. Father Andrez is coming. He'll help us figure out what to do."

Chapter 15

Ingram awoke to the sound of crying children.

He thought a wounded animal shared the room with him. The wailing pierced his ears and made his head throb. Wiping the sleep from his eyes, he realized the children were crying somewhere in the house.

He sat up and swung his legs off the bed, every bit of his body hurting. His bladder felt as if any moment it might burst. Very carefully, he put weight on his legs and found that they held, if not steadily. He moved to the bureau and searched the drawers. His shirt, pants, and underwear lay neatly laundered, folded, and mended, with tight stitches in the breast and sleeve. His jacket, shoes, and socks were missing. His keys, wallet, and a flattened package of Peter Stuyvesants sat on the bedside table.

Ingram's head pounded. The wailing of the children sounded like sirens in an air-raid. He padded out into the hall on bare feet, tucking in his shirt. The house was tremendous, opulent and foreign. To Ingram it looked like the dark mahogany insides of some

189

lost Southern dream, all scroll work, dark wood, rich paintings, and ornate carpets. Men in funny outfits stood in moody dark fields with oddly shaped dogs. Women and children posed in rigid clothes that looked elegant and uncomfortable.

Next to a painting of a chubby red-haired boy, Ingram noticed an open door and peered in. A bathroom. He shut the door and threw the latch. Cigarette dangling from his lip, he pissed for what seemed like an eternity. He shivered with the experience, and his back crackled. He flicked his butt into the toilet and flushed.

After washing his hands and examining his haggard appearance in the ornate mirror above the sink, Ingram left the bathroom and walked down the hall until he came to where the wall fell away on his left, leaving only a railing fifteen feet above a grand entryway, paneled and mirrored, possessing a massive oak door as the center piece. Stained-glass lilies and hydrangeas circled it, letting colored light permeate the room. A staircase circled down on the right, ending in a curlicue.

He walked down the staircase, his good hand firmly on the balustrade, holding himself steady. The sound of crying was fainter now, and he could hear the voices of women. He recognized Alice's deep, melodious voice. Turning to his left at the base of the stairs, he walked under the gallery he'd emerged from only moments earlier, through a large dining room, and entered a kitchen smelling of biscuits and bacon and coffee. His stomach rumbled as he ducked his head going through the doorway.

With his entry, the crying stopped and five pair of eyes widened.

"Uh... hi. Is there something wrong?"

Franny's lip began to quiver, and she turned to Sarah. "Mommy! The peafowl—something got to 'em! I think they ate 'em. Even ole Phemus."

"Baby, I'm sure they're all right. Maybe a weasel, or fox chased one, or got to a chicken or—"

Fisk turned toward her. "No! They're dead. Blood in the grass everywhere, feathers all over the yard. Serious." He put his hands on his waist and for a moment Ingram wanted to laugh; in the few hours he'd spent with her, Ingram had seen Alice do the exact same thing at least ten times. Lenora crossed her arms and looked at Sarah like it was her fault.

"He's right," Lenora said. "Something happened. We gotta go check on 'em, Miss Sarah."

Alice shook her head. "Whatever happened to 'em, we all need some breakfast. Sit down at the table and we'll eat."

Fisk started to protest but Alice cut him off, saying, "Whatever got to the fowl, they gonna get 'em again? Huh? If they been got, they been got. We gonna eat breakfast and then go investigate. You hear me, Fisk?"

The boy scowled at Alice, his shoulders setting in an obstinate pose. Alice ignored him, and began dishing up food. Though the children glared at her and Sarah sullenly, they took their plates and began to eat.

Ingram asked, "Where are my shoes?"

Alice shuffled over, coffee pot in hand. She refilled his mug.

"You only had one when we found you. You must've lost the other at the..." She looked at the children. "The fracas. I'll ask Reuben or Wilson if there's somebody on the farm with feet as big as yours. Though I doubt it."

As he ate, the children watched him keenly, eyes following his every move. After Ingram emptied his plate, he looked at it mournfully, and scraped up the last of the gravy with his fork. The children took the plates to the sink and moved to stand by the backdoor that led to the porch and yard.

"Momma, come on. We ate. Now *come on*," Lenora demanded.

Ingram stood uneasily with Sarah. She said, "It's okay, Bull. You don't have to come. Why don't you go back upstairs and get some rest?"

"I'll tag along, just to see." He lifted a bare foot. "They're tough."

Outside, the dew of the yard held silvered paths, tracks made by the feet of children, punctuated by the entrails of peafowl arranged in strange and bloody piles. Littered among the gory configurations were feathers decorating the grass in bloody streamers. Not the work of weasels, or any other predator Ingram had ever heard of. Except one. Man.

"What the hell is going on here?"

Sarah came to stand beside him, her face pale and blank. Franny stood with them, making wet, heart-broken sounds.

Ingram looked at the little girl in wonder. He squatted on his hams next to her, like a farmer inspecting a crop.

"Hey. Hey." He placed his hand on her shoulder, then tried patting. She turned to him, her eyes huge.

"It's okay, everything's gonna be just fine." He looked up at Sarah, and she had the same stricken expression as Franny.

Goddamn, this is a hard lesson. For her. For me.

Sarah cleared her throat. "I need to take her back inside the house. Away from this."

Fisk ran between piles of guts and feathers, pointing and exclaiming. Lenora stood beside Alice, arms crossed on her chest, her face furious.

"Hey, look!" Fisk called. "Ole Phemus is right here! Ain't much left of him."

"Fisk! Lenora!" Sarah called. "I'm going back inside with Franny. You two come with me." Alice looked at Sarah, nodding approval.

Fisk ignored her. "Looks like Ole Phemus finally met his match. They put his head right here with tail feathers all around it." The boy looked up, toward some of the farm's outlying houses. "I wonder if—"

He ran toward the chicken coop.

Ingram, trying not to step in the gore with bare feet, moved over to where Fisk had stood. A decapitated peacock head looked up at him with a milky eye. Tail feathers lay arrayed around the head as if in mockery of how the peacock had appeared in life.

A voice said, "Sweet Mary, Mother of Jesus."

Ingram turned to see a child dressed as a priest walking delicately through the carnage.

Sarah scooped up Franny in her arms and pressed the girl's head to her chest.

"Father Andrez," she said, rubbing Franny's back. "I'm glad you're here. It's… things have happened," she said. "Since we talked."

The priest surveyed the grounds. He shook his head.

"I see," he said slowly. "But what, exactly, has happened? This doesn't look good."

Ingram, watching his feet, walked over to where they stood. The priest looked up at him as he approached.

"This is Bull Ingram, Father," Sarah said. "He's wrapped up in…" She motioned at the world around her, the yard, the house, the sky. "All of this. We need to talk."

Franny raised her head from Sarah's shoulder. "Mommy! The birds. Why the birds?" She began to cry again.

Andrez looked around, frowning. He patted Franny's knee, and pursed his lips.

"This is a very good question." He walked forward a few paces, looking at the dead birds. He stood over the disembodied head of Phemus, then looked up.

At first Ingram though he was looking at the sun, the early morning light casting long shadows in the dewy grass. But then he realized the priest looked at the house. A window. As best he could tell, the window from his room.

"Where are the books?" The priest turned to face Sarah, holding his hands together in a pose like praying yet pointing downward. Very grave, for such a small man.

"Inside, locked in the library."

Fisk ran back, his feet making long silvery streaks in the grass.

"All the chickens are just fine. Eggs, hens, and the rooster too. All fine. Looks like what they wanted was peafowl. Maybe just ole Phemus here." He paused, wiping his hands on his britches. "Maybe the hens just got in the way." He looked at Andrez. "Who's he?"

Alice looked as though she wanted to slap the boy's head. She walked toward him, but he danced away.

"Fisk, go get Reuben, tell him to come to the Big House," Alice said. "I've got a chore for him."

The boy dashed away, between the out buildings and across the fallow stubble of corn to the field shop, where Reuben ran the daily workings of the farm.

Inside, Alice poured more coffee, then told the children to put on their bathing suits. "We're going to Old River Lake. It's still warm enough. Gonna let the big folk talk while we have a little fun." She pulled a loaf of soft, sliced white bread out of the pantry, untwisted its wrapping, and laid out twelve pairs of slices. From the ice-box, she took a pound rind of bologna, sliced yellow cheese, mustard, mayonnaise, peanut butter, and jelly and began to make sandwiches, wrapping them in waxed paper. "Sarah, will you take some breakfast up to your momma for me? And her sip this afternoon?"

"Of course." Sarah blushed. Ingram stared at her, and Andrez moved to the kitchen table. He sat down, a spill of light washing over his black suit and Roman collar, illuminating his hair. Ingram sat down next to the smaller man.

A knock came from the backdoor. Through the window, a bald man with a head like a speckled-egg stood in overalls, hand upraised, waving to the odd crowd in the Big House kitchen. Fisk moved around the man and opened the back door, an expression of amused exasperation dancing across his features. He looked at Ingram, cocked his thumb at the bald man, and rolled his eyes.

"Come on in, Reuben. I need you to rustle up some shoes." Alice pointed at Ingram. "For that man. You hear?"

Reuben bobbed his head in acknowledgement, up and down, his long wrinkled neck bunching and stretching. He stuck his hands in the pockets of his weathered overalls and examined Ingram.

"You got any paper? A big sheet?" Turning to Alice and Sarah, he held up his hands making a square with thumbs and index fingers. "Yay big?"

"Sure." Sarah walked out of the kitchen. She returned with large tabloid sheets of yellow parchment and a thick, knife-trimmed pencil.

Reuben went to Ingram, knelt before him, and put a piece of paper on the floor. He gently lifted Ingram's foot and placed it in the center of the paper, then traced around it.

He winked at Ingram. "This is just so we know bout how big your foot is. I'll get you something to wear, though it might not be pretty."

Ingram shrugged.

"Reuben, I'm taking the kids swimming. While we're gone, get one of your boys to clean up the mess in the yard," Alice said, and for a moment, Ingram thought she might add, "You hear?" But she didn't.

Reuben excused himself and left. The children tromped into the kitchen wearing bathing suits, excited at the prospect of swimming, the carnage in the yard forgotten. Alice finished packing sandwiches, pulled off a crock of potato salad, and placed it in the picnic basket along with a capped jar of lemonade.

"That's it. Let's go, kids. We'll be back this afternoon. And don't forget your momma."

Sarah went to the table and sat down with Ingram and Andrez. Once they heard the car pull away, Sarah said, "I think we need to tell Father Andrez everything, Bull. Everything you told us. He already knows most of my story, but I'll repeat mine too, just to be clear."

"Not 'Father,' Sarah. Just Andrez." He blinked, looking at her with steady eyes. "I wear that name for them, the congregation. But not for you. We know too much, you and I."

Sarah got up and refilled their cups from the pot of coffee on the stove, then sat down between them. The light spilled from the large window across her features, showing lines of care and worry. But her skin was bright, her eyes were clear, and Ingram found himself thinking how beautiful she was, especially in the morning light.

Ingram began, telling his story from the beginning as he did before for Alice and Sarah, slowly speaking, leaving nothing out.

Andrez's eyes remained focused on Ingram's broad features. When Ingram began speaking of the scene at Ruby's, he interrupted.

"You mean, you were present at that?"

"Yes."

"And you say that this Pale Man left on a river barge, the *Hellion*?"

"That's right."

"This is… troubling, to say the least. That there's a human agent mixed up in all of this." He remained silent for a bit, then waved his hand. "Continue please, Bull."

After he finished, both Sarah and Andrez sat silent for a long while, Andrez looking out the window, face to the streaming light.

"So that brings us to me," said Sarah. When she got to the point where Gregor had told her about his brother, Wilhelm, she paused and rubbed the bridge of her nose with her index and forefinger.

"I thought he was crazy. Really I did. But Gregor said I needed to know because I was the last of the Rheinharts, except for Wilhelm."

Ingram raised his eyebrows. Andrez just listened, unblinking, light on his face.

"I came home to take care of Momma and found myself drawn to the library. After a while, I began translating *Opusculus Noctis*. It's funny, but I thought I was just doing it for myself. Franny's growing up. Growing away from me, I guess, now being here with Fisk and Lenora and Alice—having family for the first time—I realized how much I've been living through her. How much I kept her from experiencing anything. I realized I needed to find something for myself, something just for me. I'd always enjoyed Latin in college, though I wasn't that good at it. So as best I could, I started translating *Opusculus*. I picked it because it was so small. Like a brochure."

She glanced from Andrez to Bull. "Finally, when I knew I needed help, I called Father Andrez—I'm sorry, Andrez. And he told me… he told me—"

Andrez reached over and patted her hands, smiling. "Maybe I should start, eh? This might be a good time for me to tell my tale."

She nodded, eyes going to Ingram.

The little man looked at them both, his hands in his lap. Then he began to speak.

∾

"I was born almost sixty years ago in Podgorica, Montenegro, in the shadow of the Black Mountain. My mother was a great lady, and men from all over came to court her despite her having two sons. Her beauty and wealth made her attractive to men, even when her charming wit and personality did not. She had bright eyes, I remember, and jet black hair with a streak of white on the left side.

"When I was around twelve or thirteen, she began acting strangely. She spoke in tongues and performed horrible acts with men, commoners and nobles alike. She was... how do you say... wanton. Blatant. Doing things in the open, doing things no son should see his mother do. But she was enraged as well. Angry with everyone, wild. Nero and I began to fear her. Fear for her. She was insane, maybe. Alienists from England came to try and help her at the behest of my Uncle Marko Knežević, a minor official at the court of Nicolas I. Nero, my brother, was quite taken with these men and their rationale for her behavior. He was always the neat one and loved order. He spent hours closeted with them, speaking of her condition, her possible chemical or mental imbalances that might cause her... wicked—it cannot be denied—behavior. But the morning we found a laborer dead in the courtyard, his pants around his ankles and his head wrenched around backward, Uncle Marko sent away the alienists and called a priest.

"The priest who attended my mother was accompanied by a man dressed in a modern suit, not the ornate clerical robes of the Orthodox Church but those of a Western Catholic priest, with Roman collar. I remember being struck by his demeanor and appearance. He had silver hair and shockingly blue eyes. He was clean shaven while his companion had a big, bushy beard. As the two men stood together, it occurred to me that our very own priest seemed little more than a... how do you say it... a witchdoctor. A shaman. And the other man, the Western priest seemed like a medical doctor. A man of science. Montenegro, at this time, was going through great changes, industrialization—the great god of industry had come to Montenegro. The old ways weren't as valued as before. And I was mad to go west to Italy, to England, to America.

"While Nero planted himself firmly at the knee of reason, a sycophant to the alienists, I became a follower of Father Guisseppi. I remained at his side. He became my mentor and... in some ways, my surrogate father."

Andrez swallowed and closed his eyes.

"My mother's health seriously declined. She broke her leg jumping from a second-story window. I was told she attempted suicide. But I believe she was trying to fly. Minutes before, she stormed through the house, ranting about ranks of angels swarming around her, stinging like the furies. She attacked me when I came into her room."

He traced a scar at the corner of his eye that Sarah hadn't noticed before. "She did this to me. Nothing horrible and quickly healed, but it's never really gone away.

"When it was decided my mother needed an exorcism, I knew what I was going to do with the rest of my life. I intended to join the church."

Andrez drew a deep breath and closed his eyes. His chest rose and fell.

"She died. Whatever possessed her, they couldn't expel it. The exorcism lasted four days, and by the end, her heart gave out. When she stopped breathing, her body began jerking and she vomited up a black bile that, despite all reason, pooled like oil and screamed obscenities at us. It took on the form of an infant... a horrible obsidian child, cursing and pulsing. When Father Guisseppi came toward it and spattered it with holy water, it laughed and hissed at us and changed its form into a long rat-like thing, fleeing out the balcony door and into the Podgorica streets. Gods save whoever it found next. Of course, Nero had been absent at the end, and when he returned, he struck me and cried and ripped his clothes. He blamed me for Mother's death.

"My uncle gave me permission to accompany Father Guisseppi

back to Rome. Nero cursed me as a superstitious fool and disappeared into the mountains with a sack of books and a rifle and whatever else he could carry. He turned feral. It wasn't until many years later that I saw him again, and by accident at that. He's become quite an unpleasant man.

"But I learned many things with Father Guisseppi. He was the curator of a special archive at the Vatican, a minor part of the Index Librorum Prohibitorum, the forbidden library, known as *Bibliotheca Occulta*. I touched on this with you, Sarah, when we spoke yesterday. The *Bibliotheca Occulta* is the most comprehensive collection of black magic and lore ever assembled by man. I became an initiate into the order of curators because of my experience. Because of my mother.

"After seminary, I returned to Rome and took up my duties there with Father Guisseppi, indexing, collating, and protecting the library. Protection was one of the main missions of my order. One of my co-initiates, a brother by the name Gord Fuseli, abandoned the order and fled with many of the most dangerous and, consequently, valuable books. Father Guisseppi and I were at a loss; we never suspected. But when we looked into his rooms, we discovered this man Gord was a slave to the poppy. An opium fiend. He'd been injured in the First World War—though we didn't think of it or call it that at the time—and apparently, he'd been keeping his addiction hidden ever since, even when he was in seminary and joining the order."

Andrez paused and reached forward, taking a cigarette and the box of matches from the center of the table. He tapped the cigarette on the back of his wrist, tamping down the loose tobacco, then crimped the edges and matched the end. He inhaled deeply.

"Not all evils are ancient," he said, smoke expelling from his mouth around the words. He held up the cigarette and looked at the burning tip. "Some evils are man-made. Such was the case with Gord. But evil calls to evil whatever the source, and the books he stole from the library made their way here. To this house."

Sarah placed her hand on the table, palm down, and stood.

"Yes. I read something about it," she said. "Wait a minute."

She left the kitchen and returned in a few moments with a stack of yellowed papers.

"These are letters from my Uncle Gregor to my father. He says," she ruffled the stack, searching. "Here he says, 'I've been contacted by a priest recently, who says he has some volumes of interest,' and he goes on to mention *Opusculus* and a volume named *Book Eibon.*"

"Yes, these are two of the books he stole from the *Bibliotheca Occulta*. And the only ones that weren't restored to the library."

"It looks as though Uncle Gregor acquired them when he was on a book-buying trip. And brought them back here."

"It does indeed."

Ingram remained silent. He didn't quite understand how these books could be dangerous, but he didn't understand how music could be dangerous either until he took this job.

Andrez nodded toward Ingram, his lips twitching with a small, remorseful smile. "Let me continue, for Bull's sake, so he can know everything. And there are things you should know as well.

"Father Guisseppi and I searched all of Italy looking for Gord. Despite his addictions, he was quite a resourceful man. He eluded us for many years, until we found him, not in Italy but living in Munich, married and quite reformed. His wife had broken him of his addiction to opiates and replaced it with another, food. The man had become quite fat. But we rejoiced to find him in good health and coherent. He told us what he could of the book buyers, but he didn't remember much and your Uncle Gregor had been circumspect in his payment and correspondence. When we learned of the advertisement placed in periodicals around Europe, we discovered they were purchased by a G. Rheinhart. Your uncle, Sarah.

"How much time and effort could have been saved if only your uncle had not possessed such a gift for languages? I cannot say. But Gord didn't realize he dealt with an American. He told us this Rheinhart—a common name—was German. So we searched in Germany for many, many years with no results. Then Austria. Then northern Italy. Hungary. Switzerland. Searching ever outward.

"Father Guisseppi grew ill and died. I was crushed. I spent nearly twenty years with this man, with the exception of my time in seminary. He was as close to family as I had ever known. After his death, I became lead curator of the *Bibliotheca Occulta*. It was then I discovered the Prodigium and the other gods. Before this, I had only thought of them as devils or demons. Father Guisseppi left me his writings, and through them, he outlined his years and years of study of the Prodigium. He kept this knowledge from me. I was shocked and not a little angry, at myself, at Guisseppi. Angry? Yes, Sarah, angry. Angry with Guisseppi because I blamed him for my mother's death. The knowledge of the Prodigium sapped his faith. How can someone have faith in a god with countless rivals? He kept this knowledge from me so that I might keep *my* faith. He had lost his long ago. But by his death, my knowledge expanded. My faith in *one* God failed.

"Bull, I can see that you don't understand. Let me explain."

Andrez cleared his throat, took a sip of coffee, and extinguished his cigarette.

"In the beginning, when the world was new and man had just emerged from the earth, there were gods—the Prodigium, which means vast and monstrous and unknowable. The Old Gods. These old intelligences moved between realms of thought, in and out of our world, between the stars and the deep blackness of night. They had countless names and countless aspects. They strode the earth, some giant, some tentacled, some with thousands of eyes, some with the shapes of all creatures fused into their flesh which was not flesh. They chose their own forms, which were as malleable as clay. Nyarlarhotep, Kronos, Cthulhu, Powaqqatsi and others. These gods enslaved man for worship or for food or even amusement. Torment and torture pleased them. A few cared for the creatures of the earth—Mithras, Cymbele, and others—and it was they who infused man with intelligence so that he might rise above all of the creatures of earth. But the other gods warred with them. Constantly, they fought, and did what they could to torment their creations.

"How? They spawned more entities—lesser gods yet still immensely powerful—to act as soldiers in this war. And the battleground of this war was mankind itself.

"The Old Ones learned to sever portions of themselves to create lesser gods. These gods—Zidus, Loki, Chernobog, Hastur, Akhkhazu, Pazuzu, and countless others—infested the earth. Some were wholly evil, reveling in the demise of man. Others were merely capricious. But being sloughed off of their masters, they gained independence. They cared less about the war raging in the heavens and on the earth, and just enjoyed their own corporeality. Some did not. Some longed to be rejoined with their makers, the Old Ones. In giving their offspring volition they gave up part of themselves. This act of... the Italian is *idago negate*... how do you say? Self negation. This act of self-negation has been the common thread of the second generation of gods.

"It is like the flow of water on terraces, or the levels of a fountain. At the top is the Prodigium, with Mithras and Cybele the sole benevolent forces. I use this term loosely, benevolent. They did not work toward the destruction of man. Their goals were indistinct and unknowable.

"Power flows from the Prodigium to the lesser gods. And from the second ranks, they inhabit man. They invest themselves in mankind. They possess us, entering our bodies. Like vermin infesting the house that is mankind. They influence our actions. They kill us for their sport. But they have their own goals and desires which can appear indecipherable to mortals, too."

Andrez stopped. He returned his hands to his lap and slumped his shoulders.

Ingram didn't know what to think. He felt confused and jagged as a shattered mirror. Thoughts and light passed through him, and he understood things vaguely. Just a little. Just a bit. It was all too fractured for comprehension.

Ingram shifted his weight in the chair. It creaked beneath him.

"You mentioned Hastur," said Ingram. "So lemme get this straight, just so I understand everything. These old gods—the Prodigium—went and had kids, and those kids are causing all kinds of trouble here for us. Is that right?"

Andrez nodded.

"So this Ramblin' John I've been looking for is really one of these—I don't know—teenager gods?"

"Not exactly, Bull. Just like the Prodigium before them, the second generation gods can spin off parts of themselves. They can infect man. They can possess us."

Ingram inclined his head toward the little man.

"And they can possess us how? Through music?"

"Yes. Through music, through touch. Some through words and thought. These books, *Opusculis*, *Book Eibon*, *Quanoon-e-Islam*—which is truly called the *Necronomicon*—these are all primers in communication with these gods, both the Prodigium and their offspring."

"So, can we kill them? Can we kill Hastur?"

Andrez looked at him strangely. "I don't know. The Prodigium? I doubt we can even begin to understand them. So killing them approaches the impossible. Can we kill these—I like your name for them, Bull—teenager gods? Maybe. We can definitely kill their agents and the people they infest. We can thwart their plans."

Ingram shifted again and raised his swaddled fist, resting it on the table. His chest, where he'd been stabbed, itched. He scratched it with his good hand.

"Jesus," he said. "I need a drink."

Andrez patted his wrapped hand. "Take heart. We are not powerless." He smiled, showing white even teeth. "And you have resisted them three times now, Bull."

"What?"

"When you encountered one on the gravel road that was most assuredly Hastur himself. And you resisted. At the radio station when you heard the music and fought the dead man. You resisted him again." Andrez tapped his wrapping with a finger. "And once again at Ruby's. You openly defied him. You killed his agent, Early Freeman, rest his soul. And you pursued the Pale Man. Then, something—*some power*—brought you here. You didn't float here by chance, that much is sure."

"I've got a question for you," Ingram said. "Why are you here? I mean, in Arkansas?"

"This is another good question, Bull. One I've been thinking about as we've been talking. At the time, it seemed like chance but now I'm beginning to doubt that. A nephew of a cardinal had fallen ill, and I was called to consult because the attending priest felt that his illness was infernal in nature. I thought it was godshatter."

At Sarah and Ingram's quizzical looks, the little man held up his hands. "Godshatter is the illness that falls on people who have been inhabited—enthralled—by the teenager gods. Often godshatter goes unnoticed because how can one diagnose the remains of a possession? Of course, the church doesn't refer to the illness as that. It was a piece of Guisseppi's personal jargon that I discovered in his papers, and it has stuck with me since.

"The young man had been institutionalized due to some violent behavior, but had been released because he had made a dramatic recovery. This alerted me to the possibility of possession. But then he fell ill. He was wracked by fever and violent palsy. Whatever god had infected him, it left the boy tainted with horrible dreams and waking visions of torment and torture. And desires. For flesh. So I brought him back to my chambers adjoining the *Bibliotheca Occulta*, so that I might study his illness further and, I hoped, restore the young man to health."

Ingram shivered. *Flesh? He's not talking about sex.*

"I intended to get the young man to join me in a very old rite. A rite of enthusiasm. Enthusiasm means, literally, 'full of a god.' *En theos*. I wanted to invite Mithras or Cybele or even one of the capricious lesser gods to inhabit him in hopes they would restore their vessel. This would take blood, and sacrifice. A finger, maybe. A tooth. Once it was done, and I had the boy deified, I planned to use an ancient rite of banishment and expel it from the boy's body.

"However, I made a mistake in judgment. I didn't suspect that the boy could still be possessed.

"I left him alone to retrieve the knife and chalice. Another mistake. When I returned, he was gone. I called for the Vatican City guards. We began searching. It was then I realized that my keys—the keys to the *Bibliotheca Occulta*—were missing. We went to the vault that held the volumes, and its door stood open like the gates of hell. The boy had set a fire. Once the inferno was extinguished, we entered the chamber that once had held every evil book known to man. All burnt. All destroyed. There was no way to tell whether he had removed any books, though I strongly suspect he did. I fear it was the *Daemonlateria*, our version of the *Quanoon*. In the original Arabic. I was assaulted by conflicting emotion: happiness at seeing so many evil books destroyed, and fear that we had been left defenseless against the Prodigium and their offspring. However silly it may sound, knowledge truly is power, and the boy—or the entity that possessed him—left us powerless.

"We found the boy's body in a neighborhood close to the Vatican. Dead and horribly burnt. It seems the entity that possessed him didn't care much for the longevity of his vessel. Which indicated to me that he had help. Either from other gods or people.

"And for all of this, I was to blame. I made the mistakes of judgment regarding the boy and consequently a priceless collection of books was destroyed. Not to mention the death of the Cardinal's nephew. The Cardinal spent the next year of his life punishing me. His final act of retribution was to send me to the most remote and god-forsaken places on the face of the earth. Tierra del Fuego. The Mexican slums. North Dakota. Ten years ago, he sent me here, to Arkansas. And here I've been. But it occurs to me now that I might have been sent here for a reason, just like you, Bull. That some other force drew me here. And that gives me hope."

"What I don't understand is why you didn't leave the priesthood? How can you know the truth and still take this exile?" Sarah stared at him.

He sighed. "For many years I asked myself the same question.

The Christian god is a myth, a bright wrapping on unexplainable events tied to other gods. But whatever the case, when I became a priest and learned Guiseppi's secret, my vocation became not to serve god, but to protect man. In some ways, I became a policeman, I think, burdened with too much knowledge of dark and terrifying things.

"I've always hoped to resume my duties at the *Bibliotheca Occulta*. I still serve the new curator in many small ways. Translations. Experience. It is sad, yes. But the cloth is all I've known. And I cannot bring myself to believe that the church is all bad. The people need hope and something to distract them from the wolves walking among them in sheep's clothing."

Sarah stared at him, this small, pitiable man. She put her hand on his.

"Is it shameful for me to say I still hope that there is a Christian god? That Jesus was not some godshattered young man? That despite everything, I still hope there might be some purely benevolent force in the world?"

She shook her head. "Of course it isn't, Andrez. Of course not. And your hope brought you here. To us."

Something occurred to her then. "In the yard, you looked up at my room. Why?"

"The piles of dead birds. They were arranged in a pattern. A pattern, it seemed, only apparent from a height. From a window, say, on the second floor of this house."

Sarah's eyes went wide. She bolted out of the door and raced through the dining room. Ingram followed fast on her heels, bare feet slapping on the floor, with Andrez trailing behind.

Up the stairs and across the gallery, Sarah ran for her mother's room. Her hands scrabbled at the doorknob, and she erupted through the door, hair flying.

"Momma! Are you okay? Momma?" Sarah was nearly hysterical.

The bed was empty. Dizzy from the burst of adrenaline, Ingram placed his hand on the doorjamb to steady himself.

"Goddamn it, Sarah." A voice came from the dark corner of the room. "What the hell do you think you're doing, coming in here like that?"

The stooped figure of a woman sat near the window on a padded bench. Her face seemed strange, dark, her white hair was wild around her face. She peered at Ingram, drawing her robes around her body.

"Who the hell is that? Who is that in my house?"

"My name's Ingram, ma'am. Your daughter—"

"I don't give a damn what your name is, sir. Get out. Now. Vacate these premises."

"Momma, this is the man who—"

"I know who that idiot is, girl. He's the stray dog you brought home."

Sarah moved further into the room. She stood by her mother, near the window. Sarah glanced out and then looked again.

"No."

"What? What did you say, Sarah?"

"I said no. He's not leaving. I don't care what you say or do. He's going stay here until we figure out what's going on. Your peafowl are all dead. Didn't you know?"

"Jesus Christ, Sarah," the old woman said, voice hoarse and sharp. "A priest, too? You planning my funeral? Well, I'm not dying today. No, madam, not today. So you can send the runt away, too."

Ingram realized Andrez stood by him. He turned back to the room. From the light of the lamp, he could see the older woman's face more clearly. A red and brown mask covered her cheeks and jaw-line. Her back was crooked, and her joints oversized. She held her body in an uncomfortable pose, hunched over like a crone.

"Momma, he's staying. And that's that," Sarah said. She turned to the door. "Bull, will you go downstairs and get the bottle of port from the library? It's on a silver tray on my desk. Just go down the stairs when you're about to enter the kitchen, take a right, and follow the long hallway. It'll end at the library. Can you do this for me, please?"

He nodded, looking from her to her mother.

"His name is Bull? I can see that," said Sarah's mother. "What's the other's name? Weasel?"

"Momma," Sarah said slowly, "you used to have manners. What happened to them? Did they get sick as well? You've always been a—"

"What? A bitch?" The old woman cackled. "It's what you're thinking."

Ingram turned. "I'll come too," said Andrez.

They found the library easily. Andrez *tsked* at the stacks of books littering the floor, but followed Ingram to the desk. There they stopped and looked.

Two books and a sword lay there, waiting for them. Andrez reached forward and touched the cover of the larger book. He picked it up and opened it. He caught his breath.

Ingram peered at the book over Andrez's shoulder. An illustration glared back at him. A grotesquely fat man sat naked in the middle of a floor marked with designs, a knife in his hand. Blood pooled around him, from the wound at his crotch. He'd severed his own testicles. In the next panel, the man crouched over a bowl and defecated into it, blood spilling onto the feces from the wound in his groin. In the last panel, the man, with a look that could be pain or joy, sculpted a creature from the shit, pushing his severed testicle inside his creation, into its chest.

Realizing Ingram looked over his shoulder, Andrez closed the book. "The *Necronomicon*. An evil work."

"What the hell was that guy doing?"

"Golem. Making a golem from his own waste and giving it power through blood."

Andrez gave Ingram a sick smile. "All power comes from sacrifice. So, in some sense we are gods too. We can create things as well. If you're willing to sacrifice, you can create. This set of illustrations shows a very foul way to sacrifice. That is all that magic is. The willingness to sacrifice, to negate yourself."

"Damn," Ingram said, resting his hand on the smaller man's shoulder. "I think I understand now what Sarah meant when she said she nearly lost her mind."

"Damned, indeed," Andrez said. "And look. The sword. Wilhelm's sword."

Ingram reached forward and took it in his uninjured hand. When he raised it high, he felt as if invisible gears locked into place. It felt good in his hand. Perfect.

Chapter 16

Sarah's mother glared at her.

"You sleeping with him?" Her black eyes shone bright, inquisitive, like polished buttons. Her tone of voice made the question light, as if she inquired about the mail, or whether Sarah had remembered to get milk at the store.

"Of course not, Momma," she said. "He's been hurt, that's all. He woke up last night."

"He's a big one, isn't he? I'll bet he'd fill you up." She chuckled. "Bull, you say? He looks it. A hoss."

Sarah gasped, a hand coming to her mouth. She felt the blood rushing to her cheeks, her neck.

"Oh, girl," her mother chuckled, a dry, rasping sound. "You can lie to me, but don't lie to yourself. If you haven't thought about it you're either dumber than ditchwater or so well practiced at self-deceit you don't even know you're doing it."

Ingram coughed nervously from the door. The old woman looked at the man, grinning.

"How big are you, Bull?" She glanced at Sarah. "Sarah here wants to know. Are you a big old hoss?"

He entered the room, padding softly on his bare feet, and placed the port on the bedside table, scowling. He looked like someone held a gun on him, shoulders high and tense. He shut the door behind him as he left.

"Don't think he likes me too much, girl." She pointed at the port. "I want my sip. Pour it for me."

Sarah brought the tray to her mother's vanity and poured a glass. The old woman slammed it back, rocking her head like a sailor on leave. She swallowed loudly, smacked her lips, and held out the small glass for another. Sarah filled it again.

Sarah looked down at the yard. Two workers, coming from the direction of the field shop, walked through the cornfield with a large drum between them. Handles of rakes and shovels poked out of the barrel. She looked back at the yard.

What would do something like that? Was slaughtering not good enough? Why make a bloody arrangement of everything?

The sign in the grass stopped the breath in her chest.

In the center of the arrangement glared the severed head of Ole Phemus, that cantankerous peacock. Up and away from the center lay a curl of wings and the torso of another bird—denuded of feathers and flayed of skin so that it glistened red and white in the morning sun—looking for all the world like a question mark. Two other lines of flesh and feathers ran away from Phemus' head; one curled around like a tentacle and the other shot straight away, ending in a flourish of tail-feathers. It was indecipherable and full of meaning all at once. She clenched her fists.

"Another, girl."

Sarah turned away from the window, back to her mother. Elizabeth held out the filigreed cup and shook it in Sarah's face. Before she realized what she was doing, Sarah slapped the cup from her mother's hand, sending it flying across the room to shatter on the crown-molding.

"Pour your own," she said, grinding her teeth. She squatted

down on her haunches so that her face was even with her mother's.

"I don't know what's happened with you, Momma, but you look fairly spry to me. I don't see why you can't start taking care of yourself."

Elizabeth Rheinhart's nostrils flared. Her eyes widened. Then she smiled.

She chuckled again, sounding like sandpaper blocks rubbing together.

"Goddamn it. I knew it. I knew you weren't just Ware's girl." She reached out a liver-spotted hand and jabbed a yellow fingernail into the flesh of Sarah's breast. Deep. Sarah yelped with pain and jerked away from the old woman.

"I've waited years for you to show a little backbone. I knew there had to be a bit of me in there, little girl. Not just the weak-willed thing you've shown yourself to be ever since you left with Jim." She laughed from deep in her throat. "Jim. You picked a winner there, didn't you. Eh?"

Again, Sarah's hand lashed out, striking her mother on the cheek. She remembered her mother doing the same thing to Uncle Gregor.

Elizabeth stood, uncoiling herself from the vanity bench. She drew her robes around her as she rose, straightening her back.

Spry is an understatement, Sarah thought. *I haven't seen her move like that since I was a girl.*

"I'll tolerate quite a bit from you, child, but not that," her mother said, each word clear. "Go. You're not fit for conversation. Have Alice bring me my dinner. When you've calmed down, we'll talk."

Once in the hall, door firmly closed behind her, Sarah began to shake uncontrollably. Her breath came in gasps and—even though she tried to press them back—tears sprang in her eyes. Her hands shook as if palsied. She leaned heavily on the wall.

"Sarah?" His soft, deep voice. She felt his hand touch her on the shoulder, warm and powerful. She didn't want him to see her tears and think her weak, but his hand turned her inexorably toward him, like the movement of the earth. She gave in, something inside her relinquishing, and she hugged his chest, pushing into the circle of his arms. Like a circle round the sun, bright and warm and massive, blotting out everything else.

"You OK?"

She held him for a long time, trying to bury herself in his body, pressing her face into his chest and breathing, taking in his scent. He smelled like horses, cigarettes, and bourbon. Arms around him, she could feel just the edges of the wide, muscular expanse of his back. And she thought about what her mother had said. Yes... he could fill her to brimming. God, now she wanted that more than anything, this giant of a man pushing himself into her.

"Sarah?"

Andrez's voice.

She released Ingram. Andrez watched from the doorway of Ingram's bedroom, a worried expression on his face. Ingram reached forward, taking her hand.

"It's gonna be okay. Right? She's got her juice. She'll simmer down."

She turned from the men, pulling her hand away, and walked back across the gallery and downstairs. She could hear them following. She didn't know where she was heading until she found herself in the library.

She sat at the desk. Opening the drawer, she looked inside, then slammed it.

"Do either of you have—"

Andrez stepped forward and handed her a cigarette, cupping his hand around the tip. He lit it from a wooden match.

Ingram removed a crystal tumbler from the disarray of glasses, the remains of Sarah's search for the sword. She looked at the desk. The *Quanoon* and *Opusculis* glared at her.

The whiskey Ingram handed her burned its way down her throat, into her stomach. She chased it with a hard drag on the cigarette.

Andrez stood in front of the desk, looking down at her. "I am, quite frankly, frightened of your mother. She's quite... how do you say... fierce. Formidable."

"She's a goddamned bitch," Sarah said, the words popping out of her mouth of their own volition. "She always has been. She'll tolerate you, let you go along with your life, until what you want and what she wants don't...jibe." She took another swallow from her glass. "Then she'll rip you apart like a damned—"

"A wolf?" Andrez inquired, looking at her strangely.

"The disease makes her face look like that. It's a minor symptom of the lupus."

Andrez shook his head sadly. "Maybe she got this disease because she resembles a wolf on the inside. Eh?"

Sarah shook her head. "No. It's just a disease. And wolves aren't as vicious as she is, anyway."

The little man smiled, then looked to the door. Reuben stood there, in his overalls, holding two large boots.

"Sorry to bust in on you like this, Miss Sarah, but nobody answered the door. I got some shoes here for Mr...."

"Ingram," the big man said. "Why're they all dirty?"

"Big Jim was a farmer, Mr. Bull. Spent his days knee deep in mud, may he rest in peace."

"A dead man's boots."

"That's right, Mr. Ingram."

Ingram laughed and took them, and Reuben nodded at Sarah as he left.

They were quiet for a moment as Ingram sat down on the window banquet and rolled up the cuffs of his pants.

"I saw something strange from Mama's window." Sarah opened the desk drawer again and withdrew a piece of paper and the nub of a well-chewed pencil. She scratched on the paper for a moment and then turned the paper around so that Ingram and Andrez might see.

"Andrez," she asked, placing one finger on the paper. "Do you recognize this?"

He nodded. "It's Hastur's sign. The yellow sign, but in this case, not yellow but bloody. The question is why? The sign usually appears at a place where there's a covenant in effect. Or, more likely, a territorial marker to let any other entities know that he has possession of this place or person. But I don't understand how it could be either in this case."

Andrez looked at the *Quanoon* and *Opusculus* on the desk. "Unless..." The little man's hand went to his chin, as if he had a beard there to stroke. He sat like that for a long time, then shook his head.

"I don't know, but we must be on our guard. It's no small matter when gods—even this one that Bull has faced down—start meddling in the affairs of men."

There was nothing Ingram could say to that. He refreshed their drinks, pouring the whiskey with a large, unsteady hand. He took Sarah's glass, and she turned her head from staring at the *Quanoon* to smile at him. He set the bottle back down.

"Don't scratch, Bull. You're gonna make them worse."

"What?" He looked down, realizing that his good hand fretted at the wound on his chest. "Oh." He dropped his arm and took up a tumbler.

He raised it up to the light coming from the window. "Well, here's to weird shit and dead birds."

Andrez *tsked*. "No, Bull, don't toast to the bad." He took up his own glass. "Here's to the strength of new friends."

They raised their glasses, and drank.

Chapter 17

I n the late afternoon, when the yellow light slanted into the library, the children returned from swimming at Old River Lake with far less noise than their departure.

Franny went to her mother, her bare feet making soft slaps on the hardwood. She leaned into Sarah's chest and looked at Ingram. The exhaustion showed on her face, her body. Sunburnt across the nose, she held her index and middle fingers in her mouth and sucked at them busily, an old habit Sarah thought she'd broken her of.

Franny popped her fingers out of her mouth and asked, "Is he staying here, Mommy?"

She smiled and said, "Yes, baby. For a little while."

"Good," the girl said.

From the door, Alice said, "Sarah, I'm gonna take Lenora and Fisk on to the kitchen, get 'em some dinner. Send lil Fran in when she's ready."

Franny turned to Ingram.

"How tall are you?"

"Tall."

"How tall is that?"

He held a hand flat on top of his head.

"This tall."

"That's not what I meant."

"I don't know really. Pretty tall. I gotta duck going into most rooms."

"I wanna be that tall when I grow up."

He thought about what she said. Sarah and Andrez watched him. The awkwardness he showed around others disappeared as he spoke with the girl.

"Why would you want to be as tall as me? People look at me funny. People make fun of me for being so big. They call me animal names. It's not that swell, believe me."

"If I was that tall, what do you think they'd call me?"

Ingram rubbed his chin, looking at the ceiling. "Beanpole, maybe. Giraffe."

She laughed, her body hitching. "Stilts," she said.

"I like giraffe. You ever see one?"

"No."

"They're from Africa, and they eat the leaves from the top of trees. They're beautiful. If you grew as tall as me, you'd have to be part giraffe."

Franny pushed away from her mother and approached Ingram. He kneeled.

She reached out and touched his chest above his heart, where the bandages were visible under his shirt.

"Does it hurt?"

"Franny, don't ask such personal questions," Sarah said.

Ingram glanced at Sarah, frowning. He turned back to Franny.

"It hurt when it happened, but it just itches now."

"Were they really mad?"

"Who?"

"The people who hurt you."

"Yeah. I guess they were. But don't ask me why."

"Why not?"

"Because I don't know why they were mad. Maybe they just stay that way, mad at everybody. All the time."

Franny frowned. "I wouldn't want to be them."

"Me neither."

"I'm glad you're staying with us, Bull."

"Me too, Franny. Me too."

She patted his good hand, like a parent patting a child's. He seemed surprised by the gesture. He grinned.

"I'm hungry. Are you hungry, Franny? Why don't we go get some dinner with Alice?"

"And Fisk and Lenora. I'll bet you were really hungry once you woke up. You slept for a really long while."

"Yeah. I had funny dreams."

Franny took Ingram's hand, pulling him away from the library into the hall.

"I have funny dreams too. Crazy dreams. Really. About dogs that live in the attic. Some are nice *and* funny. Some are mean."

After they left, Andrez chuckled and said, "That's an odd couple."

"She wants a father. She hasn't said anything about her own since we came back to the Big House, but she wants a dad." Sarah drained the last of her drink then stood, smoothing the front of her dress. "Bull just had more of a conversation with her than Jim ever did." She looked down at her wedding band. "I don't need a lecture."

"I'm not going to give you one. But you like him, don't you?"

Sarah looked at the priest, unflinching.

"He's quite possibly the loneliest person I've ever met. But I do like him. It's strange, but even before he awoke I felt... I don't know. Confused. I felt like I knew him. I was afraid of him. But drawn to him too."

He nodded. "Does that scare you?"

"It makes me wonder if I'm crazy. Everything is happening all at

once, and I don't understand anything. The world, my... reality...
is shattered. I'm terrified and excited all at once."

"Sarah, your reality hasn't changed. Your perception of it has,
and that is what's important."

She bowed her head, thinking. "Let's go get some dinner. It's
getting dark soon and, quite frankly, I'm not inclined to drive you
back to Stuttgart. So we need to figure out where you're gonna
bunk down."

"I don't sleep much. Maybe two hours a night. I never managed
to sleep well after... after what happened to my mother. I can just
remain here, in the library, if that's all right. I'd like some time to
study the *Quanoon* and look into the *Opusculus* a little more." He
waved his hand toward the stacks of books littering the floor. "I'd
like to do a little indexing as well. Your father and uncle amassed a
pretty unique collection here. If you don't mind?"

As she left him, she heard him open the *Quanoon*, gasp, and
then turn the page.

Chapter 18

C ap Hap stood on the deck of the cruiser bound for Tulagi in the dress armor of a Roman centurion. His breastplate shone silver in the Pacific sun, embossed with a scene of a bull surrounded by priests in togas. A scorpion stings the bull's testicles. A snake and a dog drink from a wound at its throat.

Hap stood with his hip cocked, one hand on his sword, grinning at Ingram.

Ingram saluted and Haptic returned it, bringing his hand sharply to the helmet with red horse-hair plume.

"At ease, marine."

Ingram relaxed, spreading his feet and keeping his hands at the small of his back.

The captain walked around him, inspecting him.

"Goddamn, son, looks like you been through the fucking grinder."

Ingram nodded.

"Hastur. Pissant son of a bitch. He's the sorriest whore's son ever to walk this earth."

Haptic sat on the canon's base, unsnapped the leather strap to his helmet, and pulled the helmet from his head. He set it down beside him, the bright red bristles of the plume jutting skyward, and rested his hands on his knees.

"You know why you're here?"

Ingram shook his head. He realized they weren't on the ship's deck but deep in the Tulagi jungle. Water dripped around them, making *plat-plat* sounds on the oily leaves. Cap Hap sat on a log now.

"Sit, Bull. Sit down, son. I said, at *ease*."

He sat on the log.

"There's some fucked up shit going on out there." Cap Hap waved at the brush and undergrowth surrounding them. "It's about to get even uglier, and I need you to do something for me."

Ingram tried to speak, but his voice wavered, like he'd been smoking all night and just woke up to find his throat raw.

"What?"

"I need you to open yourself up to me."

"I don't know what that means."

"It means you'll let me inhabit you when the time comes. Hastur must be checked. Must be stopped. He's working to bring the Old Ones through."

"Old Ones?"

"Goddamnit, son, haven't you been fucking paying attention to what's been going on around you?"

Cap Hap stood and paced in front of the log. It began to rain. More soft *plats*. Off in the green dark of Tulagi, gunfire sounded, accompanied by the faint screams of dying men.

"The woman summed it all up when she called them the Prodigium. The Titans. The fucking *Old Ones*." He stopped in front of Ingram and put his hands on his hips. "The Old Ones. They want to eat this world. Devour it. You. Her. The girl. The priest. But not just that. People can die and be remembered, you can keep the ones you love alive in your heart and memory. These fuckers devour love and light. And the memories of love and light. Replace it all with worship and sacrifice to the dark. You won't remember your mother, your fellow soldiers, your best friend. They'll be dead, and it'll be as though you never knew them. Do you want that to happen?"

"Who are you? You're not Cap Hap. He died." Ingram looked around at the jungle. "He didn't even make it this far. At Guadalcanal."

"Bull, I've been with you ever since you went to war. You know me of old, son."

"That's not telling me anything."

"You are the stubborn one, aint'cha?"

Cap Hap patted his breast plate as if it had a pocket, looking for cigarettes. He grinned a bit sheepishly, then dug in the gap at the top of his left greave and pulled out a pack of Pall Mall's. A book of matches was stuffed inside the cellophane.

He shook out a cigarette and offered it to Ingram.

They smoked in the jungle, the wet foliage pressing in close, water dripping from the dark canopy of trees overhead, the sounds of far-off battle filtering through the thick brush.

"Does it really matter who I am? I've been working with men like you for the last three thousand years. I'm for the soldier defending his homeland. I'm for the family. I'm for the child. That's all. Pretty fucking simple, even for a jarhead to understand."

"What'll I get out of it?"

"Five bucks and a hand job."

Ingram stood, dusted off his slacks, wiped moss from his ass.

"You'll be rewarded. I don't even know why I'm having this conversation with you, Bull. When the shit starts hitting the fan, you're gonna have to act, and you'll need my help. Don't look at me like that, marine. I've buried men better than you. Not many fucking stupider, though."

He took a deep drag off his cigarette and then flicked it away.

"When you need me—and you will need me—just say Mithras. In answer to your earlier question, that's my name. I'll come and— I'm not gonna make any bones about it—possess you. Take over. You'll go away for a while, you might be able to see and feel depending how strong willed you are, but I'll be driving and you'll be in the backseat. But I'll take care of what has to be done."

He exhaled a large cloud of smoke, bluish white, swirling, then stepped away from Ingram and the log. The *gahn-gahn-gahn* of .50 cals cut through the jungle foliage, cut through the air, and when Mithras died, it was almost beautiful, the body arcing, the pop pop pop of gigantic bullets perforating the silver breastplate, a red mist rising up, borne on smoke and bullets, into the air and into the trees, into the green.

Chapter 19

He woke in the guest room, sheets pooled in a sweaty mass around his waist. With his good hand, he rubbed his face, his eyes, trying to clear his head of the dream of Mithras. Sarah stood at the foot of the bed, watching him.

She was in the room and he had no idea she'd been there, watching him sleep. She came around the side of the bed and placed a hand on his chest, on his heart, where Franny had touched him earlier.

Slowly, she slipped out of her nightgown and dropped it to the floor, her skin prickling in the cool night air.

Ingram's eyes widened. He brought his good hand to her waist, resting it on the curve of her hip where she might carry a baby. Her skin felt warm to the touch.

He felt himself rise. Not speaking, she looked at him with lidded eyes. Her hand moved down his chest, pulled back the sheets at his waist, and found him.

Hissing, he drew her tight and twisted sideways, kissing her rib cage. She turned, one hand still on his erection, putting a breast in his face. He sucked, taking the nipple in his mouth and teasing, rolling it around. Now it was her turn to hiss, drawing air through clenched teeth.

She put a knee on the mattress and rose up, swinging herself on to the bed, keeping her hand on him. Leaning over Ingram, hair falling forward and wreathing her face, breasts swinging, Sarah kissed him. Their lips met, and she sensed his confusion even as his cock pressed hard into her stomach.

"We shouldn't be doing this," he breathed. He kissed her again and pressed her close to his body.

She kept her arm between them, gripping him tightly and working her hand up and down.

"Ssssh." Her shushing sounded loud in the room. "We need to be doing this. I don't think either of us has needed anything as much as this. Ever."

She kissed him again and they twined their tongues, losing themselves in the wet sensations of each other's body. She pulled away, rose up, positioning herself over him, placed his head right at her center, and sank down. She rose and sank. And again.

"Damn," she said. "You're—"

Words failed her. He strove underneath, pushing upward into her, pushing in, coming to grips with her body, the heavy sway of her breasts, the slimness of her waist, the thickness of her ass, her thighs. His eyes like saucers, he took her in, the softness of her face, the blurriness around the edges. The wariness that inhabited her since they met was gone, and she gave over the part of herself she'd reserved. He cupped a breast in his hand, and she brought it to his mouth again, riding him, breath coming in little gasps, faster now. She made a sound in the back of her throat. With every slap of their bodies coming together, she made a chuffing sound, in time with the movement of his pelvis and legs against hers.

She lay on his chest flattening her breasts—he felt the hard nubs of her nipples against his sternum—then he rolled her over onto her back, taking charge, establishing his own rhythms. His wounded hand was forgotten. The slapping sounds grew louder as he increased the tempo. She closed her eyes, giving herself over to sensation, head back, still breathing heavy, the cords of her neck standing out as he moved above her.

She spread her legs wide, as wide as she could, grabbing her ankles.

"Deep," she said. She opened her eyes and leaned up, taking his nipple in her mouth and biting. He hissed again. "Go deep, Bull."

He withdrew from her completely, took himself in hand, and ran his length up and down her seam. She squirmed and opened her eyes to see what he was doing to her, looking down her body at where they almost fused. Almost.

"Deep, Bull."

At the end, she bit her lip to stop herself from screaming.

They smoked, afterward.

He said, voice rumbling in the low light, "Are you gonna regret this?"

She turned, resting her head on her arm, looking at him.

"No," she said. "Why should I?"

"Your husband. Franny."

"My husband is gone. He might as well have died in Bastogne, or Normandy, except for Franny. He lasted a few years at home, and now he's drinking and working himself to death in a slow suicide. Even having a child wasn't able to bring him out of his... self-absorbed—" She waved her cigarette hand, painting with the smoke. "Whatever you call it. He's withdrawing inward and nothing, no one, can get through his wall." She took a deep drag and turned to ash her cigarette in the tray on the bedside table. "I'm filing for divorce."

He nodded.

"Not for you, Bull. I hardly know you."

"Wouldn't have dreamt it."

She laughed and he did too and the bed shook again. He put a hand on her hip. She watched his face.

"I didn't realize how much I needed... contact. Human closeness, maybe. Until I met you. I feel like I've known you all my life. Like we are supposed to be together. Does this make any sense to you?"

"When we found you in the boat, I... I knew. I knew you were here for a reason. And since I was the only one to know it—except maybe Franny, I think she may have sensed something too—"

"You scare me a little, too."

She snorted. "What? I scare *you*?"

"The feelings I'm having. Like they're beyond my control. And with everything that's happening..." He took her cigarette from her hand and took a long drag. He handed it back. "Sarah, I've seen the dead *rise*. And every time I try and think about it, well... I'm getting distracted."

"I've had the same feeling. You woke up and my mind's been occupied solely with you. You and your body. I haven't had a chance to think about everything I've learned."

She shook her head, a frown crossing her brow.

He rubbed the bridge of his eyes. "I had a dream before—"

"We got distracted?"

He ran his hand across her flank, watching the goose bumps break out across her flesh. "It was a dream of my old captain, Cap Haptic. He died in the war." He frowned and looked away. "It was strange. He was dressed as a Roman soldier, a gladiator or something. The dream was clear, not like a dream at all, but like I had seen him only yesterday and just remembered. I can remember the conversation we had perfectly."

"What did he say?"

"He said Hastur has to be checked. To be stopped. And that he wants to possess me. Him, not Hastur. To 'inhabit' me. That when the shit hits the fan, if I call on him, he'll help me do what needs to be done."

"Call on him? Did he say how?"

"He said just for me to say his name."

He opened his mouth and then grinned sheepishly.

"You don't want to say it?"

"No. Not really."

"OK. Spell it."

He pushed her back on the bed and traced a letter on her stomach.

"A double-u?"

"No."

"An em?"

After a while she knew the name and he was hard again. He grazed her nipples with his fingers. Leaning forward, he took her breast in his mouth, and her hand sought him out.

Later, Ingram fell asleep and she slipped from the room, padding down the hall. She stopped at her mother's door, listening. Nothing. Back in her room, she realized Franny was gone again. *Snuck off to Fisk and Lenora's bed.*

She ached as she climbed into bed. Her legs felt rubbery, and her thighs and buttocks burned with the exertion. Pulling up the covers, she sighed and went to sleep and did not dream.

Chapter 20

I t began raining in the morning, the patter of drops on the roof stirring Ingram slowly. He stretched, reached for Sarah in the bed, remembering the previous night. He felt good—amazingly good. Humming, he peeled the bandage off of his chest and threw it in the trash can. Gingerly, he set his great bulk on the settee and unwrapped his injured hand. A whiff of spoiled meat hit him, and he realized he smelled himself, the unaired flesh of his ruined hand. He dressed again in his dirty clothes—no help for it—and went across the hall to the bathroom, washing what he could of his hand and forearm. Purple and yellow streaks went down his forearm to his pinky and that side of his hand was swollen to twice its regular size. His fingers looked like sausages. When he flexed his hand, he felt bones grind inside, but it seemed like he still had mobility. The swelling impeded his hand's flexibility more than the actual break.

He went back to his room and replaced the brace and rewrapped his hand. He slipped on the dead man's boots and thought of Cap

Hap, dressed as a Roman soldier. Mithras, he'd told him.

All I have to do is say his name.

In the kitchen, the percolator burbled and Alice pulled a tray of toast out of the oven.

"Hey, Bull," she said, looking him up and down. For an instant, Ingram worried that she'd heard his and Sarah's frantic lovemaking the night before. He considered being embarrassed, then shrugged. Fisk and Lenora burst into the kitchen, arguing.

"No we ain't, fool. Tell him, Momma! We ain't gonna get any more peafowl."

"Don't call me fool, fool. I know just as much as you. And if Franny asks Missus Rheinhart, you know she'll get some more."

Alice looked at the children, and placed her hand on her hip. They stilled and looked at her.

"Franny ain't in charge. You know I don't like that fighting this early in the morning. Go sit down."

Sarah came padding in, tying her robe. She looked at Ingram and then quickly to Alice.

"Where's Franny?" She moved over to the counter, pouring herself a mug of coffee and chasing it with two spoonfuls of sugar. "She sleeping late?"

Alice, plucking bacon from the cast-iron skillet's popping grease, looked at Sarah curiously and said, "I don't know. She didn't sleep with Lenora and Fisk last night. I thought she slept with you."

The mug shattered, sending streaks of scalding hot coffee shooting across the kitchen floor.

"What? Where is she?" Sarah turned and ran through the house. Ingram ran after her.

"Franny! *Franny!* Answer me, baby!" Her voice pitched into registers of panic. "*Franny!* Godammit, answer me!"

She stopped in the atrium, hair wild, and turned in a circle.

"Sarah, wait a second—"

"Momma's room. She's with Momma." She turned to the stairs and vaulted up, taking two steps at a time, her robe fluttering behind.

Ingram kept close on her heels. She burst into her mother's room.

"Franny!" She flipped on a light then went to the window and pulled back the curtain, filling the room with a thin gray light. Empty.

"Your mother's gone. Maybe they're out walking."

An irritated look passed over Sarah's face, and she began biting her fingernails.

"No. No. Franny's terrified of Momma. She'd never go with her." She turned, not looking at Ingram. "Where is she?"

She turned and raced out the door and back down the stairs, yelling, "Alice! Alice! Get Reuben! Franny's gone, and Momma is too. Get Reuben to start looking!"

Alice came to the atrium with Fisk and Lenora behind her. The two children looked scared.

Father Andrez appeared behind them, peering over reading glasses. He looked rumpled and tired.

"What's this? Your daughter is missing?"

Sarah brushed past Alice, the children, the priest, heading toward the back of the house.

"Franny! *Franny!* Answer me right now!"

She bolted through the kitchen door, slamming it behind her.

Ingram followed. Andrez grabbed his shirt as he passed.

"Bull, stop. Sarah's mother is gone too? Is that right?"

He nodded, chewing his lip.

"You have to get Sarah calmed down. We don't have much time. We have to find Franny quickly because—" He rubbed his face. Exhaustion marked his features. "I think you know. Get Sarah and bring her to the library."

Ingram nodded and went after Sarah. Outside, he ran to the field shop, where Reuben and his field hands sat on barrels, eating cornbread and drinking buttermilk. They looked startled to see Ingram.

"Franny. She's missing. Get up and start searching the farm. I gotta find Sarah, she's running around like a—"

"Yessir. Right now, boys. You heard the man."

"One of you get a car and drive the highway. Put one man on the roof if you have to so you can look down into the ditch."

Reuben gave a sharp nod, then bellowed orders.

Ingram turned and ran back to the house. He went around the side and looked in the old peafowl roost. From the corner of his eye, he saw a flutter of white against the gray gloom of the morning. Sarah. He turned and ran.

He caught her as she entered the dark woods, on the way to the river.

"Sarah! Stop."

She whirled, her hair limp with rain. Her robe was open, her nightgown plastered to her body.

"I can't! Franny might be in the river!"

"No, Sarah. She isn't. Come back."

"I have to find her, Bull. I..." Her face looked drawn and pale. Her hands shook. He came closer, put his hand on her shoulder. The wind whipped through the wood, bringing with it another quick burst of sideways rain. His shirt stuck to his back and the cold water ran down the backs of his thighs, down his legs.

He tried to draw her to him, to hug her, give her comfort.

She jerked violently away.

"No! I can't." And then her face crumpled, and she slumped down to the muddy ground, leaving Ingram standing above her, hands useless at his sides.

She sobbed, hard inhalations that wracked her body.

"Franny... It's my fault..."

Ingram knelt, put his hands on her shoulder and tried to draw her up.

"No, goddamnit. It's my fault, Bull. Don't touch me."

He brought his hands back, but stayed kneeling in the mud.

She hit the ground with her hand. "I was *fucking* you and I should've been taking care of her. It's my fault. You're just a goddamned distraction."

"Sarah, listen to me. Something's going on here we don't understand. If we don't act quickly... I can't say what might happen to Franny."

She stared into the mud, rain streaming down her neck, dripping from her hair.

"*Sarah!*" he bellowed, putting all of himself into it. She jumped involuntarily. "We don't have much time! We've got to go back to the library and talk to Andrez. He knows what's going on here."

She didn't resist him when he drew her up.

He kept his arm around her on the way back to the Big House. Alice waited for them at the back door, holding towels.

"I sent Reuben to look for her. He and his boys are searching the farm and the roads."

"That's good. The little priest's waiting for us in the library."

Andrez looked up from the *Quanoon* when they entered. He came around the side of the desk, took Sarah's hands in his, and looked at her sincerely.

"We have to move quickly, Sarah. I know what's happening now." He let go of her hands and walked back around the desk. As he moved he took on a magisterial posture, a straightening of the back, a precision of his gestures that Ingram hadn't seen in him before.

Alice went to stand by Sarah, rubbing her shoulders and whispering in her ear. Sarah began to nod. Her hands stopped shaking.

"I had a suspicion yesterday but now we know. The slaughter of the peafowl was a sure indication of either territory or possession. But it's also a sign of a bargain. And Hastur made a bargain with someone in this house yesterday."

He let the words sink in.

Sarah's eyes became large, and she said, "Momma."

Andrez nodded. "Yes. She bargained with Hastur for health and longer life. That's why she's missing now."

"That bitch," Sarah muttered. She looked up. "She took Franny! She bargained away my daughter! How could she do that?"

Andrez looked pained. "She does have a claim to your daughter, at least as far as Hastur is concerned. There are very few rules that the gods adhere to, but the significance of blood is undeniable."

"But why? Why would Hastur want Franny?" Ingram's own

voice surprised him. He could hear the tension.

"He's trying to get back to his parents. He's trying to bring the Old Ones through."

"What will they do to her?" Sarah asked in a very small, soft voice.

Andrez looked pained.

"Sarah…"

"What will they do to her?"

"I think you—"

"*What will they do to her?*"

The priest sat down in the desk chair, slumped his shoulders.

"Violate her. Kill her. Violate her corpse."

A high-pitched keening came from Sarah's throat. Alice gripped her tight, trying to pull her head down, but Sarah resisted.

"No no no no no no—"

"But we can do something," Ingram said. "We can find her. Can't we?"

Andrez shook his head, and said, "I've been reading the *Quanoon* all night. When I heard that Franny was missing, I came back in here to see if I could find something to locate her. The best I could find is a spell to discover if someone is dead. And it requires… sacrifice. Nothing to locate someone who is missing."

"Wait a sec. I know where she is."

Sarah whirled on him, hands drawing up like claws. "What? Where is she?"

"On the *Hellion*. The boat from Ruby's. The barge I saw leave with the Pale Man. This has to be connected. It's all connected. She's on that fucking barge."

"The boat! The one we found you in. We can use that to find her." Light came back to Sarah's eyes, and suddenly she moved again with vigor. "Alice, get Reuben to bring gasoline. The boat did have a motor on it, didn't it?"

From the doorway, a child's voice said, "Yep. Sure did. Johnson 15 horse. It's enough for the river, that's for sure."

They turned to see Fisk and Lenora standing in the doorway.

Alice barked, "Get your butt in the kitchen. This is adult talk."

Fisk began to cry. Lenora looked defiant and wounded.

Their mother went to them. She said more gently, "Honeys, I know you're scared. I want you to go in the kitchen and wait for me there. Mr. Bull is gonna figure out how we can get back Franny. Go on, now. It's gonna be okay."

Ingram turned back to Alice. "You have a gun in the house?"

She nodded and went to get it.

His eyes fell on the sword resting on the table. He picked it up, and again he had that feeling of wheels locking into place. In his hand, the sword felt light. For a moment, Ingram just looked at the sword in his hand, admiring how good it felt there, how it completed his arm. He'd been missing something before then.

"We might want a little more than a gun when we get there," he said, looking around the room. Andrez and Sarah stared at him.

Alice re-entered the library carrying two pistols and stopped.

"What in the world?"

"What?" He turned to Sarah. "What's going on?"

"You look different, Bull. You look... I don't know... right. Like you were meant for that sword. Have you said his name?"

Surprised, he shook his head.

Andrez said, "What? Whose name?"

"Bull had a dream last night—"

"That's neither here nor there." He turned to Alice, taking the pistols from her. "You get Reuben?"

"I called the field shop. One of his boys answered. I told him to get that boat ready for you. Gas. Everything."

He looked at the Andrez. "Are you coming with us?"

"Of course." Andrez pushed away from the desk and stood up. "I'm ready."

"Sarah, go change your clothes. We can't do this with you in your night gown. Put on good shoes. And I can use that time finding a flashlight." He turned to Alice. "Get a bag. Something sturdy. Put some water, a towel or bandages in it. Some booze. Any extra ammo you have. And rain gear."

He looked back at Sarah.

"Girl, we have to hurry. Run, now. Run."

She ran, and Alice followed.

"Come on, Andrez. Let's go wait in the kitchen."

Minutes later, the women returned. Alice carried a small canvas duffle bag with two plastic ponchos, two flashlights, a bottle of brandy, a roll of hurricane tape, two towels wrapped in a plastic trash bag, and a few rolls of gauze.

Ingram looked up from where he inspected the pistols on the kitchen counter. "Sarah, you and Andrez get into the ponchos. I'll be fine."

He picked up one of the pistols and handed it to Sarah.

"This is a twenty-two magnum revolver. You've got six shots. If you need to use this, don't waste it on a gut shot or body shot. Only headshots will drop them."

He took the other pistol and tucked it into the front of his pants.

"I'd tell you to stay here, but I know you wouldn't have any of it."

"I'm going."

"So, let's go."

Chapter 21

S ince the moment she realized that Franny was missing, Sarah
thought she was going mad.

Her thoughts careened around her head without any direction. Focusing for any time was painful. It was as if her mind was
trying to distract her from the reality of situation, that her daughter was gone, ripped from her and in mortal peril.

But when Bull raised the sword her mind calmed down and
she allowed herself to hope that Franny would be okay. The
idea that they could be violating her daughter now, killing her,
filled Sarah with a cold fury she hadn't felt since she'd slapped
her mother. Looking at Ingram calmed the rage but didn't ex-
tinguish it.

She watched Ingram as they walked through the woods toward
the river. His shirt was plastered to his skin and his back rippled
with muscles, crisscrossed with a fine lattice-work of scars from the
war visible even through the fabric.

I guess the Marines prepared him for this. I hope so.

As she had followed Ingram and Andrez out the door, Alice had stopped her.

"I'd go with you but—"

"Alice, you've got to stay with the children."

She nodded. "I got something for you." She removed a folded straight razor from her blouse—her bra, Sarah realized—and handed it to her.

"Put it where I had it. It's something you keep to yourself and pull out when you need it."

She hugged Alice, then kissed her on the cheek.

"I love you."

The other woman looked at her, tears welling in her eyes. "Get your girl, Sarah. Bring her back."

Sarah nodded, and dashed out the door to catch up with the men.

The day darkened. Inside the wood, the mud sucked at their feet, and branches scratched at their clothes, faces, eyes. Ingram moved in front of them, huge and predatory.

The brown waters of the Arkansas River swirled and whipped past them when they reached the shore. One of Reuben's boys sat at the rear of the boat, bailing the accumulated rain out of the back. The motor buzzed, idling in the current and sending a small stream of smoke curling away.

Ingram stopped at the rise looking down on the shore. He motioned for the field hand to come up. After the boat sat empty, Ingram led them down the steep bank, treacherous with mud.

Sarah smelled the scent of burning gasoline from the flat-bottom's motor. A seagull shrieked above them, plying the river's dark waters. Standing there on the rise above the men and the rushing current, she felt very small and frightened. Everything she'd learned in the past days came crashing in on her in a very personal, very small cataclysm. She began to shake with the cold and the pure futility of what they were about to attempt. On the river in the rain to hunt down a god.

Ingram stepped into the boat. It sank three inches with his

weight. He turned, held out a hand for Andrez, who took it and hopped almost gracefully on the middle seat, setting the duffel bag containing the gear on the middle seat. Ingram turned and looked up the bank at Sarah. Water streamed down his head and onto his chest and back.

Sarah slipped down the bank and found a seat in the boat.

"Y'all get forward," Ingram yelled over the buzzing of the motor. "I weigh too damned much. Get on the front seat so the boat won't tilt."

Sarah realized that the prow of the little flat-bottom rose two or three feet from the river's surface. She swung a leg over the middle seat.

"Keep your bodies low! Flat-bottom's will tump real easy."

"Tump?" Andrez's voice cut through the buzz.

"Tip over. Into the fucking drink, professor! Get your ass up front."

They moved forward, dropping the prow a foot. Ingram moved from his crouch to the seat by the motor. He adjusted the outboard, twisted the throttle, and revved the engine. Behind him, the motor sent white plumes downriver, lingering in wisps on the surface. He looked at the tank in front of him. He reached forward and rocked it, causing gas to slosh inside. 20 GAL was stenciled in white paint on the side.

Ingram looked up.

"One of you is gonna have to untie us and shove off. Push us away from the shore! Not downstream!"

Andrez started to move but Sarah reached it before him. The boat tilted crazily, yawing back and forth.

"Goddamnit! Slow in these boats. Go slow! Keep your body down! Keep it low!"

Despite his words, Sarah noticed, he looked happy.

She untied the slimy rope from the deadwood.

The boat fell away from the Rheinhart property into the muddy river. Strange eddies and currents rippled beneath them, and for a moment, Sarah felt unbalanced and confused at the ever-shifting balance of the little boat. She sat down heavily. Ingram, twisting in his seat, flipped the outboard into gear and cranked the throttle. The boat lurched and veered into the middle of the river.

"Watch for logs! If one's under the surface and we hit it—"

The boat made its way back upstream, to the west. The wind rippled their hair, and the rain drops stung their skin, coming in sharp bites.

Ingram veered the boat back to the shore. They turned in front and looked at him quizzically. At a clear run of muddy beach, he cranked the throttle and rushed the flat-bottom up on the shore and cut the engine.

"What? Why are we stopping?"

"Wait a sec. We haven't thought this through." He wiped the water from his face, and Sarah realized how cold he must be. The rain pattered off of her poncho.

"Which way do we go? Upstream or down? The *Hellion* could be anywhere. And what do we do if they start singing? Go mad? Start ripping each other to shreds?"

Andrez said, "We could stuff our ears like Odysseus' men."

"I don't know what the hell you're talking about, but stuff them with what?"

They looked at one another blankly.

Sarah said, "Mud? Clay from the shore?"

"I think," Andrez said, slowly, "that we know enough to prevent the worst. Never before, in the history of man, have three people gone against gods as informed as we are. They are powerful, yes. But they are not *all powerful*. And we are not helpless."

"And we don't have time for anything else but…"

"Faith."

For a moment, Sarah was confused, staring at the unbelieving priest. "Faith?" she asked.

"In ourselves. In me. In Bull. In *you*. We will do what it takes, yes?"

"Yes." It was all she could manage. It was true.

"So that leaves the direction," Ingram said. He put his hands on his knees and looked at the two in the front of the little boat.

"Bull, do you think," she said hesitantly, "you might want to say his name?"

Andrez looked at her.

"What do you mean, Sarah?"

"Bull had a dream last night. About Mithras."

Ingram shook his head. "Hell, no. I'm not gonna let him take me."

Andrez looked between the two.

"What exactly are we talking about here?"

"Bull had a dream of Mithras. He wants to possess Bull. What did he say to you?" She looked at the big man.

"He wants to inhabit me. The motherfucker."

Andrez's eyes went wide. "He asked to 'inhabit' you?"

Ingram nodded, scowling.

The priest laughed and said, "Gods don't *ask*, Bull. Most gods just take what they want."

"A big fuck-all it makes to me. I'm not gonna let him in."

"So what are we going to do?"

"Why don't *you* ask him?"

Sarah glanced at Andrez, then looked back to Ingram.

"What do you mean?"

"I mean, yeah, he wants to inhabit me and I don't intend on letting him, but that don't mean he won't help us."

"It can't hurt to ask," Andrez said.

Before she knew what she was doing, Sarah stood, turned upstream, into the wind, and opened her arms. "Mithras!" Her voice came louder and shriller than she intended. She cleared her throat. "Mithras! My girl is gone and we need help. Please, give us some signs which way to go. We're just... mortals, and you're a god and we need help. It's your job to help! And if you can't... or won't... then what are you good for? Die. Or go away."

She turned, sat back down heavily on the seat, and buried her face in her hands.

Andrez murmured, "Not quite as I might have phrased it, but—"

Upstream, a huge flight of crows erupted from the trees lining the bank, took air, and like a black cloud, flew downriver, passing over the shored boat and cawing madly.

"Well, folks," Ingram said, "that pretty much cinches it, don't it?" He turned, crouched, then twisted around and yanked the cord on the outboard. It buzzed back to life.

"Push off!"

Sarah—needing to act and not think—hopped out of the boat, put her hands on the cold metal prow, and shoved as hard as she could. The boat hissed, sliding along the grit of the shore, and she took two steps in the water before she pulled herself back into the boat.

Ingram cranked the throttle. Again, she sat heavily, and Andrez put his arm around her.

Ingram steered at the back of the boat, eyes restlessly searching the waters before them. He steered the boat in a big loop, heading southeast with the flow of the river. The flat-bottom, pushed by the current and the outboard, whipped past the shore and flew downriver, following the crows. Sarah and Andrez huddled closer, keeping their backs to the rain and wind and looking backward, upstream, watching their wake and Ingram.

Once, the boat lurched horribly and the outboard jumped in Ingram's grip, pitching drastically upward and to the right. Sarah's hands darted out and caught the sides of the boat.

"Log!" Ingram bellowed. "Under the surface!"

He righted the boat and pointed it back downriver. The rain increased and the wind pushed at their backs, even with their forward speed.

The buzzing of the engine lulled Sarah, dampening her senses, blotting out all other sounds. The boat rocked and yawed on the water in a hypnotic rhythm and she found herself becoming dazed, lost in a thousand yard stare at the far shore, just a black ink stroke on the horizon slanted with rain. Andrez pressed closer, and she could feel his shivering through the ponchos.

Finally, Ingram's swaddled fist lanced out, pointing, and he yelled, "There! The *Hellion*!"

They turned to look and spied a long, low-slung rectangular barge without the massive flats of cargo. One tall stack pushed smoke into the sky and bristled with antennae. Tires ringed the gunwales, and the boat itself had doors and windows lining the deck.

Ingram yelled, "They broadcast the signal from the boat!"

The buzzing of the motor lulled, and Ingram turned the boat around, pointing it into the current to stop their forward movement.

"This is about to get messy." He looked down at his wrapped fist.

Keeping his good hand on the throttle, he ripped the bandages from his maimed hand with his teeth and threw the splint into the river. He held up his hand and flexed it, twice. His skin was yellow and purple, bruises streaking the discolored flesh.

Ingram looked back at them.

"OK, folks. Here's how this is gonna go. I'm gonna aim our little boat somewhere we can tie on. There's tires ringing the barge, so we should be able to tie on almost anywhere, but it'd be nice if I could find a spot that will make boarding easier. I've been on lots of boats, mostly military, but it's been a while. Sarah, I want you to tie us on as fast and securely as you can, then I'm going to grab the duffle, throw it on the deck, and come right over you two. So once we're tied, make yourselves as small as you can. Once I'm on deck, I could be a bit busy before I can help you up. Got it?"

They nodded. Sarah began shivering uncontrollably. She couldn't tell if it was from the wind, or water, or the fear that overcame her.

"All right, Sarah, grab the rope and get ready."

She got on her knees in the front seat and faced forward. With white-knuckled hands, she gripped the boat's tie and grasped the rim of the flat-bottom.

Ingram wrenched the throttle again, revving the motor, and turned the boat to the side, pushing them in a sharp arc, dashing back downstream toward the waiting black hulk of the *Hellion*. As they approached, the low throb of the barge engines shook the small flat-bottom from the water up. The *Hellion* loomed closer, grimed with oil and mud and the white streaks of seagull excrement. The flat-bottom rocked in the wake of the barge.

Ingram steered them down the length of the barge, searching for a place to moor their smaller boat. The *Hellion* throbbed with the sound of the diesel engines deep within. Finally Ingram cut the motor, falling back toward a tire resting a few feet in front of the barge's wake.

He angled the flat-bottom inward. The *Hellion* filled Sarah's view. Her heart leapt in her chest, throbbing in time with the diesels. Her hands shook, and the stench of diesel fumes overwhelmed her.

"Grab on, goddamnit! Grab the tire!"

She grappled with the makeshift mooring. From upriver as they approached, the tires ringing the barge seemed small, like car tires. But up close, they were enormous.

Andrez lent a hand, holding on with all his might as she leaned far out over the prow of the flat-bottom and worked the rope around a tire. The movement of the boats made the exercise harder, and as they rocked in the water, the tire slammed against the hull of the *Hellion*, catching Sarah's hand there. She exclaimed wordlessly with the pain, giving a startled yawp.

Franny. Sarah ground her jaw and forced the rope around the tire.

Andrez snatched up the ends and quickly tied a knot. Ingram cut the motor, and suddenly the *Hellion* dragged the flat-bottom. The little boat pitched crazily, banging against the grimy side of the larger boat.

"Out of the way. I'm coming through."

Ingram dashed to the front of the boat, sword and pistol tucked into his belt. He threw the duffle bag onto the barge, climbed up the tire, and hauled himself over the wooden gunwale, flopping on the deck, hidden from where Sarah and Andrez rocked on the river.

Sarah saw his movement through a small porthole in the gunwale. For a long breathless silence, Sarah and Andrez stared at the lip of the barge, worried that a dead face would peek over the rail and stare down at them with lidless, white eyes.

Ingram's face appeared over the rail. He leaned forward, reached down, and extended his good hand. Sarah grasped it, and he yanked her forcefully out of the boat, up past the tire. She grabbed the gunwale and pulled herself the rest of the way.

"Deserted, looks like. A damned ghost ship."

She regained her feet on a narrow gangway leading to the stern of the barge.

Ingram lifted Andrez out of the boat and onto the deck.

"We need to be quick. Gotta search the whole boat, and there could be—"

"Dead."

"Yeah. The corpses. Take the pistol," Ingram said. "This sword is better for me. I'm a crappy shot with my left anyway." He pulled the gun from his waistband and handed it to Andrez. "Like I told Sarah, shoot 'em in the head. Put it in their face if you have to."

Andrez nodded.

"All right, I've never been on a boat like this before, so we're gonna move as fast as we can." Ingram shook his head and half-muttered, "I didn't think this bastard would be so damned big."

He slung the duffle over his shoulder.

"We move from stern to fore. Quickly. Last place we check will be the pilot's roost, there." He jabbed a finger at the cluster of antennae behind a stack. "There'll be someone in there, steering, but that might not be where they have Franny. But if we hit the roost first, they might have time to sound an alarm. Let's go."

Ingram held the sword loosely in his hand and walked on light feet. He balanced his weight, placed one foot in front of the other. She tried to imitate his movement, but her heart hammered in her chest and she could only think of Franny. She wanted to scream and rush from door to door, flinging them open. Her Franny was here somewhere. This foul boat. Twenty feet to the stern, they came to a door leading into the interior of the boat. Ingram tried the handle, shoving the door open.

Inside, there was only darkness. And the stench of the dead mixed with rotten fish.

Ingram shrugged the duffle from his shoulder and handed it backward, still keeping his eyes ahead. Then he looked back at Andrez and Sarah and mimed holding a flashlight.

He stepped inside. Sarah held her breath. Blood throbbed at her temples. Her legs felt weak, rubbery. She ripped at the duffle, hands shaking, while Andrez watched her. She handed him a flashlight, and he flipped it on. She turned on her own, and they moved through the door and into the interior of the *Hellion*, shining faint lights in the dark.

"Here. Wait a sec."

The room flooded with light. Three bulbs in mesh cages mounted on the bulkhead burned brightly, showing ranks of tables. A small galley. Foodstuffs were spilt on the floor, flour and spices making grainy sprays near the oven.

"Here. Blood."

It was black and crusty and covered the far half of the room. The walls were smeared in it. Painted with it. Looking at the bulkhead, Sarah could almost read the bloody story the smears told, like some strange violent language distilled down to an essence of bloodstrokes and hand prints. Like an illustration in the *Quanoon*.

Ingram turned around in a circle, cursing. He looked from the stern door to the one at the fore. "This is gonna be engineering, most likely." He pointed at the stern door. "We check that first, then we'll know no one's behind us. Right?"

Sarah nodded because she didn't trust herself to speak. Andrez spoke for her. "We must hurry, Bull. Now."

Bull went to the door, forced open the latch, and swung it open. He stepped through. They followed.

A small open aired space. Still no one appeared. Just the thrum of engines and the smell of fish and muddy water and diesel fumes. Before them stood a door marked in black stencil, ENGINE ROOM. Ingram yanked open the latch.

As Sarah followed Andrez through, she was assaulted by sound.

The dynamo that turned the massive screws that drove the *Hellion* was louder than the sound of creation. The bulwarks shook with the noise, and the vibrations shook Sarah through the floor. The room smelled of oil, and wet rodents, and something else.

Ingram found a switch and flipped it. More bright bulbs burning in mesh cages.

A single figure stood at the end of the room, facing the engine, the wall of gauges and valves. He was slight, and dressed as a child.

He turned, as though sensing their presence.

A tow-headed boy. Wearing jeans and a dirty shirt. His face, though gray, wore an expression of surprise, mouth caught in an O, his eyebrows high.

For an instant, Sarah was back in the orchard, among fallow fields and the whole world smelled of burning tires and rang with the caws of crows and the Alexander boy had gripped her too tight and pushed his erection hard against her and she'd shoved him away. She hadn't been mad, she hadn't been terrified as she was now. But she'd wanted him to stop. He did and that look of surprise crossed his face, just like this boy's here, when he saw Alice watching him with murderous eyes, holding the cudgel. He'd ran away, crying, and Sarah had felt so bad for him. She'd never seen him again. This boy, this boy before her, looked the same, surprised, and so similar he could be the same child. The Alexanders lived on the far side of Altheimer, by the river, she knew. And suddenly, she was sure of it, that this boy *was* an Alexander. Maybe even the son of *her* Alexander boy. *Franny.*

Ingram moved forward, raising the sword.

"Bull. Wait." Hearing her own voice, Sarah realized she sound shrill, on the verge of hysteria.

He stopped. "What?"

"I know him, I think."

He looked at her for a long while, too long, as the dead boy walked down the long room toward them. Bull dipped his head in acknowledgement and waved them back.

Andrez touched her lightly on the shoulder, his soft eyes searching her face. "Come, Sarah. We will wait for Bull out here."

She looked back at the boy. He was closer now, and in the light. His gray skin looked waxy, mask-like. The open O of his mouth was as black as the opening of a well, and his eyes were pure white. As she watched, his waxy skin shifted, as if something beneath the skin was moving. The mask of the boy's face reassembled itself into one of pure hatred.

Somehow the boy was even more pitiable now that some dark thing inhabited him, forced him to move.

They take. That's all they do, these petty gods. They take from us and give nothing back.

The realization did not give her the fire of outrage, the strength of the desperate. She felt only an overwhelming sadness.

She let Andrez pull her through the open door, and he held his pistol tightly, knuckles white, as they waited for Ingram.

There was a loud grunt and a bellow, and then Ingram was back, holding his hand. It dripped with blood.

"Mercy didn't work too well," he said. He tried to laugh but it failed in his throat, and he opened his hand to show them the ruin of it.

His smaller fingers were missing and the two stumps pumped blood. Ingram shrugged, raising his big shoulders and letting them fall. "Get the tape."

They wrapped his hand in gray hurricane tape, and Ingram stood and switched the sword to his left hand.

"We still have more boat to search."

They moved forward, back through the galley, and forced open the next door, exposing a musty barracks. The lights didn't work in there and Sarah, the stink of carrion filling her nose, desperately searched their duffel for a flashlight. When she found it, the beam was pitifully small in the darkness.

A bed held a graying, fly-swarmed corpse. And the light revealed another door on the port bulkhead.

The latch moved stiffly under Ingram's hand. Using his weight, he shoved down on the handle and shouldered it open.

Brightness from the room streamed out over them, casting a wedge of light into the ranks of bunk beds. The room was lit from grimy round porthole windows and the soft yellow glow of electronic equipment. Wires crisscrossed the small chamber floor in a morass. The cables fed through a porthole, leading to the fore of the boat. A table held a microphone and turntable, still spinning. Sarah's heart leapt in her chest. *The music!*

Ingram stood over the turntable and, with one hand, swept the electronic gear from the surface onto the floor in a barrage of sparks and smoke. The room filled with the stink of ozone and burning rubber.

Andrez moved into the room further, walking toward the door in the far wall. Passing the table, the priest looked to his side and jumped, jerking away from the corner hidden by the table.

Sarah moved around the table and saw what—who—was there.

Elizabeth Rheinhart huddled in the corner, hair white. Any remnant of sanity had been driven from her. She gibbered silently, her glazed eyes roaming the corners of the room, her bleeding fingers tracing bloody doodles on the wall.

Stepping forward, Andrez moved to Elizabeth and put his hands on the woman's shoulders, as if to comfort her.

She whipped around and sprang from her crouched position, fastening bleeding hands on the priest's neck. He bowled over, crashing into Sarah and sending her reeling into the wall, banging her head on the porthole's rim. Elizabeth ripped violently at the little man, fists flying. Her hands fell with such a preternatural speed Sarah, head spinning from the blow against the wall, had trouble following her mother's movements. She saw, through what felt like gauze, her mother leaning forward and biting into the priest's cheek while Andrez's hands beat a frantic tattoo on her face, her head, desperately trying to fend her off.

Behind Elizabeth, the wreckage of Sarah's mother, she perceived Ingram moving glacially, his sword coming up. Sarah threw herself in front of the man, even as her mother ripped at the priest. Ingram swept Sarah away with his wounded arm, pushing her once again against the wall. He grabbed a handful of her mother's hair and yanked her viciously off Andrez. Throwing her as easily as he would a rag-doll, he tossed her across the table that had held the microphone and electronic gear.

Sarah's chest heaved.

"Mother!" Her voice boomed in the close confines of the radio room. It had a strength she didn't feel.

"If there's anything left of you in there, stop! Listen!"

The thing that had been her mother paused, cocked her head like some sort of predatory bird, and blinked slowly, her mouth dripping with Andrez's blood.

"You bargained away Franny, Momma. For that, I can never forgive you. But if you stop now and help us get her back, maybe—"

"Maybe?" Elizabeth voice was like gravel, harsh and hoarse. But even then, recognizable. Full of contempt.

"It takes the end of the world for my miserable daughter to show real strength. Or offer me forgiveness."

"You could go to your grave without this terrible thing on your soul—"

Elizabeth chuckled, a harsh phlegmy sound. "My soul? Have you been listening to this little priest?" She pointed a clawed finger at the Andrez. Sarah's mother's face curled into a smile. A smile full of sharp teeth. "Have you? Did he not tell you?"

She laughed again. Slowly, she turned her bloody claw and tapped her chest. "There is only this. *Only this!* The flesh! Nothing else. Why do you think they war over us, the godlings? Because the living is all there is! They must infest us to assure their own survival. And I'm not ready to leave this husk."

Giving a bloody grin, Elizabeth vaulted onto the table as if to defy gravity and landed with her legs spread wide, arms out like a wrinkled and desiccated wrestler. Her tongue flicked in and out of her mouth, snakelike. Then, cackling, she leaped over Ingram's grasp and landed on top of Andrez. His limbs jerked like a marionette with its strings cut.

Sarah's arm acted of its own accord, lancing out and hitting her mother with the flashlight. Batteries, glass, and metal flew in all directions. Elizabeth whipped her grisly head around and fixed her eyes on Sarah.

Something in Elizabeth changed. Her skin darkened and her face began to elongate. She jumped backward, away from Andrez, then climbed the wall and hung upside down from the ceiling.

She was becoming a wolf. A hideous black thing, with snout and hands, nude of fur but obsidian and oily, thick with muscle. And deadly teeth. An image of the obsidian child that screamed obscenities and fled into the streets of Podgorica, a world away in Montenegro, flashed in Sarah's mind.

"He is coming." The new shape of her mouth made the words indistinct. "You can't stop him. The world devourer. The lover of destruction. Coming. I will be his whore. His wife." Her tongue flicked in and out. "His *servant*."

Lightning fast, she leapt at Sarah, who stood, dumbfounded as her mother transformed into this *thing*.

Ingram's fist slammed her to the floor of the cabin. His foot lashed out viciously, catching the black thing that had once been Sarah's mother in the chest.

Ingram moved before she could begin another attack, grabbing the thing by the neck and hoisting her into the air. She clawed frantically at his arms, drawing furrows in his already bloody skin.

He slammed the pommel of the sword into her face, and she went limp in his hand. He tossed her across the room, back into the corner they had found her.

"*No!*" Sarah screamed. She scrambled to where her mother had fallen.

"Momma!" she screamed, cradling her mother's limp form. Blood streamed from Elizabeth Rheinhart's nose, her eyes, her ears. Her form mutated, changed. Her skin became pink and white once more. Her body vibrated, shaking and spasming. After a while she stilled, the tremors leaving her limbs.

Sarah closed her eyes and wept.

Ingram went to Andrez and helped him up. A quarter-sized hunk of flesh was missing from his cheek, pumping blood. The priest's eyes and cheeks had already swelled horribly, turning purple. Andrez spat blood to the floor, and two teeth pinged off the metal.

Woozy, unsteady on his feet, Andrez gripped Ingram's arm. Sarah looked at the priest, his gory mouth, then back down to her mother.

No more tears for this… this… thing. She sold my baby to become some Old God's whore. She deserved to die.

She shoved her mother's corpse away and stood.

She looked at Ingram. Gore covered his torso. Blood streamed from wounds on his right arm. The bandage covering his missing fingers was no longer spotted with red, it was soaked. Sarah reached out and touched his shoulder, concern in her face.

Ingram's eyes searched hers. He leaned forward.

In her ear, he whispered, "Don't cry for me. I *chose* to be here. And so did the priest. And so did you, and so did your mother, for that matter."

He swallowed, glancing at the priest who was touching his face gingerly, lost in his own pain.

"Just so you know… being with you, with Franny has been… it's changed me. I feel like I could become a good man with you. We could be good together."

Andrez cleared his throat. His voice sounded different, the plosives coming strangely. "It's been hours now. We have to move."

Ingram straightened. "You're right."

He moved to the door, and peered through the porthole.

"Looks like we're right under the pilot house. There's the stairs leading up." He turned back to them. "It's time to finish this. Whoever's steering this damned boat will be in the pilot house. We're gonna go in there and get Franny back."

At that moment, the boat lurched, sending them bouncing off the metal hull.

"Feel that, Bull?" Andrez asked, eyes wide.

"Yeah. We hit something, submerged tree probably."

"No, do you *feel* it?"

Sarah nodded. "Yes. Something's changed. Something's happened."

Andrez shook his head. "We have to hurry. They're trying to bring something through. This feels like Godshatter. But worse."

"Let's go." Ingram lifted his sword.

"I can't find my gun, Bull. I must've dropped it."

He faced Sarah and shook his head. "Well, it's too late to go back in there." He looked down, as though checking himself one last time. "Stay behind us, Sarah. If you see anything you can use as a weapon, pick it up. When we go out this door, you'll both need to be right on my ass. I'm going out and up the stair and through the door, even if I have to knock the bastard down."

"Let's go get Franny," Ingram said.

Ingram turned, opened the door, and moved quickly into the gray light of day. Andrez scrambled behind him, and Sarah followed as best she could, keeping close behind the little man.

The shore was nearer now—brown and green foliage whipping past, thirty yards off the starboard bow—as the barge took a large crook in the river. The wind ripped through Sarah's clothes and she smelled the river, like dead fish and dead men and river mud.

The three raced around a short dividing wall and mounted the stairs to the pilot house. Ingram took the stairs two at time, sword out, the muscles in his back rippling.

At the top of the stairs, he stopped and looked at his companions.

The instant he turned, she saw everything about him, his pain and loneliness, his determination and viciousness, his wounds and fiercely beating heart. She felt her heart swell and rise to meet his.

Ingram nodded to her, then wrenched the handle down and shoved open the door. Andrez pushed his body into motion after him, and Sarah followed.

Her senses slowed, and she felt as though she moved through water, everything happening with a dreamlike intensity. Her perceptions became almost mechanical, ticking off details as if she was inventorying a still-life.

A room. Two men—both living—one by a table and the other at the pilot's wheel, backlit by river and sky. The light streaming through the windows, thin and bloody. Ingram stepping forward, filling the space with his presence. Andrez moving toward the pilot, raising his pistol. The blood spattering the walls and windows glistening in the weak half-light from outside. The room smelling of iron and incense and...

She felt her pulse throbbing in her temples, her chest heaving. A panic filled her, suffusing all of her awareness, senses distilled down in to short, sharp shocks. Her mind registered what was in the middle of the room.

Franny lay splayed on the table, surrounded by candles and incense. Her once bright blue eyes shone wide and horrified and dim, her mouth gaped in a rictus of pain and fear. Her flaxen hair ringed her face in a soft halo, darkened in places by blood. Her delicate fingers—once so chubby as they grasped Sarah's fingers—curled inward towards the nails that fixed her to the table.

Too late. They were too late.

They'd split Franny from vagina to throat and spread her ribcage to display her organs in gory loops. She died terrified. Her corpse gleamed red in the low light of the pilot house. Sarah could feel her mind breaking as she gazed on the remains of her daughter.

Where Franny's heart should have been was a swirling blackness like a whirlpool. And in the instant that Sarah's mind comprehended her daughter's fate, the darkness grew. It pulsed, expanding, sending small tendrils of blackness spilling over the edges of Franny's chest cavity. At its edges, phantoms twisted like tentacles coalescing from smoke and vapor and blood. It grew.

The Pale Man stood beside Franny's body chanting and moving his hands in obscure patterns. His nakedness didn't register on Sarah immediately, the blood caking his body—his legs, chest and flaccid penis—gave the impression of clothing. He looked up at Sarah with blue, piercing eyes that held her. His lips withdrew to show yellowed teeth and a black tongue.

Oun tulu ia denu fin ia.

Everything happened all at once. From the corner of her eye, she saw the silhouette that stood at the pilot's wheel turn and bat away

Andrez's gun as it fired. The priest fell backward and the pilot—a dark-skinned man with tight kinky hair and a well-groomed mustache—raised a pistol and snarled at them, firing. In the flash of Andrez's gunfire, Sarah saw that the pilot was as naked as the Pale Man.

The pilot's gun barked three times quickly, flashing in the room, deafening her. Sarah stood tranfixed. Red flowers blossomed on Andrez's back and his skull. A bloody mist remained in the air as the priest slumped to the floor.

Ingram bellowed wordlessly and lurched toward the pilot. The pilot wheeled, brought the gun up into Ingram's stomach, and fired again. The larger man jumped, his body jerking with the gunshot. Another bloody flower blossomed, this time from Ingram's back.

Oun tulu ia denu fin ia!

Bringing up his mangled right arm, Ingram grabbed the pilot's throat. Before the man could pull the trigger again, Ingram raked the sword across the man's face, cutting deeply into the pilot's cheek and peeling off the man's features—his nose, his lips, his brow—like a butcher denuding a pig of skin. A high-pitched scream pierced the air. The air whistled and burbled in the open wound of the pilot's face. Where his nose had been was now only white cartilage and blood. Sarah couldn't tell if the sound was the pilot's screams or her own.

As Ingram raised the sword again, to drive it into his eye, the pilot squeezed the trigger convulsively, and Sarah saw Ingram's body jump once more. He screamed and shoved the sword home, impaling the man through the mouth. Spattered with red, Ingram fell.

"Bull!" Her voice didn't sound like her own anymore. He toppled over as she reached him. He hit the floor heavily, coughing crimson at the impact.

"Get…" The words burbled in his throat. "Get the Pale Man."

She realized that the chanting had stopped. She stood and whirled. The Pale Man watched her over the body of her dead daughter.

"Now, at the end of all things, it would be a Rheinhart to thwart me," the Pale Man said.

Sarah gasped.

"Wilhelm!"

The Pale Man grinned and flicked the black tongue in his mouth.

"Yessss," he hissed. Then suddenly he coughed, a deep hacking sound coming from someplace further than his chest. Blood darkened his lips.

"I was once Wilhelm Rheinhart. And you are my blood. And so was she."

Sarah's eyes burned with the gunsmoke in the room. She brought up her hands to her chest and glanced wildly about, looking for something to use as a weapon. In the smoke, she couldn't see Andrez's or the pilot's guns. Ingram must have landed on his own sword as he fell. She clutched her chest, felt hardness there, and remembered.

"She was..." The Pale Man smiled, bloody lips like heated and fluid wax. "She was blood of my blood? My niece. My great niece. Ah. That explains why it was so *sweet*. Her pain... exquisite." He shook his head. In the light, his skin looked like paraffin, waxy and inhuman.

"But it's too late now. He's coming over the threshold."

Sarah looked down at Franny's remains. The blackness spilled over the sides of her daughter's chest cavity like water flowing from a high place. It spread out from the table and lapped at the walls. Sarah felt the cold of the darkness touching her legs. As she watched it, her perceptions skewed, tilting sickeningly. For an instant, she felt like she stood at the precipice of a gigantic vortex, massive and unknown. The rim of the abyss. At the center, she sensed something vast and monstrous moving through limitless dark spaces.

"No," Sarah said, raising her eyes from her daughter's corpse. "No."

She withdrew the straight razor from her breast, and flicked it open.

"No. He won't come through when you're dead. I know that much."

Before she realized what she did, Sarah vaulted the edge of the table and crouched in front of the Pale Man, swinging the razor in short, sharp arcs.

His pale-blue eyes grew large, surprised. He brought up his hands in time to meet her swing. The razor sliced through his flesh as though it truly were wax, drawing a dark line down his forearm and palm. A manic strength overcame Sarah, and she knocked his hands to the side, lashing him with the straight razor again.

A line of black beads crossed the skin of his face, his hands. She reversed her swing, as she'd seen Ingram do with the sword. The Pale Man threw himself backward and jumped to the side. He backed away, trying to keep the table between him and Sarah.

"Wait! We can be… *exalted*! When he comes past the threshold, he'll grant us anything!"

She rushed forward, swinging the razor in bright steel arcs. The Pale Man feinted, then lashed out with a long white arm, his fist impacting with her cheek, and she reeled back, bright tracers swimming at the edges of her vision. She righted herself with difficulty.

Rage unlike any she'd ever known filled her. She regained her balance and advanced again, keeping her body low, hands up, not swinging blindly now but waiting for an opportunity to strike.

"Blood of my blood! We will wed and be king and queen over the world! Multitudes will beg for our mercy! We will never die!"

As he spoke, he kicked out at her. Pain erupted in her knee and she fell heavily into the table, half on top of her daughter's corpse.

As she fell on top of her daughter, the faintest scent of Franny remained, despite the slaughter, despite the gunsmoke and candles and incense. For the briefest moment, Sarah smelled her daughter, her baby, the scent of her hair fresh from the bath, the smell of her body as they lay together in bed.

She righted herself. Ignoring the pain, she darted forward, ducking under the Pale Man's swing, and swiped his chest with the razor.

When he screamed, it sounded like the whine of a ball-bearing burning itself out, high and grating. He swung his fists wildly, but

Sarah crouched low and the blows glanced off her skull. She lashed out again with the razor, opening the Pale Man's cheek.

He jumped backward, trying to get more distance between them. "We can live *forever*! We can give your little girl back her life!" Sarah slashed again, and he moved backward once more.

He stopped and smiled.

"But this is better now. His entrance will be faster if I have your body lying beside your daughter's. Maybe you possess a bit of innocence yet."

As she watched, his blood-caked penis began to rise.

"You might even enjoy it, niece, when I stab you. But I'll bring you back." His smile grew and grew, past any human's capacity for joy. "And do it again, just to teach you not to interfere."

Like a snake striking, he was over the table and upon her, forcing her down to the floor. Hands like a dead man's grabbed her wrists, pinioning her. He opened his mouth and his tongue, black as night, emerged, longer and more grotesque than anything she could imagine.

His eyes became obsidian. Hastur inhabited him. The god had come to partake.

She was screaming now, but his grisly head lowered to hers, black tongue snaking, and he placed his mouth over hers, blocking all sound, and she had no breath anyway. She could feel his tongue growing tendrils that burrowed into her flesh. The Black Kiss. His skin felt like oil upon her, invading her most secret spots.

She thrashed. She writhed. She felt her hand fall on something hard. The smooth, ivory handle of the razor. But she couldn't move.

The god that inhabited Wilhelm thrashed in response, thrusting as far inside Sarah as his flesh would allow. And then, just as it seemed it couldn't get worse, that the darkness pushing in from all sides would shut her mind off like the turning of a light switch and she'd go gibberingly, totally insane, Wilhelm's eyes blinked and they were no longer black but watery blue.

His eyes grew wide as a huge fist grabbed his neck and yanked him away.

Ingram. Still alive. Bellowing.

Sarah felt him withdraw from her mouth. And suddenly, where she'd once been filled with something hideous, now she was filled with rage like some incendiary light firing in her chest.

Ingram screamed. He pulled Wilhelm to him, struggling to hold the thing that had once been a boy. Wilhelm exploded into movement, thrashing and screaming wildly, each limb moving frantically, jerking, spasming, trying to injure the inexorable grip that held him. With his good hand, Ingram began raining blows down.

"*Sarah!*" Ingram screamed, struggling to hold the white thing in his grasp. "You've got to—"

She lurched forward, flicking open the razor. Wilhelm's fists caught her on the temple, on the jaw, and darkness closed in on her. She fell forward, through the barrage of fists, landing heavily on his chest.

Face to face, once again, she brought the razor up. With the blade, she entered him.

She raked his neck once, twice. She sliced his eyes.

His hands went to his mouth, which opened and closed soundlessly. He began to cough as the black line of blood on his neck widened, then opened, spilling ichor down his front. He coughed, blood spattering Sarah's face and arms.

He coughed, the sound dying away into a burbling hiss. Then he lay still.

On top of him, she could feel the life leaving his body. His eyes grew dull.

The boat lurched violently, rolling Sarah away. The floor of the pilot house wasn't level anymore.

She crawled over to Ingram. Blood pumped from his stomach in horrifying amounts. It was hard to tell where his body ended and the floor began, so much blood covered everything.

Weakly, he said, "Sarah, you've got to... got to... get the sword."

Too much. Too much had happened, and all she felt was grief. All she saw was death.

She stared at him, unblinking.

"No time. The boat's hit something. You have to get... have to get Franny and yourself off the boat."

She sat, unmoving.

"Sarah! Goddamnit!"

"Bull, Franny's dead," she said with a dull voice. She didn't care whether she lived or died now either.

"No. Not gonna—" He coughed a huge gout of blood. "Not gonna let that happen. Get the sword."

"What? Why get the sword?"

"Get the—" He took short, shallow breaths now, his chest rising and falling quickly.

He swallowed. "Get the... *Get the goddamned sword!*"

Sarah jumped at his words. She frantically searched the floor around his body. Under the lip of the pilot's wheel, the sword had come to a rest as Ingram fell. She grabbed its sticky hilt and drew it to her.

She turned and knelt over Ingram, holding the sword in both hands.

"Good... good. I don't have long." He tapped his chest, on the sternum. "Right here. Put the point right here."

"Bull, I... I can't. We'll get you a doctor. Just hang in there."

"No, no. I'm dead. But I've got... I've got one last thing I can do."

"No, we'll get a doctor. He can— " Her tears disappeared into the pool of his blood.

"Sarah. Sarah. Remember the book. The book. You have to take out my heart. Cut it out."

She shook her head. Closing her eyes as tightly as she could, she shook her head and denied it.

"The... the *Quanoon*, Sarah. Cut out my heart and put it in Franny. Do it."

"No, Bull, you'll die before it even—"

"No, I won't. Take it out. I give it to you freely. To her. Save her."

Tears burned her eyes.

"I give it to you. It's mine to give, and by giving it, it will—"

Finally, she nodded once, understanding.

"Do we need to say anything?"

He closed his eyes and didn't open them for a long while.

"Just goodbye. And—"

She leaned forward and kissed him.

"*Mithras*," Ingram said.

His face went white. His eyes snapped open and grew to the size of half-dollars. His pupils darkened to black.

Then, every cord, every sinew, every ounce of Lewis Ingram's body thrummed, filling with light. Blinding white light.

Ingram's eyes—enormous and swimming in light—turned on her, and he spoke to her with the voice of a god.

"*Now, Sarah. Do it now.*"

With all her strength, she drove the sword into Ingram's chest, splitting his sternum. Light streamed from the wound instead of blood. His flesh tore with a ripping sound. All the way to his pelvis, she worked the blade. She screamed as she pulled, closing her eyes to the brightness.

She threw the sword to the side and stuck her hands in the gash, gripping the edges of his ribcage. With a great heave, she opened his chest. It split with a crack.

Nova. A bright explosion of light.

And then Ingram's body dimmed, the god's eyes went vacant, and in her hands was a pulsing, living heart made of light.

She rose on trembling legs, turned, and went to Franny's body, horribly maimed and broken.

She set the heart in Franny's chest.

❧

Epilogue

They watched the children from the shore.

Lenora and Fisk danced around the shallows, splashing each other. Franny sat on the beach, observing their water fight. Fisk ran in circles, high stepping in the shallows, chanting, "I'm a preacher man, I'm a preacher man! Gonna baptize you!"

Franny smiled wanly at his antics, and Lenora came and sat down by her. She took Franny's hand in hers and put it to her cheek. They sat like that for a long time, Lenora holding Franny's hand to her face, watching Fisk dance around. After a while, he noticed and joined them, sitting to the side.

Sarah tried to hear what the children said, but the lapping of the water blanketed any sound. A buzz grew in the air. A flat-bottom passed their vantage, two men with fishing rods heading south, into the cypress. They waved, and the children waved back. Eventually, the wake reached where the children sat, casting miniature breakers onto the muddy beach.

"Do you think she can remember any of it?" Alice asked, pouring a cup of coffee from a thermos.

New leaves wreathed the shore of Old River Lake, and the water had a film of pollen on the surface. As the children sat, the water stilled, the yellow film creeping back in like a noose tightening.

"Yes. She remembers everything." Sarah took the cup Alice offered. "At the end, Momma…"

She stopped, rubbed the bridge of her nose, blinked back tears. "At the end, Momma said that they war over us because there's no such thing as a soul. That this is all there is."

Alice snorted. "She always was a damned fool, your mother, with no sense of place. The evil bitch."

"I have to wonder if it is true."

"No, goddamnit, it ain't."

Sarah watched the children. She stayed very still and did not move.

"How are you so sure?"

"I feel it. Here." Alice tapped her chest. A strange echo of her mother's gesture. "And your proof is right there, in front of you."

"What do you mean?"

"Franny came back. She was gone, but now she's back. How could that happen if there wasn't no such thing as a soul?"

"I don't know."

"Shee-it. I can't imagine what that must be like for her."

Sarah remained quiet, thinking. She had an idea of what it must be like.

"Sometimes…" Sarah couldn't cry anymore. Word had come the day before that Jim had died of asphyxiation. He'd choked on his vomit. Sarah planned on leaving Franny with Alice and the kids to attend the funeral.

"Sometimes, I almost wish I hadn't… I hadn't brought her back."

Alice gasped. "Shut your mouth. Never say that. Never."

"No, Alice. She remembers it all. Every bit of it. The rape. The murder. Beyond maybe, I don't know. How can you live after that?"

"Just like she's doing. One day at a time. She's just a little sad, maybe. Shocked, like them war vets. Like Bull was."

"No." Sarah sipped at the coffee. "But she does smile occasionally, with the kids. Never to me. I can't say I blame her."

"You brought her back. You brought her back from the…" She trailed off, uncomfortable speaking of it.

"Yes. But I didn't keep her safe to begin with. And she knows it."

"That's a load of horseshit. You was fighting with… gods. Gods, goddamnit. How can you contend with that?"

"I'm her mother. I'm supposed to protect her."

"Shit."

Fisk jumped up and ran back in the water. He splashed for a while, then turned and dove into deeper water.

"Fisk! Stay close to shore now, you hear me?"

He dove underwater and disappeared. When he resurfaced, he had two hands full of mud. He put them on top of his head, and Lenora squealed with laughter. Franny hugged her knees and smiled.

"Boy, don't you got no sense?" Alice yelled. She stood up and went to the car, retrieving a large picnic basket. Her breath whooshed out as she sat back down on the blanket.

"Kids, it's lunch time. We got meatloaf sandwiches!"

Fisk jumped up and raced over to the blanket. Lenora stood and, taking Franny's hand, pulled her to a standing position. A faint seam ran from the hollow of Franny's throat down her chest, disappearing into her bikini bottoms.

When she sat down, Franny put her hand on Sarah's leg, gave a little squeeze, and leaned into her mother.

Sarah swallowed, put an arm around her daughter, and ran her fingers through white hair.

❧

The black thing came out of the forest wearing the shape of a man. It stood in the clearing nearest the dark wood, behind the old peafowl house.

Franny rose from her bed and went to the window. She cocked her head and looked at the creature.

I can make you powerful.

She put her hand on the window.

"I'm already powerful. I don't need your promises."

I will make you wise and strong beyond imagining.

The girl shrugged, making the hem of her nightgown swing.

The black thing didn't move, but she could feel its anger growing.

I will rip down this house. I will devour everything and everyone you love.

She snorted. Her shoulders shook with silent laughter.

"I am the doorway now. You cannot pass. *He* cannot pass. You can't do anything to me that hasn't already been done. So go away, and leave us alone."

She watched it disappear into the wood. Then Franny smiled, turned, and climbed back into bed with her mother.

❧

Acknowledgements

Writing is a solitary pursuit.

Publishing, however, is not. This book might have been conceived by me, but it was brought to term and born into the world through the steadfast friendship, love and support of many people. To you I give my thanks.

Thanks to my wife and children who remain excited for me even on those days when I am not; to my agent, Stacia Decker, for accepting me as her client—it's a good thing we both have great taste; to Jeremy Lassen and Ross Lockhart, my publisher and editor at Night Shade Books, respectively, for their guidance and forbearance to a young author if not young man; to Dr. Terrell Tebbetts of Lyon College for instilling in me a wonder and joy at the English language—and for reminding me to murder my darlings; to Joe Howe, for unflinching, reasoned and well-thought advice and pep-talks; to John Rector, whom I hated at first, but who I have now come to hate like a brother; to Erik Smetana, Kevin Wallis, and C. Michael Cook, Steve Weddle, Shanna Wynne, Stephen Blackmoore, Ronald Kelly, Doug Winter, Gary Braunbeck, Kate Horsley, Christopher Ransom and all the folks at the K.A.O.S. board. And of course, Lewis Dowell, my brute of a friend without whom Bull Ingram would never have been born.

Each of you, in your own ways, have guided and encouraged me.

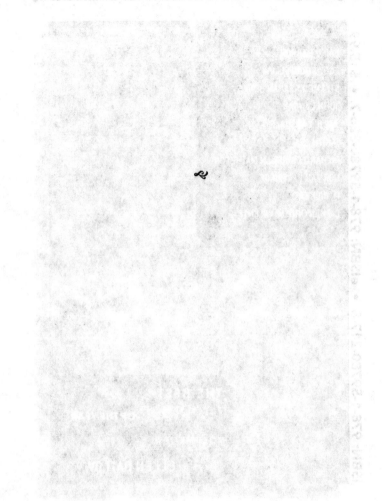

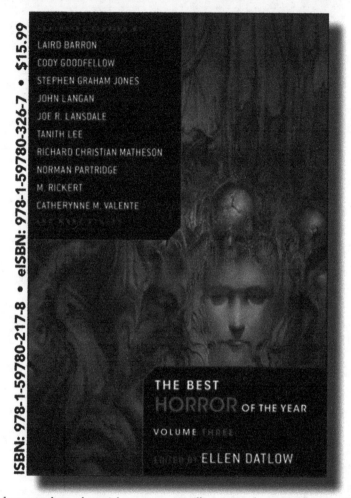

ISBN: 978-1-59780-217-8 • eISBN: 978-1-59780-326-7 • $15.99

LAIRD BARRON

CODY GOODFELLOW

STEPHEN GRAHAM JONES

JOHN LANGAN

JOE R. LANSDALE

TANITH LEE

RICHARD CHRISTIAN MATHESON

NORMAN PARTRIDGE

M. RICKERT

CATHERYNNE M. VALENTE

THE BEST
HORROR OF THE YEAR
VOLUME THREE

ELLEN DATLOW

A doctor makes a late-night emergency call to an exclusive California riding school; a professor inherits a mysterious vase... and a strange little man; a struggling youth discovers canine horrors lurking beneath the streets of Albany; a sheriff ruthlessly deals with monstrosities plaguing his rural town; a pair of animal researchers makes a frightening discovery at a remote site; a group of horror aficionados attempts to track down an unfinished film by a reclusive cult director; a man spends a chill night standing watch over his uncle's body; a girl looks to understand her place in a world in which zombies have overrun the earth; a murderous pack of nuns stalks a pair of Halloween revelers...

Legendary editor Ellen Datlow (*Lovecraft Unbound*, *Tails of Wonder and Imagination*), winner of multiple Hugo, Bram Stoker, and World Fantasy awards, joins Night Shade Books in presenting *The Best Horror of the Year, Volume Three*.

Night Shade Books is an Independent Publisher of Quality Science-Fiction, Horror and Fantasy

ISBN: 978-1-59780-146-1 • $16.95

To the long tradition of eldritch horror pioneered and refined by writers such as H.P. Lovecraft, Peter Straub, and Thomas Ligotti, comes Laird Barron, an author whose literary voice invokes the grotesque, the devilish, and the perverse with rare intensity and astonishing craftsmanship.

Collected here for the first time are nine terrifying tales of cosmic horror, including the World Fantasy Award-nominated novella "The Imago Sequence," the International Horror Guild Award-nominated "Proboscis," and the never-before published "Procession of the Black Sloth." Together, these stories, each a masterstroke of craft and imaginative irony, form a shocking cycle of distorted evolution, encroaching chaos, and ravenous insectoid hive-minds hidden just beneath the seemingly benign surface of the Earth.

How to Make Friends with Demons

Graham Joyce

"Anyone who isn't reading Graham Joyce is doing themselves a huge disservice. No matter what kind of story he takes on, his work immediately becomes the standard to which all others have to be compared. The only disappointment with a Joyce book is that, at some point, it has to end."
— Charles de Lint, World Fantasy Award-winning author of *The Mystery of Grace*

ISBN: 978-1-59780-142-3 • $24.95

William Heaney is a man well acquainted with demons. Not his broken family—his wife has left him for a celebrity chef, his snobbish teenaged son despises him, and his daughter's new boyfriend resembles Nosferatu—nor his drinking problem, nor his unfulfilling government job, but real demons.

For demons are real, and William has identified one thousand five hundred and sixty-seven smoky figures, dwelling on the shadowy fringes of human life, influencing our decisions with their sweet and poisoned voices.

Marked by his trademark lucid, flowing prose, powerful atmosphere, and impressive storytelling, Graham Joyce's *How to Make Friends with Demons* is an ambitious and captivating novel of emotional endurance and psychological horror.

Night Shade Books is an Independent Publisher of Quality Science-Fiction, Horror and Fantasy

ISBN: 978-1-59780-189-8 • $15.95

STORIES OF THE DEVIL BY

ELIZABETH BEAR	KELLY LINK
HOLLY BLACK	CHINA MIÉVILLE
MICHAEL CHABON	CARRIE RICHERSON
CHARLES DE LINT	CHARLES STROSS
STEPHEN KING	SCOTT WESTERFELD

AND MANY OTHERS

Edited by Tim Pratt

The Devil is known by many names: Serpent, Tempter, Beast, Adversary, Wanderer, Dragon, Rebel. His traps and machinations are the stuff of legends. His faces are legion. No matter what face the devil wears, *Sympathy for the Devil* has them all.

Edited by Tim Pratt (*Hart & Boot & Other Stories*, *The Strange Adventures of Rangergirl*, *Blood Engines*), *Sympathy for the Devil* collects the best Satanic short stories by Neil Gaiman, Holly Black, Stephen King, Kage Baker, Charles Stross, Elizabeth Bear, Jay Lake, Kelly Link, China Mieville, Michael Chabon, and many others, revealing His Grand Infernal Majesty, in all his forms.

Thirty-five stories, from classics to the cutting edge, exploring the many sides of Satan, Lucifer, the Lord of the Flies, the Father of Lies, the Prince of the Powers of the Air and Darkness, the First of the Fallen... and a Man of Wealth and Taste. Sit down and spend a little time with the Devil.

Night Shade Books is an Independent Publisher of Quality Science-Fiction, Horror and Fantasy

The Winner of the Shirley Jackson Award Delivers Another Stunning Collection of the Weird and Fantastic

OCCULTATION

AND OTHER STORIES

LAIRD BARRON

Laird Barron has emerged as one of the strongest voices in modern horror and dark fantasy fiction, building on the eldritch tradition pioneered by writers such as H. P. Lovecraft, Peter Straub, and Thomas Ligotti. His stories have garnered critical acclaim and have been reprinted in numerous year's best anthologies and nominated for multiple awards, including the Crawford, International Horror Guild, Shirley Jackson, Theodore Sturgeon, and World Fantasy awards. His debut collection, *The Imago Sequence and Other Stories*, was the inaugural winner of the Shirley Jackson award.

Pitting ordinary men and women against a carnivorous, chaotic cosmos, *Occultation*'s eight tales of terror (two never before published) include the Theodore Sturgeon and Shirley Jackson award-nominated story "The Forest" and Shirley Jackson award nominee "The Lagerstatte." Featuring an introduction by Michael Shea, *Occultation* brings more of the spine-chillingly sublime cosmic horror Laird Barron's fans have come to expect.

"Stina Leicht is one of my favourites among the new writers we have today. She writes with depth and heart and tells a story with all the resonance of an old whiskey: dark with an edgy flavour."
— Charles de Lint, author of *Forests of the Heart*

STINA LEICHT

of BLOOD and HONEY

A BOOK OF THE FEY AND THE FALLEN

ISBN: 978-1-59780-213-0 • $14.99

Fallen angels and the Fey clash against the backdrop of Irish/English conflicts of the 1970s in this stunning debut novel by Stina Leicht.

Liam never knew who his father was. The town of Derry had always assumed that he was the bastard of a protestant—His mother never spoke of him, and Liam assumed he was dead.

But when the war between the fallen, and the fey began to heat up, Liam and his family are pulled into a conflict that they didn't know existed. A centuries old conflict between supernatural forces seems to mirror the political divisions in 1970s era Ireland, and Liam is thrown headlong into both conflicts.

Only the direct intervention of Liam's real father, and a secret catholic order dedicated to fighting "The Fallen" can save Liam... from the mundane and supernatural forces around him, and from the darkness that lurks within him.

"Terrifying, darkly hilarious, tougher and meaner and faster than a .45 hole-in-the-head—Roche delivers a fast-paced, gripping thriller where the showdowns make other zombie novelists look like they're playing with dollies."

—Violet Blue, author of *The Smart Girl's Guide to Porn* and many others

THE PANAMA LAUGH

THOMAS S. ROCHE

ISBN: 978-1-59780-290-1 • $14.99

Ex-mercenary and pirate interdiction specialist Dante Bogart knows he's the one who handed his shady employers the virus that makes the dead rise to devour the living while laughing their asses off. Whether they were using it to create super-soldiers, build biological weapons or live forever, he hasn't got the foggiest. But he knows it escaped. Dante even tried to blow the whistle on the nightmare via a tell-all video that "went viral"—but that was back before the black ops boys deep-sixed him at a secret interrogation site on the Panama-Colombia border. So he wakes up in the jungle with the five intervening years missing from his memory and his hippie ex-girlfriend married—to Dante's best friend, no less—he knows he's got to do what he can to cure the laughing sickness that's slaughtering the world. Doing that will take a trip over the nightmare that was the Panama Canal, then around Cape Horn in a hijacked nuclear warship to San Francisco, where a crew of survivalist hackers have holed up in the Moorish castle known as the Armory to resist laughing corpses and corporate stooges alike, taking Dante's whistle-blowing viral video as their underground Gospel.

About the Author

John Hornor Jacobs has worked in advertis-
ing for the last fifteen years, played in bands,
and pursued art in various forms. He is the
cofounder of *Needle: A Magazine of Noir*. He
is also, in his copious spare time, a novelist.